T0293891

SANATAN

सनातन

SANATAN

सनातन

A novel

SHARANKUMAR LIMBALE

Translated by

PAROMITA SENGUPTA

VINTAGE

An imprint of Penguin Random House

VINTAGE

Vintage is an imprint of the Penguin Random House group of companies
whose addresses can be found at global.penguinrandomhouse.com

Published by Penguin Random House India Pvt. Ltd
4th Floor, Capital Tower 1, MG Road,
Gurugram 122 002, Haryana, India

First published in Marathi as *Sanatan* by Dilipraj Prakashan, Pune, 2018
Published in Vintage by Penguin Random House India 2024

10 9 8 7 6 5 4 3 2

ISBN 9780143465768

Typeset in Adobe Garamond Pro by MAP Systems, Bengaluru, India
Printed at Replika Press Pvt. Ltd, India

www.penguin.co.in

Contents

Author's Note vii
Translator's Note xi

Sanatan 1

Glossary 223

Author's Note

I don't know how many people will like my writing. Honestly, I don't really care. I never write keeping anybody's likes or dislikes in mind. I simply state whatever is directed by my conscience and my intellect. And this conscience of mine—well, it is a kind of experiment; my conscience has emerged from Indian culture and traditions. Indian culture is like a complex yet compassionate chemical compound; it is a site where several religious and non-religious groups of people coexist. Talking about any one of the several religions in India is certainly not equal to talking about India as a whole. This novel, *Sanatan*, is specially focused on the Dalits in India. All religions, regions, languages and cultures in India have kept the Dalits at a 'safe distance' from themselves and their social existence. Considered them untouchable. And the distance was such that discrimination against the Dalits was but an inevitable fallout. The Dalits were isolated, disenfranchised. And it is exactly this situation that this novel tries to illustrate. It serves as a statement against the gross and omnipresent discrimination, and attempts to oppose it. It is only when these counter-discourses, these statements against the discrimination, grow and increase in number, that the upper-caste culture shall find itself being questioned, find itself in trouble. And it is this very idea that I want to underline in my work, because it seems to me to be the only good antidote, a means of creating healthy mass social awareness—of not just past events but also future possibilities. Borrowing from the imaginary resources of the past, I have made an attempt to unveil our fiery present.

The age-old varna system in India was a kind of reservation. Knowledge-based power was reserved for the Brahmins, political power for the Kshatriyas, business power for the Vaishyas, and the burden of serving these three upper varnas was inflicted on the Shudras. There was no thought at all given to the plight of the untouchables and the Adivasis. And this system was revered and followed for ages; it was accepted as a system created by God himself. However, what it resulted in was social imbalance. After India gained independence, an effort was made to end this social imbalance through caste-based reservation for the untouchables and the Adivasis. On the one hand was that section of society which had enjoyed the benefits of reservation for thousands of years, and on the other was that which had suffered neglect, deprivation and poverty throughout that time. This, sadly, is the grim but true picture. And even today, the regretful reality is that the reservation for Dalits is yet to reach and benefit all those who are in dire need of it.

While reservation has brought about positive changes in the lives of the untouchables and Adivasis, it has caused grievances among the upper castes, who cannot accept this change. The revolution has, however, reached into the deep recesses of social structures, such as education, law and our political democracy. Our social consciousness has awakened, and a new way of thinking is on the rise. Educated Dalits are now in a position to question and rethink the history and tradition that has caused terrible suffering to them and cheated them. There have been a few historical texts on the Mahar, an untouchable caste, but those are not enough.

I was inspired to write this novel after reading about the Mahars. This novel does not narrate the history of the Mahars; it divulges their present condition. When Babasaheb Ambedkar embraced Buddhism, a religious reformation was initiated within the folds of Hinduism. The Hindu religion has caused unimaginable harm to the Adivasis and the untouchables, the extent of which has not yet been accounted for. In such a scenario, how can we even expect any kind of compensation or restitution? This book talks about such irreparable damage. Compensation is given to people who are struck by some disaster. In this case, however, it is a matter of people suffering from poverty and ignorance for hundreds of years. It is absolutely imperative that we evaluate and account for their displacement. We must go to the very depths of this problem. This situation cannot, should not, must not be ignored any further. This is what this novel signals at.

There is no intention here to be disrespectful towards the towering personalities of history; Mangal Pandey and the Rani of Jhansi, Lakshmibai, are inspirational, ideal personalities. The complaint is, however, that the Dalits and Adivasis have also loved this country a great deal and made sacrifices. No one, however, has paid sufficient attention to these sacrifices. This novel does that. But it has not been written only for the Dalits. It has been written with the intention of building a new and progressive social order; it has been written with the idea of a new human formation, the creation of a great country; and one hopes that the reader's attention will go towards these suggestions and ideas.

There exists a group of progressive people who want to focus on positive transformations and creative developments in society, and who have faith in the democratic system of governance. This group or generation is well aware of the social injustices but wants to move on with the times. From ancient times, humanists have sided with the underprivileged and the weaker sections of society. Is the humanist tradition/way of thinking in some danger today? It is time to think about these things.

I used the myths and Puranas as source texts/resources for this book. Google and Wikipedia have eased access to much information. I express my heartfelt gratitude to all of the above.

Sharankumar Limbale

Translator's Note

Translation is a serious matter. The global dominance and use of the English language is a complex postcolonial phenomenon, remarkable for the diversity of cultures and peoples who use it, each negotiating it in singular ways and each leaving their unique stamp on it. No matter what Macaulay's intentions were in 1835, English has been taken over, owned, used and abused, tossed and turned, grilled and barbequed, tawa-fried, chutnified even, by its users. Not only in India, but wherever it went. And how did it respond? It responded with a comic resilience like that of Viola in Shakespeare's *Twelfth Night*: when she finds herself in unfamiliar territory, she first exclaims, 'What country, friends, is this?' But then, pretty soon, she finds herself in a situation where she admits, 'Whoe'er I woo, myself would be his wife.'

In spite of the fact that the *Oxford English Dictionary* now recognizes more than a thousand Indian words as part of standard English, not every Indian experience sounds quite the same when narrated in this 'official' Indian language. For instance, kinship terms and terms of address—in which age, gender, status and family relationships are marked by a highly specific vocabulary—cannot be translated, quite simply because there are no direct equivalents in English. This lexical gap can only be filled by using particular Indian terms. Again, the specificity of the traditions, values and norms of various Indian local cultures mandate that the English language must accommodate Indian words.

Thus, this English translation of a Marathi novel is called *Sanatan*, for if 'Sanatan' were to be literally translated into English, as 'Tradition' or 'Eternal', it would carry none of the cultural and religious connotations associated with the original.*

I must get a little personal at this point. I must tell you my story. I must tell you my story because my story is inextricably intertwined with the way I have translated this book. English-language proficiency was a privilege thrust on me. I found myself in a bilingual situation from birth—actually, even before it! I was in a bilingual environment from the moment I was conceived, at a 'hill station' built in the foothills of the Himalayas by the sun-baked British, who wanted to periodically escape from the scorching heat of the then capital of British India, Calcutta. My father, a linguist with the Government of India, was posted at one such hill station (someone had named it 'Scotland of the East'). I was born about thirty years after the English left India, and English would be the language I would speak, write, dream, think, feel and even make a career in.

Little did I know as a child that there are many 'Englishes', that one day I would be researching 'Beginnings of Indian Writing in English in Nineteenth-Century Bengal' for my doctoral dissertation; or that I would some day land in Ireland (where English teachers are high in demand), managing an English-language school that teaches 'English as a foreign language' to people from Europe, South America, the Middle East, Asia—basically, people from all over the world. To a child whose birthday gifts were *David Copperfield*, *Tales from Shakespeare* by Charles

---

* Sanatan is an endonym used by Hindus to refer to Hinduism. It refers to what is regarded by Hindus as the 'eternal' truth and teachings of Hinduism. 'Sanatan' can also be translated as 'the natural and eternal way to live'. The term is used in Indian languages alongside the more common 'Hindu Dharma' to refer to Hinduism. Sanatan Dharma can also denote the list of 'eternal' or absolute duties and practices.

and Mary Lamb, and *Malory Towers*, rather than *Thakurmar Jhuli*, *Nonte-Fonte* or *Shera Satyajit*, it was not just linguistic but cultural orientation.* What was happening, essentially, was linguistic acculturation.†

To a child who was made to feel embarrassed by her lack of adequate knowledge of the 'mother tongue', English as she knew it, or as she was learning it, in all its alienness, and perhaps because of it, became a source of comfort. The language of fairy tales and princesses. The language of cottages built of cake and gingerbread. A language that was like a foster parent to a forlorn, alienated child. Yet, somewhere, it was all an act of constantly shifting between languages, constant translation. Looking back on my childhood in multilingual India, and looking around now, as I am 'outside' India at present, I realize that I had always been (as I am even now) constantly translating among the three languages that make me—English, Hindi and Bengali. But the fun fact is that today, though I know more words in English than I do in Hindi or Bengali, English is and will remain designated as my 'foreign language', at least so long as I am in a 'foreign' country. Honestly, I would not have realized the 'foreignness' of it until I came to a foreign country and started making my living teaching this foreign language to foreigners.‡ In India, English is simply 'my' language.

---

* *Thakurmar Jhuli*, *Nonte-Fonte* and *Shera Satyajit*: The first is a classic Bengali collection of folktales by Dakshinaranjan Mitra Majumdar, the second an iconic Bengali comic strip created by Narayan Debnath and the third a collection of short stories by Satyajit Ray.

† The theory of linguistic acculturation posits that a language learner's success is determined by the extent to which they can orient themselves to the culture of the target language. This may often be at the cost of the erosion of the indigenous culture.

‡ 'Foreignness', I personally think, is a lot in one's mind. One can feel/be 'at home' anywhere in the world or nowhere at all. But here I have used the

A good translator, like a good editor, is supposed to be invisible. Why, then, am I talking about myself and not about the translation? Could it be anxiety? Or could it be that I am trying to forefront the politics of language acquisition and use?

Well, I must say that though I have tried to remain 'invisible' in the English translation of *Sanatan*, I don't think it is really quite possible to be completely 'invisible.' And by that I mean that this translation of *Sanatan* bears my imprint—the stamp of my tryst with the English language, my negotiations with it, my way of looking at it. Thus, you find in this story 'Lal Dongar' and 'Kaala Wada' and not 'Red Hills' and the 'Black Palace'; thus you find in this story 'Maharwada' and not 'Mahar settlements', 'roti' and not 'flat bread', and so on and so forth.*

Language determines audience, and the looming presence of an audience might affect the semantic choices and connotations in a text. The trappings of the ideological base of the intended and imagined audience aren't easy to escape. Who is the English translation of *Sanatan* intended for? Is it intended for the outcast who still carries shit on his head (manual scavenging is now banned in India, but let's not pretend that it does not exist)? Or is it intended for the widow and children of the man lynched

---

concept of being foreign in a practical, material sense. On another note, I now have a standard answer when an Irish person compliments me, 'Oh! But you have such great English!' 'It comes from the same place as yours,' I say. 'We are both products of a similar colonial past.' It is, however, a fact that Indians have managed to hold on to their indigenous languages better than many other cultures swallowed whole by the colonial monster.

* Marathi words pepper this translation. Generously. Unapologetically. A glossary has been added keeping in mind the intended broad audience, but then the brief glossary descriptions are expected to lead the unfamiliar but serious reader to explore and research more about the word/concept, its connotations, its deeper significance where necessary.

for eating or carrying a dead cow? In all likelihood, this book, translated into English, is going to be read by those privileged enough to have been born into English because of political, economic and sociocultural circumstances. The question, then, is: Does it matter to bear the agony and anxiety of translation, to have spent hundreds of hours translating this story? Let's hope so! Let's hope so because this act of translation facilitates the access of the privileged like me into the lives of the Mahars and the Adivasis, whose stories were not written for a very long time, whose role in our history was neither acknowledged nor documented, and in whose misery we were and are complicit. This is one of those texts that open up new worlds. Worlds where eating a dead rotting cow is a celebration. Worlds where even death brings no relief, and the sorrowful spirit roams the earth as a ghost. Worlds where such ghosts ride on whirlwinds to avenge their miserable lives and unjust deaths. Worlds where changing their religion or going away to work in a sugar plantation in the Caribbean does not free the untouchables from the shackles of caste or give them even a brief respite.

A translation such as this once, then, is making use of the form as a vehicle to articulate and broadcast appalling experiences that have been glossed over for centuries and have been philosophically justified. It tells the truth untold. This is a text that is rewriting history rather than just telling a story. In fact, there are multiple stories here and hardly 'a' protagonist. And these multiple narratives are woven like a braid and tied with threads of historical events.

Will *Sanatan* find a place on the bookshelves of the English-reading general audience? Time will tell. But this book is hard-hitting, intense, provocative and rebellious. *Sanatan* cares very little for any conventions of the novel; it is genre-defying. Neither does it care for popularity. Sharankumar Limbale clearly, and rather boldly, states in the author's note that he never writes to please anyone; he simply follows the dictates of his consciousness. This is a story that must be told, he says. And that is exactly what I felt about it as a reader—that this is a story that must be translated into as many languages as possible, so that it reaches a wider audience.

This translation, one must remember, is the translation of a translation. The original text was written in Marathi. It was translated into Hindi, and I have used the Hindi text as a kind of bridge. I have tried to be completely faithful to the Hindi *Sanatan*. Sharankumar Limbale has worked closely with me, attentively reading the English text, providing explanations when needed. At times the syntax may appear crude or jolting, but that is essential, inherent to the narrative themes and style. A story such as this needs to be a bumpy ride. There is little place for comfort.

I would like to end this note by quoting the Adivasi poet Abhay Flavian Xaxa, whose shocking death at the age of thirty-seven was a huge loss to Dalit and Adivasi activism and literature. As Xaxa mentions at the end of one of his poems, some writers must indeed 'invent' their 'own grammar':*

I am not your data, nor am I your vote bank,
I am not your project, or any exotic museum object,
I am not the soul waiting to be harvested,
Nor am I the lab where your theories are tested,

* I remember an incident from a few years ago when I was teaching in India. A first-year student came up to me with his notebook. He had written something. I looked at it and appreciated his efforts. He went away, happy. Two days later he was back. Dejection was writ large on his face. He came up to me. 'Ma'am,' he said, 'I showed this piece of writing to my sir, and he said that there were grammatical mistakes. He wondered why you hadn't pointed them out to me, ma'am.' I couldn't help smiling. 'I care more for your ideas, my boy,' I said. 'The grammar will eventually take care of itself. Don't let it get in the way of your ideas and self-expression.' I'm not sure what he understood then, but I am happy to say that he eventually went on to do a master's in English, runs his blog and is himself an English teacher today.

I am not your cannon fodder, or the invisible worker,
Or your entertainment at India Habitat Centre,
I am not your field, your crowd, your history,
Your help, your guilt, medallions of your victory,
I refuse, reject, resist your labels,
Your judgments, documents, definitions,
Your models, leaders and patrons,
Because they deny me my existence, my vision, my space,
Your words, maps, figures, indicators,
They all create illusions and put you on pedestal,
From where you look down upon me,
So I draw my own picture, and invent my own grammar,
I make my own tools to fight my own battle,
For me, my people, my world, and my Adivasi self!

And perhaps that is how we find ourselves 'at home' in a 'foreign language'. That is what we do with the cultural invasion. That is how we speak, we write. That is how we translate. And that is how we do language.

Limerick, Ireland — Paromita Sengupta

One

The Mahars were screaming. It was a special kind of noise—one that could only be heard on the day of Holi, the festival of howls. The children of the untouchables were howling with joy. On any other day, these screams would have been regarded as unholy, and people would have crouched in fear. But today it is a holy scream, for it is Holi today. Holi, the carnival of jubilation, of rapture. The Mahars were exulting in that rapture. They were all laughing loudly, screaming loudly.

Bhimnak Mahar was busy scattering the dry grass and useless fodder around the site of the Holi pyre. Sidnak Mahar was preparing the holy fire. Bhimnak and Sidnak—both in the prime of their youth. The best of friends. Children paid them heed; they were their heroes.

The Mahar women had started filing in with their offering plates. The elderly Mahars sat under the old tamarind tree and got busy talking to each other. 'This year the Holi pyre is too high,' said Yesnak Mahar, scratching his back against the tree. He used to play the trumpet, and so people called him the Trumpet Player.

'Keep a safe distance or you might burn yourselves,' Ambarnak Mahar warned the youths lighting the pyre. His chatter continued for a while. Bhimnak and Sidnak were trying to ward off the children who came too close to the fire.

The Holi pyre was scorching, just like the relationship between the Mahars and the Brahmins. It was now blazing, raging uncontrollably. Children were having great fun in the bright light of the burning Holi. Their merriment was just like the flaming fire, which had now reached the rendi leaves. The sky was full of smoke. Women were rapt in their worship rituals, and the children screamed their hearts out.

The children had spent the whole of the preceding month gathering dung cakes for Holi. Every year, they would do the same. They would pilfer dung cakes for days. It was part of the fun. Some seven or eight kids were specially designated for this job. They would run around the village, stealing dung cakes whenever and wherever possible. Sidnak, with his ragged blanket, led the group. Bhimnak would be behind him, and behind Bhimnak the flock of children. They would store the stock—a big heap of dung cakes—near the temple of Mari Ma, their goddess. The rest of the day would be spent debating the next move, deciding on the next target. The night would see actual action. If the pilferers were sighted by an angry villager, they would have to run away. And as they ran, some would fall, while others would hurt a knee or a thumb. But their excitement was unabated. They would resume their job with great enthusiasm the next night. This was how they came to steal some dung cakes from Arjun Khatal one day.

The next morning Arjun Khatal came fuming into the Maharwada. He was mad with rage. He abused the children. He confronted Sidnak. The children kept staring at him in their innocence. He said menacingly, 'If you dare steal from me again, I will . . .' His bearded face looked even more sinister than usual. But the moment he turned to go the children burst out laughing. And so loud was their laughter that the vultures resting on the nearby neem tree all flew away.

'We should now teach him a lesson.'

'Forget it. Let's put this behind us.'

'There are dung cakes in Krishna Javde's fields.'

'How do you know?'

'His cattle are kept tied in the field all day!'

'Fine! Let's go tonight!'

Such was the gang of children in the Maharwada of Sonai village. There was also a pack of dogs in the Maharwada. In fact, there were loads of dogs and pigs there. The Mahars were required to stick animal bones to their roofs so that their huts may be identified as those that belonged to the Mahars. Sidnak's roof displayed the bones of a buffalo's leg, while on Bhimnak's lay the ribs; Ambarnak's hut was marked by the bone of a cow's leg; Bhootnak's had the jawbones of an ox, while Dhondamay had an ox's horns.

The hide of a buffalo had been laid out to dry in front of the Mari Ma temple. Sidnak lifted a stray dog, Champi, on his shoulders. Parbati emptied a pot of water on the stairs of Mari Ma's temple. Today she had kept a fast—she did so on Tuesdays and Saturdays.

Sidnak began playing with Champi. The children were hustling each other. By now, they had forgotten Khatal's abuses. They knew very well how to look at the upper castes. What they did not know was how to look at their own lives. They had human bodies, but their minds had become like that of animals—numb! From their very birth they knew how to live by forgetting the abuses thrown at them. They firmly believed that their fate had caused them to be born as Mahars and were silent about it. Even if someone were to tell them that this silence, which had persisted for thousands of years, needed to end, they would not have paid heed to it. This system was based on violence, after all. The Mahars did not know such words as 'opposition' or 'retribution'. They had never opposed the village. All they knew was that they would live here and die here, in this very village. They believed that if they opposed the village, the villagers would spit in their mouths! Never did they try to revolt against their fates.

Crows perched on the hide drying in front of the Mari Ma temple. Bhimnak drove them away. A few pebbles were enough to do the job. The hide was secured to the ground with the help of babool thorns. It was still wet. And red! Stained with blood. Some mud was sprinkled on it, so that the crows and vultures would not claw at it. Ambarnak was on duty, keeping watch. Flies swarmed near the hide while vultures hovered above. Ambarnak opened his pouch, took out a mango leaf and made a hookah of it. He placed some tobacco in it. He then took out some cotton and flintstones, which he rubbed together, and a flicker lit the cotton. He placed his mango-leaf hookah on his lips and inhaled the tobacco; smoke billowed from his nostrils and mouth.

The sun had done its job for the day and gone off to sleep in its mother's lap. Ambarnak had pointed out the site of the Holi—it was the same place where they had burnt the Holi the previous year. Sidnak cleared the area. Bhimnak sprinkled some water. They drew a circle on the ground. Sidnak kept building the Holi; Bhimnak kept mounting dung cakes on it. The children had brought twigs from the rendi tree. Bhimnak placed them right at the centre of the Holi and scattered some dung-cake powder around it. The Holi had become narrow towards the top. The upper part of the rendi-twig structure was left open while the dung cakes covered the rest of it. Ambarnak Mahar performed the Holi Puja. Yesnak lit the fire. The children began to scream.

> Holi! Holi!
> A Brahmin has died
> This evening
> In the village lanes.

The Holi flared up. Sparks began to fly all around. The fire spread far and beyond. The air was filled with the crackling sound of the flames. The fire blazed. The smoke spread. Bhimnak's sister, Kera, Ambarnak's wife, Masai, Bhootnak's wife, Parbati, Yesnak's wife, Satvai, Sidnak's sister, Tukai—they had all come to worship Holi. Children jumped around the Holi joyously. Birds abandoned their nests in the trees and disappeared because of the smoke and commotion. Night descended, darkening the branches of the tamarind tree, and yet the animal hide lay there!

The sound of horses' hooves drew near. Krishna Javde, Arjun Khatal, Babruvan Kharate, Navnath Jakikore and Sidram Kore had come riding their horses. They stopped near the Mahars' Holi. 'Pass them the fire of our Holi,' Ambarnak said loudly. Some of the children put a spark of fire on a dung cake and placed it on Sidram Kore's palms. The villagers left with this spark of fire from the Mahar's Holi. Ambarnak proudly proclaimed, 'The village Holi can't be lit without the fire from the Mahar's Holi. This is a matter of pride for us.' The Holi fire burnt brightly. The flames and smoke from it seemed to touch the sky. The dung cakes glowed red. The sound of screaming could be heard from the village. The village Holi was now lit. The Mahars were satisfied.

It was quite late now. The fire had started to die down. The Holi had now been razed almost to the ground. The Mahars started going home one by one. The Holi was all alone now, left to itself. The solitary tamarind tree also fell asleep, all by itself.

* * *

Dhuli Vandan, which is celebrated the day after Holi, also went by. Bhimnak and Sidnak had come near the bank of the fast-flowing Falguni River. Walking carefully along the bank, they reached the cliffs. The banks were rich with the grass that grew on the fertile soil, and the crystal-clear water sparkled as it flowed. The river made its way around the cliffs. The water was deep, and the current was strong here. Wild date trees gave this place the look of a forest. One gular tree lay prostrate over the river. Herons lined the tree trunk. Next to the gular stood a jamun tree. A flock of waterfowl rested in its shade. Whirlpools swirled in the sharp deep outfall made by the sudden drop. The two banks of the river looked like expanses of a sandy landscape. The Falguni flowing near Sonai village was a sight to behold.

Sidnak was standing on a rock on the cliff. Champi played near his feet. Sidnak playfully pushed Champi into the water. She swam back to the cliff and shook the water off her body. Bhimnak was swimming in the water. Holding his nose, he ducked into the water and sprinkled himself with it.

Sidnak jumped into the water. The water splashed. The fish were alerted. The gurgling sound of the water made the fish move towards the muddy water. They surrounded Bhimnak and Sidnak from all sides. Sidnak swam towards the cliff, climbed out and sat there with his feet dipped into the water. Crabs inhabited the clefts in the cliff. Sidnak hit the water with his feet. Sparkling drops splashed all around. Champi began to bark. Then, Biru the shepherd came to the water with his buffaloes. His dog stood there and seeing it, Champi began to bark. Sidnak rubbed his body with a stone.

No matter how many times he bathed, Sidnak would remain impure and untouchable. The upper castes become pure when they dip themselves into the river. They wash off their sins and become holy. But the untouchables, they are not purified by the holy river. If anything, they make the river water impure. They make pilgrimage sites unholy.

Sidnak entered the water again. He began washing himself rigorously, as though he were washing off the cynical gaze of others. He felt a vain satisfaction at the thought that the water with which he had washed himself would soon reach another village and that the upper castes of that village would drink this water. He jumped out of the water. His body was untouchable! He was untouchable! His shadow was impure! His words were impure! If he touched the corpse of an upper caste, that corpse became impure. Even the burial ground became impure.

During a flood, this rock would be submerged under the waters of the Falguni. No one entered the river at that time. Not until the rock became visible again. As Bhimnak stood on the rock, Parbati came along to get some water. She washed her earthen pot and filled it. She brought it up to her knees, but it was heavy. She asked Bhimnak for help. He was only too eager to help her place the pot on her head. Her face glistened with the drops of water that had dripped off the delicately balanced pot. She was soon on her way, and Bhimnak was left staring at her receding figure. Her thin shanks shone like the fibres of golden maize in the sun. His gaze lingered covetously on her bare back. She was wet, with her sari clinging tightly to her figure. Bhimnak's mind was a whirlpool of desire; the outfall was deep.

Bhimnak had caught a crab. It was trying its best to escape. Bhimnak wrenched its claws. And then its legs. The crab watched helplessly. Bhimnak cut open its belly and removed the gut. He washed the dead crab in the water. The river water was replete with fishes. Sidnak and Champi were staring at Bhimnak. Parbati didn't come again. They both turned to leave. The river flowed on; the wind blew. Bhimnak's mind was not at rest. He remembered Parbati, and also Bhootnak, her husband!

He remembered an ancient lore. Goddess Parvati, wife of Mahadev, was bathing in a river. She saw a trifoliate bel leaf floating in the water. She kept gazing intently at it. Carried by the current, the leaf came closer to her. On the leaf was a red dot—a drop of blood. She touched the leaf. A baby was born on the leaf. Parvati hugged the infant; she was excited and overjoyed. She took the baby home and showed it to Mahadev. She narrated the story to him, and he was happy with what he heard. He accepted the baby, who started living in their house.

One day, the child came out to the yard. There was a dead cow lying there. The child began eating the cow's flesh. When Mahadev saw this, he was furious and cursed the child: 'You will stay outside the village. You will eat the flesh of dead animals. People will disregard and humiliate you, and even your shadow will be treated as untouchable.' The child started living outside the village. He had to eat the flesh of dead animals. This was how the Mahar caste was born.

A thorn pricked Bhimnak's foot. It was stuck in his heel, looking like a black mole. He had been unmindful of his surroundings, thinking of the story of Goddess Parvati as narrated to him by Parbati. Sidnak was angry: 'Can't you walk carefully? Watch where you put your foot?'

One blazing midday, Bhimnak had gone to Parbati's place. She was alone. His knees were scraped. Her back was heavily bruised. The vein of his penis was torn. He touched his cut gently. His fingers were smeared with blood. A red dot of blood! 'I am the only child of my mother! Born after fourteen years! I will have the same fate!' She touched her hair as she spoke. He kept quiet, and wondered if the thorn had pricked his foot or his heart. He limped on.

Crows were cawing in the Maharwada. There were about a couple of dozen huts there. Two or three families had become Muslims, so their huts were empty—those converted Mahars now lived in the Muslim neighbourhood. Sonai was a village in the Bahmani Kingdom, so the Muslims were proud citizens there, with a strong voice and presence in spite of being a minority community. The Muslim pride heightened during the reign of the nizam. The Hindus, in spite of being the majority, remained subdued in front of the Muslims. There were only ten Muslim houses in the village. The Mahars who had changed their religion put up their huts behind those ten houses. The Muslims of the village remained aloof from these converts. The village was clearly divided between Hindus, Muslims and untouchables.

* * *

Wherever there is a village, there is a Maharwada. The Maharwada is always outside the village. The Maharwada of the Mahars! Of the dogs! Of pigs! Of donkeys! Of garbage! Of dirt! The Mahars had to do all the menial work of the village. And what they got in return was refuse and waste. Ambarnak, Bhootnak, Yesnak and Dhondamay—they were the four Padewar Mahars of Sonai. Dhondamay, neither man nor woman, had taken Bhimnak's and Sidnak's help to do the menial work—a job she had inherited from her father. Dhondamay lived by herself.

Some of the Padewar Mahars did domestic work in the houses of upper-caste Hindus. They worked in distinguished houses. They were called 'Raabta Mahars' or 'House Mahars'. Those who were Padewar Mahars would get these jobs by dint of inheritance. This work was not given to the Mahars who came from outside the village. Every year, only these four houses got this job. Once the duties were assigned, these Mahars would be given a stick with bells attached to it. They would have to enter the village with it, so that the sound of the bells would warn people of their approach. This stick and the sound of the bells were a symbol of pride for the Mahars, but for the other villagers these were associated with the untouchables—a warning that they should keep away from the approaching Mahar and even their shadow. There were other marks, too, of a Mahar—the black thread around their necks and hands, the black thread around their waists and, above all, the look of helplessness on their faces. It wasn't just the Mahars' attire or appearance, even their language marked them out.

The Mahar who was assigned domestic work would be regarded as the Padewar Mahar for a given time. The village would assign him jobs which he would then divide among other Mahars. This was the way the Maharwada and the village functioned. The Mahars were proud of this tradition.

Collecting rent and debt from defaulters, following up with them, making arrangements if a big client happened to come to the village, taking care of horses—arranging fodder for them and massaging their bodies—patrolling the village, being the drummer when required, looking after the fields, crops and the threshing floor, being the watchman, showing the way sometimes, protecting the trees and the forest, killing dangerous wild animals, patrolling the mountain passes, keeping an eye on strangers and intimating the Patil if someone's presence in the village was suspicious, finding thieves, keeping the village roads clean, carrying dead animals from the village, collecting firewood for the upper castes . . . and in return for all this, begging for food. The Mahars could not say no to any of these jobs. They would be tortured mercilessly if they refused. They would be boycotted, and all their food supplies would be cut off. If a Mahar man refused to work, his wife and children would have to fill in. The Mahars mostly accepted their condition with the thought, 'This is our fate. How can we possibly fight it?' In the discriminatory Hindu religion, the Mahars were on the lowest rung. The Hindu religion was based on segregation between the upper and lower castes. Inequities were the very basis of the caste system. The untouchables were at the foot of this hierarchy. This was because they had sinned in their previous lives and their present lower-caste birth was their penance for those past sins. This was the tradition. This was the belief.

Restricted from access to public spaces. Separate hutment. Separate well. Even separate crematorium. The Mahars could never step outside the limits set for them. They would have to stay put where they had been placed—at the very bottom. The Mahars had to lick the spit of the upper castes and suffer a slave's life, and their predicament was to be content with this life. The Hindu religion sustained itself not on the valour of the Kshatriyas but on the manure generated from the carcasses of the Mahars. The Mahar—a two-legged animal. And he was used to lifelong slavery.

The Mahar would skin dead animals and sell the hide to the Dhor. The Dhor would dye the hide and sell it to the shoemaker, the Chambhar, who would make shoes and sell them. The upper-caste people made the Mahar drag and skin dead animals!

Ambarnak was sitting under the tamarind tree. He would be watching over the village at night. Keeping an eye on the hide of dead cattle by day and watching over the village by night—he knew no other life. Sometimes he would introspect. He would stare at the Chand Minar. His grandfather had built it. Mehmood Gvan, the wazir of Bidar, was returning victorious after the Konkan mission. He had put up a rest camp in Sonai. The army halted for two days there. The victorious army had received a royal welcome from the king of Jhol. Ambarnak's grandfather Bidnak was in charge of the grand black horse of the wazir, and the wazir had personally inquired after Bidnak!

The horsemen roamed the village, each choosing a house in which to spend the night. As night fell, the men of the house carried their mattresses and pillows to the *chawadi* or to one of the temples. Back home, the women prepared food. The horsemen reached. The beds that the women had prepared were ready. Decorated. The horsemen spent the night in the houses they chose while their horses stood outside and while the men of those houses slept in the chawadi or the temples.

It was at this time that Bidnak became a Muslim. He came to be known as Chand Ali. He was a mason. He got the minar built. It was taller than the Mahadev temple in the village. The minar lent a grandeur to the village. Chand Ali's grandson Akbar Ali would sometimes invite Ambarnak over to his house, especially on Eid. Sometimes, Ambarnak would go over to deliver beef. There was an invisible but firm bond between the two men. The bond of blood. And that was why Ambarnak often thought of becoming a Muslim. But he kept the thought to himself. He both loved and loathed the Hindu religion. Whenever he had time, he would gaze at the minar. He was proud of his grandfather. A sense of pride and gratification overwhelmed him.

Ambarnak saw Sidnak running after a dog. The dog had some rotis in its mouth, and Sidnak seemed desperate to catch hold of it. Sidnak was hurling stones at the dog, but nothing could stop it—not even Ambarnak when he joined in. The defiant dog ran towards the Mari Ma temple. Sidnak and Ambarnak ran behind it. The dog was tired by now. It stood for a moment to catch its breath, panting. The rotis fell from its mouth. Sidnak aimed a stone at it. The dog began to growl. Ambarnak hit it with a stone and drove it out of the temple. The dog ran to the back of the temple and stood there staring. Sidnak picked up the rotis that the dog had dropped and came out of the temple. They sat under the tamarind tree. Sidnak was happy that the rotis were still warm. His mouth was watering.

The dog's saliva had wet portions of the rotis. Sidnak threw them towards Champi, who eagerly gobbled them up and sat beside Sidnak, wagging her tail. Sidnak and Ambarnak shared the food. 'Champi must be taught to pinch rotis,' said Sidnak with a laugh. 'That would be great for us,' agreed Ambarnak, joining in Sidnak's laughter. Champi's tail began to wag faster!

Leaves were falling from the tamarind tree. The branches looked dry. Birds twittered. Sidnak showed Ambarnak a green snake on a twig. As thin as a sprig of onion. The birds were louder now. The snake had caused the alarm. Ambarnak changed the topic. 'Have you heard?' Sidnak shook his head. 'Then listen,' said Ambarnak. 'Do you know what people are saying? Mahadev and Parvati roam the skies at night. Many have seen them. Even I saw them yesterday. Parvati keeps crying with the little Ganpati on her lap. Mahadev looks desolate. They come out on the southern side. People are terrified. If the gods themselves are crying, surely some misfortune will take place. Bad days are ahead.' Ambarnak was speaking earnestly.

'Yes, Bhootnak told me. The world is going to drown in a deluge. But how does it matter to us? Let the landowners worry. What have we to lose?'

Sidnak appeared untroubled. He added, 'How long will this persecution continue? Sin reigns supreme. The earth will drown. I might survive. For I know how to swim. But then how long can I keep swimming? What if alligators eat me? Perhaps I shall get wings! The Brahmin will die. The Mahar too. As we keep swimming, we will turn to fishes. Mahar fishes!' Sidnak began to laugh at his own fantastical imagination.

Ambarnak stood up. He pulled down the cattle hide he had laid to dry on the branches and tied it up properly. Kera was on her way to wash the clothes. A monkey had wandered into the village. Children were running after it. The monkey climbed up the neem tree. The branches of the neem tree swayed, and crows began to caw. It was after many years that a monkey had come to the Maharwada.

* * *

Bhimnak brought Dhondnak Mahar home. Dhondnak had come all the way from the town of Jhol. He was the elder brother-in-law of Bhimnak's sister, Khoklayi. Dhondnak had brought news of a death. Biru shepherd's mother-in-law had died. Dhondnak stood before Biru's house. Biru's wife began bawling loudly. Cursing. A Mahar messenger from her parental house surely meant bad news—far from being able to offer customary courtesy to her guest, she went berserk in anticipation of grief.

When Biru returned from the forest, Dhondnak told him that Kashibai was dead. Biru went inside with the news, but he didn't come out again. Dhondnak headed towards the Sonai Maharwada. On the way, he met Bhimnak, who was chopping wood. Krishna Javde's wife arrived with two stale rotis and some vegetable curry; she kept the food on a stone in the courtyard and went back inside. Bhimnak shared the rotis with his guest. Dhondnak felt somewhat resuscitated. Bhimnak shouted, 'Give us some water, mother!' placing a pitcher on the same stone. It was a while before Krishna Javde's wife brought water. She poured it into the pitcher and went back in. Bhimnak and Dhondak helped each other drink the water, pouring it out by turns.

Bhimnak had two sisters. Khoklayi was the elder one, married to Dhondnak's brother, who lived in Jhol. Bhimnak's younger sister was Kera, who could not be married off because of her eye disease. Bhimnak's mother was very old. So all the housework fell on Kera. Bhimnak's father had died, after being struck by lightning, a long time ago. Their mother, Kondamay, had single-handedly raised the children. Life had been unkind, and she was rather exhausted now. Dhondnak looked in on her. He assured her, 'Khoklayi and her children are doing well.' She heaved a sigh of relief. It was now time for Dhondnak to leave. Bhimnak and Dhondnak went to Ambarnak's place. The Dhor in Jhol had sent money for the cattle hide. Dhondnak counted the money carefully before handing it over to Ambarnak. Ambarnak then carefully counted the money and asked Dhondnak to convey a message to the Dhor. He placed the money in the folds of his dhoti. They started talking.

Dhondnak: 'I met Khunya Pardhi on the way!'

Ambarnak: 'Yes! I heard that the Pardhi are roaming around.'

Dhondnak: 'This Khunya Pardhi! Well, they do not give trouble without cause!'

Ambarnak: 'I know him.'

Dhondnak: 'Kill the poor hungry Pardhi if he steals some food from the fields while the horsemen go about looting people in broad daylight. The poor have no protectors.'

Ambarnak: 'Khunya Pardhi's eyes are wild like the tiger's. It's impossible to even look at him. Even his laughter is like that of a ghost!'

Dhondnak: 'The Pardhi are very smart. The one I met showed me a tunnel. One can cover the distance from Jhol to Rampur in four hours through the tunnel. He knows every nook and corner of the bamboo forest.'

The donkey tied in front of Ambarnak's house had begun to wail. They chatted a while longer. Dhondnak lifted the bundle of hide. Flies were buzzing around it, and they scattered as he lifted the bundle. Shaking off his laziness, Dhondnak said, 'I must reach before it is night.' Ambarnak agreed, 'Even the donkey has signalled!' As Dhondnak placed the bundle on his shoulder, the flies came back to swarm over his head. He had started for Jhol from the field of Navnath Jakikore.

Hides, bones, animal flesh, dogs, donkeys, pigs, heaps of rubbish, worn-down slums, worn-out faces—signs of a Maharwada. Like the Buddhist caves struck by fanatic Hindus! Creaking! Exhausted! Bent! With no future! No relief! A cursed lot haplessly breathing in an atmosphere of terror. Bhimnak and Ambarnak walked towards the tamarind tree—the place of rest for every Mahar.

'We got money for the hide. Let us feast in the name of Mari Ma. What say you?' asked Ambarnak.

'It has been such a long time! The temple hasn't been attended to for a while now. If Mari Ma gets incensed, an epidemic will follow!' replied Bhimnak.

On their way, Ambarnak and Bhimnak were shocked to see Parbati. They stood rooted at the spot. This was not the first time this had happened—some goddess or some ghost would often possess her like this, and she would shout and scream. Her hair was unkempt, haywire. She was burning. Drenched in sweat. Children and women had gathered to watch the dreadful spectacle—there was a huge crowd in front of Bhootnak's house. It seemed impossible to go near or get Parbati under control. She was shuddering.

'Hey, someone should move a lemon in a circular motion before her!'

'Hold her by the waist!'

'Women, come ahead to help!'

'Try to control her, Bhimnak!'

'Run away, children! Don't crowd here!'

Parbati was now slamming her feet against the ground. Bhimnak crept up from behind and grabbed her by the waist. She wriggled to get free. Bhimnak strengthened his grip. Women stood with folded hands. Kera came ahead. She tried to arrange Parbati's sari. The delirious Parbati was violently shaking her head.

Ambarnak despaired. Bhootnak was away at work. Someone in the crowd shouted, 'Lay her at Mari Ma's feet. That will calm her down.' Parbati neighed like a horse. Bhimnak pushed her ahead. Parbati's limp body was glued to Bhimnak's. The tender touch of her body aroused him. As they moved ahead, the crowd followed them. Parbati's feet hardly touched the ground. Tukai whispered to Satvai, 'What do you think? Is she possessed by the deity or by the devil?' Many of those present thought that Parbati was possessed by a ghost!

When a Brahmin dies, his soul takes a new body through a new birth. He finds salvation. But a Mahar has no soul! His spirit wanders endlessly. He never finds salvation! When a Mahar dies, he becomes a ghost. He keeps thrashing about in rage. An incomplete, unsatisfied life roaming the earth even after death. Trying to fulfil incomplete desires. Taking revenge on those who had tortured him when he was alive. A ghost never rests until its demonic desires are satisfied.

Parbati had loved Parshya Mahar, but they could not marry. Parshya died by suicide. He had hanged himself, become a ghost. When the new bride Parbati was on her way to her in-laws, Parshya's ghost took control of her. The turmeric on her body caused the ghost to get a quicker grip. As they were crossing the village border, she was jolted, as if someone had crept up from behind and engulfed her in a tight embrace. Parbati came to her in-laws. She dreamt that a big fat dark man was lying over her. He held her hands and pinned her feet to the bed with his feet. His chin pressed on her chin. Parbati woke up with a shudder. She sat up. Terrified. Panic-stricken. Beside her,

Bhootnak was snoring. Parbati wondered about the dream—that huge dark body, naked! She could not even move. That leaden dream remained a burden—she could feel its weight long after it was gone.

Bhimnak laid Parbati at the feet of Mari Ma. Ambarnak rubbed some holy ash on her from the worship. She came out of the trance like one wakes up from a dream. Her senses were restored! The storm had subsided. People gazed in awe at her face. It was the countenance of a ghost.

* * *

Ambarnak was mending his axe. He occasionally checked the blade's sharpness by running his thumb across it and then began sharpening it again on the stone. The sound resonated across the courtyard. After a while, the blade glinted in the sun. A crow perched nearby seemed to have a lot to say. 'Whose arrival are you announcing?' Ambarnak wondered aloud. A black cat sat beside Ambarnak. A donkey waited at the gate. The Mahars were out for the day's work. Arjun Khatal came in unannounced. Ambarnak stood up immediately.

'Yes, master! What is it?'

'A cow has died. Dispose of it!'

'How did it die?'

'Someone may have poisoned its food!'

'Why would anyone be an enemy to a mute animal?'

'What can I do? But I won't let this go easily! I'll find out who is behind this mischief or my name isn't Arjun Khatal! Bring the Mahars! Carry the animal!'

'Yes, sir! I'll be there shortly!'

Arjun Khatal's coming was big news. The news of his cow's death became the talk of the Maharwada. 'It was a young cow! The meat will be delicious,' the Mahar women were telling each other. The death of an animal was a festival for the Mahars. Ambarnak sent for Bhootnak. He was on his way to work. Bhootnak sent for Sidnak, Bhimnak. Yesnak was headed towards the river. Sidnak whistled to signal him. Bhimnak called out. Yesnak replied with a whistle but carried on.

Ambarnak: 'Bring the sticks and rope!'

Bhimnak: 'I have a rope. I'm bringing it!'

Sidnak: 'I will bring sticks.'

Bhootnak: 'I just sharpened the knife blade.'

Ambarnak: 'Arjun Khatal is in a rage. He says someone has poisoned his cow. He will see this matter to the end!'

Bhootnak: 'Whatever happens, the Mahars will be blamed!'

Ambarnak: 'Come, bring your sticks and ropes, we must go now. Don't waste time. The cow will start stinking. It died of a bloated stomach.'

Bhootnak: 'It has been a while since the vultures came. We'll see them now.'

Ambarnak: 'We'll get the cowhide.'

The Maharwada was highly excited. Parbati brought out all her knives. As soon as Yesnak came back from the river, Ambarnak broke the news of the cow's death in one breath! 'Arjun Khatal's cow is dead. We have to get it.'

Bhimnak brought a rope. Tukai wanted the liver. She was waiting with bated breath for the dead cow. Children were playing in front of the Mari Ma temple. Ambarnak recalled Arjun Khatal's threats. He thought of his bloodshot eyes. Sidnak brought sticks. Champi was at his feet, showering him with her deepest affection.

'How shall we bring the dead cow?'

'Shall we carry it?'

'Shall we use a bullock cart?'

'Khatal is fuming. He won't give us a cart.'

'The cow is huge. Can't carry it in one go.'

'Let's go now. We'll see what can be done!'

It was as though they were going to battle. Excitement coursed through them. Vultures were perched on neem trees. They had smelled the news! Masai began to think: 'I will store some dried meat. Good that the cow died. My stock of dried meat has run out.'

Dhondamay was happy too. 'Good,' she thought. 'It has been days since I tasted meat. How I missed it!'

'Stale rotis can be fried in the cow's fat,' Kera said while washing utensils. The vultures on the neem tree screeched impatiently. Parbati had come to the Mari Ma temple. Kera joined her. They were best friends.

'The temple floor needs to be daubed! It has become all flaky now.'

'There is some cow dung lying on the way to the river.'

'I have already brought some.'

'Do you need water?'

'The dead cow will arrive soon!'

'I want the tongue. For my mother.'

'Take it! What I want is to make some dried meat.'

'I love cow meat. Not buffalo meat.'

'Sit!'

'So much work to do.'

'I have work, too! But sit with me. I don't want to be sitting here all alone.'

'Mother is sick. She has lost her appetite.'

'Sit! I'll tell you cow stories.'

'You know so many stories!'

'My grandfather used to tell us stories.'

'Okay.'

'If we don't keep retelling the stories, we forget them.'

'Tell me, then! I will listen.'

'A cow had four children. She loved them equally. One day, the cow asked her children, "How will you honour me after I die?" The three elder boys had the same answer: "We will respect you like god." The cow was happy. She asked the same question to her youngest son. He said, "I was born of your abdomen. So I will keep you in the same place." The three elder brothers became infuriated. They turned on the youngest, "You will eat the dead cow? You glutton!" That's how we are Mahars: ones who eat (*ahar*) something great (*maha*). Maha plus ahar equals Mahar.'

'You have told me this story four times already.'

Parbati was respectfully narrating the cow story, and Kera was in such haste! Parbati held her hand and said, 'Come, sit! The dead cow will arrive any moment! How will I sit alone? I feel scared of these vultures. I feel afraid even when I am in my house. Every night ghosts haunt my dreams. I have no peace of mind. I keep fasting for Mari Ma, but nothing happens to lessen my fears.' There was despair in Parbati's voice.

Helplessness and despair—it had become the lens through which the Mahars viewed life. It had become the Mahars' philosophy, their existence and their reality, their idea of life. Living under the constant threat of violence, a precarious life, they were never able to stand up to their oppressors. The upper castes kept them subdued. They forgot all self-respect. Every question had but one answer: 'They are upper caste and we are lower caste.'

'Look! The dead cow is here!' The children were jumping with joy! Bhimnak and Bhootnak were at the front, and Ambarnak and Sidnak were at the back. The front legs of the cow were tied and a stick was made to run through them—one end of the stick was shouldered by Bhimnak and the other by Bhootnak. The hind legs were also tied together in a similar way, and a stick ran through them too. One end of the stick rested on Ambarnak's shoulders, while the other end lay on Sidnak's. The four of them together were carrying the dead cow. The cow's feet rested on the Mahars' shoulders, while its back, tail and head hung close to the ground.

Yesnak was following them. The cow's eyes were wide open. Its teeth had popped out of its jaws. Flies were buzzing around its ears. Arjun Khatal's wife had worshipped the dead animal. The Khatal children had cried. Arjun Khatal's wife had given the Mahars some jowar grain. Yesnak had tied the grain in a corner of his dhoti; the jowar was visible through its thin fabric. Yesnak stumbled. Drops of blood oozed out of his toe. He put some soil on it and began to limp again.

The dead cow rocked this way and that from the movement. It was lowered on the ground for a moment's relief, as the carriers were out of breath. But they picked it up again quickly. The Mahars were heavily perspiring under its weight. But they could not afford to delay any further. The cow's tail and stomach were stained with its dung. Crows hovered over the procession. Dogs trailed behind it. The Mahars took the cow behind the Maharwada.

It was there that the dead cow was unburdened from their tired, aching shoulders. Behind the Maharwada lay the garbage dump. Heaps of rubbish. Litter. Dead animals were brought here to be skinned. Pigs roamed here. Sidnak loosened the sticks. Bhimnak removed the ropes. Bhootnak and Bhimnak were too tired to stand any longer. They squatted on the ground, trying to catch their breath. Parbati had brought the knives. Yesnak gave her the jowar. A crow perched on the cow's horn. Dogs circled the carcass. Sidnak shooed away the smaller children. They didn't like that at all, and kept coming back to the scene. The crow began to scratch the cow's eye with its beak. The cow's legs had stiffened; its belly was bloated. Flies buzzed all around. The upper-caste women who had come to defecate were in trouble—they would have to find a place farther off. They began cursing the Mahars.

The Mahars were getting ready. The cow was laid on its back. Its feet were up. Ambarnak took the knife and looked at it. Bhimnak held up the front right leg of the cow. 'Hold it up firmly,' cried Ambarnak, who sat near the cow's neck. The blade shone. The cow's neck was free. It would now be skinned—starting from its neck, down to its very tail. Bloodstains! Ambarnak now moved to the right leg. Bhimnak held it tightly. Ambarnak loosened the skin around the hoof. The skin from the hoof up to the belly was ripped off. The legs were free now. 'Pull hard!' he screamed. The cow's front right leg came apart; the flesh was visible. Bhimnak threw the leg on the ground and went to the right hind leg. Ambarnak removed the flesh. The right hind leg was skinned and freed. He skinned the jaw and neck. They dragged the cow on its back. Bhootnak loosened the skin from its belly up to the back. Sidnak and Bhootnak pulled at the skin with all their might. Half the cow lay skinned. Ambarnak grabbed the knife again. He freed the front and hind left legs, and loosened the tail skin further. The whole body was skinned.

Bhootnak ripped open the cow's belly. He removed the filth inside. Intestines. Gut. He emptied the air in the entrails. A terrible stench rose from it. Sidnak threw the intestines in the rubbish heap; the dogs made a dash for it, diving in hungrily; they began to fight and bark loudly. Crows hovered above, waiting for their turn.

Bhootnak began chopping the meat and distributing it among the Mahar women who had come to take it. The women seemed happy. Bhootnak was now tired from cutting the meat. His hands were wet and sticky with blood and flesh. Some of the blood was on his body too. Bhimnak and Sidnak folded the hide and left. The crows and dogs now made a go for what remained of the cow. The vultures joined them.

'There is no hole in the hide. And it came off quite easily too.'

'The cow was good! The meat is fresh!'

'Everyone took their share of the meat!'

Bhootnak rubbed salt on the hide. He laid it out to dry. Sidnak's father sat to tend the hide. The rest of them went to the river to wash themselves. Ambarnak, Bhootnak and Yesnak were full Padewars. Sidnak and Bhimnak were Padewars for Dhondamay, so the crop was divided among them. Half belonged to Dhondamay; the other half was divided equally between Sidnak and Bhimnak. These Mahars were responsible for looking over the Mari Ma temple and the *takya*, which lay in ruins. Tall grass grew all over the place. No one really bothered much about the Mari Ma temple either.

The Mahars washed themselves in the Falguni River. They washed their bloodstained knives. Tani was washing clothes. No one in her house ate meat. Her house was different. Though the Mahars were very tired, the excitement of eating meat kept them on their feet.

Stoves lit up in the Maharwada! The meat was being cooked. Its delicious aroma filled the air. Women were engrossed in the cooking. Ropes were strung inside the houses—some of the meat was going to be dried. Soon, chunks of meat hung from those ropes. Flies swarmed around them. Every house reeked of cooked and raw meat.

Some were waiting for the meat to be cooked, while others were already chewing on half-cooked pieces, and some others were trying to clean their teeth, as they had pieces of meat stuck in there.

It was dark outside. Insects and flies from the garbage pile now thronged inside the huts. Outside, insects like grasshoppers and crickets made their various noises. After a heavy meal, the Mahars lay down on their beds. Each house was now filled with meat that had been laid out to be dried, and so the people had to find themselves some corner to lie in or to stretch. Cats and dogs were now sluggish too, after a filling dinner.

The moon came up in the night sky, its light filling the air. Ambarnak and his wife, Masai, lay near the door of their hut. They felt uneasy and were unable to sleep. Ambarnak could not forget Arjun Khatal's threats.

'Parbati keeps repeating the same story.'

'She is mad.'

'Why? She seems fine.'

'The ghost got into her.'

'I am afraid of ghosts too! Sometimes, when I walk down the street, I feel scared that a ghost will stop me there.'

'There were more ghosts in here earlier. Not so many these days.'

'But why do I see all those things that are used for scaring the ghosts away, lying just behind our house?'

'Ghosts don't appear to all and sundry. They appear only to those who are meant to see them.'

'I am scared!'

'Keep a shoe or sickle close to your head. Ghosts won't come near.'

Masai and Ambarnak kept chatting as they lay. Masai was drowsy; she answered languorously with, 'Yes-yes.' Soon she began to snore. A mouse jumped on Ambarnak. Dogs began to bark. Ambarnak paid heed. Someone was approaching. The sound came closer. Ambarnak became alert.

Soon Arjun Khatal and Sidram Kore were at the door. They held lathis in their hands. Sidram Kore held a lamp. Ambarnak stood up.

'Come to the chawadi! Patil has called for you.' Patil was the head of the village. Arjun Khatal's voice was menacing. 'Come with the Mahars!' he reiterated.

'Yes, I'm coming!' This was all Ambarnak managed to utter, shocked and dazed and half asleep.

'Come fast. Patil is waiting!' Sidram Kore yelled threateningly.

Ambarnak was a mute listener. The two of them left. Ambarnak stared at their retreating figures for as long as the lamp was visible. He was terrified. The moon hid behind the clouds. But Ambarnak had nowhere to hide. He woke Masai, asked her to go sleep inside and left promptly.

Then, Ambarnak woke Yesnak, Bhootnak, Sidnak and Bhimnak. Parbati was scared. They assembled at the Mari Ma temple. Vultures called from the neem trees. The dog that was sleeping in the temple ran off. Every face wore a look of exhaustion. The night had decayed. Ambarnak was the only one speaking. 'Don't confess! Even if they threaten with knives on our necks, don't take names. They might beat us up to get the names. Don't be scared. Mari Ma is with us. Later, we will give her an offering.' Ambarnak folded his hands to Mari Ma in utmost devotion. The others followed suit. The donkeys began to bray. All were terrified. Darkness spread. The moon had set. They left for the chawadi. Ambarnak was at the front. Their legs felt lifeless. Their minds were frozen like ice, like a sacrificial goat lying wounded in front of the deity. Yet somehow they dragged themselves along.

A smoky, misty footpath, barely visible under the glittering stars. Shadows of the walls of old houses on the footpath. Slithering feet of the Mahars in the silent night. Street dogs howling—breaking the silence because they had caught scent of the Mahars. The sound of an old man coughing in one of the houses. An infant bawling in its mother's lap. Crickets and grasshoppers chirping. The heavy minds of the Mahars. The dismal light in the chawadi. Darkness had woken up from its sleep. Fear engulfed the Mahars. The chawadi appeared like death itself, waiting with its jaws open.

The Mahars greeted the village folk. They stood with folded hands, bowed heads. Devrao Patil stood like Yamraj himself—his arms folded across his chest. Menacing *mashals* burnt bright.

Navnath Jakikore and Babruvan Kharate tied the Mahars' hands. Untouchability did not seem to be an issue for them now. The Mahars were very afraid. Who knew what would happen next? Bhootnak was trembling in fear. Ambarnak, saying 'We have done no wrong', begged forgiveness. Arjun Khatal cudgelled Ambarnak. He screamed, expressing extreme anger. Navnath Jakikore hit Bhootnak on his back and shoulders. Bhootnak fell to the ground. Sidram Kore held Bhootnak's feet, and Navnath Jakikore struck his legs till the lathi broke. Arjun Khatal then turned to Sidnak and beat him up mercilessly. Babruvan Kharate turned to Bhimnak to beat him up. They all spat on the Mahars' faces. The Mahars were shrieking in pain and humiliation. Sidram Kore pushed Yesnak to the ground and urinated on him.

A crowd gathered in front of the chawadi. The cries of the Mahars entertained the crowd. They laughed. Scoffed. Mocked.

Bhootnak's skull cracked. Blood oozed from it. Sidnak's eyes were bruised. Blood dripped from Bhimnak's nose. The Mahars' shrieks had shaken the chawadi. Their distressing cries woke the Muslims sleeping in the nearby mosque.

'You have slaughtered a cow!' Devrao Patil's voice thundered.

Ambarnak managed to gather some courage and say, 'What is our fault? We merely carried away the dead cow.'

'The cow died because you poisoned its food!' screamed Arjun Khatal.

'The cow is a holy animal. Thirty-three crore gods reside in its body. How dare you kill the holy mother? How dare you eat its flesh? You hurt the sentiments of all Hindus. Aren't you afraid of anyone, anything? You are taking undue advantage of our silence . . . ? You have become too smug, too complacent!' Devrao Patil screamed loudly, and the crowd was excited. 'Beat them! Beat them black and blue! Show them their place! Beat the smugness out of them!' The crowd demanded for more.

The Muslim people in the nearby mosque could not understand what was happening. But sensing something was wrong, they ran to the chawadi. 'Something is amiss. Come and see quickly.' Their leader was Akbar Ali. The plight of the Mahars made Patil feel proud of himself. Devrao Patil had thought that he could keep the village in his control by beating up the Mahars. Beating up the Mahars would make him a hero in front of the villagers and prove how great he was. By beating up the Mahars he was looking after the collective security of the village.

The Muslims reached the chawadi armed with lathis. They held considerable influence over the village. The ruler, after all, was the nizam. Seeing the Muslims, Devrao Patil slipped away. Sidram Kore also slipped away with him. The whole issue of eating cow meat and killing cows would incense the Muslims. Devrao Patil knew this and had thus departed stealthily. Babruvan Kharate and Arjun Khatal untied the hands and feet of the Mahars. Navnath Jakikore closed the chawadi doors. The crowd dispersed. Mashals were extinguished.

'What happened? Why did they beat you up?'

'Cow slaughter.'

'But wasn't the cow already dead?'

'They thought we poisoned it.'

'They beat you so much!'

'Because we ate the beef.'

Akbar Ali was making inquiries. The Muslims were enraged. 'Who do they think they are to decide what you will eat or what you won't eat? If the cow is their mother, why can't they dispose of it themselves after it dies? Why do they ask the Mahars? The cow is an animal. How can an animal be a human's mother? If thirty-three crore gods reside in the cow's belly, why don't those gods protest when the cow is being killed?' Akbar Ali was filled with rage. The Mahars left the village, and soon their shadows dimmed in the night. It was as though darkness itself was limping on.

Where the untouchables must live, what they must eat, what they must wear, in what kind of houses they must live, what ornaments they must wear, what language they must speak, what language they must hear, what names they should call themselves by, how they should be punished, everything is well documented in the Hindu scriptures. Untouchability is the worst part of the Hindu practice. The untouchables will have the courage to reject these rules only when they understand the scriptures. But they have been kept away from the knowledge they need. The Hindus don't and won't let them get the wisdom they need.

The untouchables can only earn their freedom by rejecting the Hindu scriptures.

The Mahars reached the Maharwada somehow. Limping. Stumbling. The Maharwada was fully awake at midnight. There was so much anger there that the darkness had begun to crumble.

* * *

Today is an auspicious day. A day of worship and celebration. A ritual is to be performed for Mari Ma.

The responsibility lay on Ambarnak. It was due to Mari Ma's wrath that the Mahars had been beaten up that day. The whole Maharwada was of the same opinion. Still, the Mahars were happy because of the celebratory feast. The daughters of the Mahars who had been married off had returned to their parents from their in-laws' houses. Khoklai and her husband, Ramnak, and Ramnak's elder brother, Dhondnak, had come from the town of Jhol. Bhimnak's house was also full of guests. Every house had guests. Everyone had decked up their houses. Clothes and bedding lay scattered everywhere.

The Mari Ma temple had been daubed already. The idol's eyes were newly made. Her whole body was smeared with blood-red sindoor. A buffalo had been brought from Pitapur to be offered as a sacrifice. Dhondnak had brought a cook from Jhol. The *potraj*, devotees of Mari Ma, had gathered from neighbouring villages. The potraj entertain people with their song-and-dance performances—they also whip themselves while performing. Kera, Masai, Parbati, Tukai, Satvai—they had ground some jowar, about half a sack. The music cast a peaceful aura across the village. It had been several years since such a grand festival had been celebrated in the Maharwada, and thus all the Mahars glowed with excitement.

Drums were being beaten before Mari Ma. The potraj began dancing. Six potraj were doing the aarti. The merry sound of the *ghungroo* tied to their waists and feet, the crackling sound of the whip on their bodies, the sound of the daflis, the chorus of the aarti singers and the intermittent call to Mari Ma—'Come, oh, Mother . . . oh, Mother, come'—and the noise of the shouting children. The Maharwada was in the grip of festive fever. The aggressive calls of the potraj to Mari Ma were not in vain—she was waking up from her slumber, she was coming alive!

The very appearance of the potraj was menacing—blood-red sindoor on their foreheads, dishevelled hair, fabrics of various colours dangling from their waists, dark, half-naked bodies drenched in sweat, bloodshot eyes, screams. Mari Ma was but a jet-black rock! On this rock was layered sindoor, year after year. And when a wish, *navas*, came true, silver eyes were cast on it. This was a faceless goddess—the gods and goddesses of the untouchables are faceless! Meat-eaters! They do not rest at peace until animal sacrifices are made. The gods of the untouchables force them to beg. Possess their bodies. Virgin untouchable girls have to be sacrificed to please these gods and goddesses. Young boys are sacrificed, too! In the name of 'Vaghya', 'Potraj', 'Jogtya'. Upper-caste girls or women never become 'Murli', 'Jogteen', 'Aaradhi', 'Devadasi'. Never. Nor does any goddess ever possess them. The gods and goddesses of the upper castes have beautiful, attractive faces. They are vegetarian. Mari Ma's temple was nothing but a garbage dump of the fate of the entire Mahar community.

The sound of the dafli had the Maharwada in its grips. Parbati ran out of her house screaming; reaching the temple, she began dancing. The potraj danced with her. She was in a trance again. Mari Ma had possessed her. Bhootnak came running and, grabbing her by the waist, tried to control her movements. She thrashed her legs violently. The Mahars gathered in front of the temple. Tuknak was hurling haldi on the potraj. The sound of the daflis rose further. The potraj were dancing tirelessly. All eyes overflowed with emotions.

Ambarnak and Dhondnak reached the temple with the buffalo. It was then bathed. A garland of mango leaves was put around its neck, and its forehead was smeared with haldi–kumkum. The loud noise of the daflis scared the poor animal. Ambarnak and Dhondnak held it tightly. Bhimnak held the dagger, Sidnak had the rope in place. Sidnak tied the buffalo's legs with the rope. Then Sidnak and Yesnak pulled the rope. The buffalo fell to the ground. Ambarnak tightened the bridle. Dhondnak raised its head and gave it a sip of water. Bhimnak handed the dagger to Dhondnak. The women and children were asked to pull back. The time had come for the sacrifice.

Sidnak and Yesnak tightly held the bridle. The buffalo had started bellowing now. Bhimnak and Ambarnak held its neck tightly. Dhondnak sat near its neck, dagger in hand. Some water was smeared on the animal's neck. The buffalo was squirming in fear, its eyes half open. Dhondnak placed the dagger on the buffalo's throat. 'Don't let it move!' screamed Dhondnak and plunged the dagger into its throat. Fountains of blood erupted. The buffalo's legs slammed. Ears shivered. The loud sound of the daflis drowned out the painful screams of the dying animal. No one heard its sorrowful shrieks. Parbati was still in a trance, dancing in a frenzy. Her head swayed hysterically. Her body was drenched in sweat.

The buffalo's neck had been severed. It looked like a ripe watermelon. Dazzling red. Blood was all around, coagulating. Dhondnak dipped his hands in the blood. He then made an impression of his bloodied hands on the door of the temple. The impression looked sinister. The potraj were still dancing in full frenzy. A dancing potraj came near the dead buffalo and drank its blood. His mouth was stained with blood now. He resumed his dancing. His face looked portentous, ominous. Ambarnak gathered some of the blood and sprinkled it on Mari Ma. Sidnak had untied the legs of the dead animal. Crows cawed on the temple rooftop.

The sound of the daflis died down. The dance of the potraj stopped. Parbati calmed too. The crowd near the temple dispersed. The Mahars were headed to their homes. Rotis were being made in the houses. Ambarnak and Bhootnak began to clean the buffalo. Dhondnak was busy making preparations for the cooking. Wood was brought. A large handi was brought too. The fire was burning, ready to cook the meat. Spices were ground. The cooks were waiting for the meat. Everything was ready. Kera and Kachra brought water from the river and filled the reserves. A long queue had formed outside the temple. Mahars had gathered for a darshan of Mari Ma. The potraj went behind the temple to get dressed properly. Devotion and piety bubbled in all who were present there.

'Forgive us, O Mari Ma
Forgive us our sins
We are your children
Accept our prayers
Let the animals in the village die!
Bless us so we may eat meat and mutton!
Let the people in the village die
So people will need wood for the funeral pyres!
And our children won't go hungry!
Let our stoves remain burning
Let those who torture us be destroyed
Hail Mari Ma! May your glory prevail!'

Men sat down for the feast. Each had brought his own plate. Bhimnak and Sidnak distributed rotis. Ambarnak and Bhootnak served the meat and its broth. Fingers glistened in the rich fat and oil-laden broth. Women were impatiently waiting their turn to feast.

The men finished eating.

The women finished eating.

The cook and servers had eaten too.

The remaining food was now shared among the Mahar houses.

Mari Ma was appeased!

The day had come to an end, the sun had set. Dogs ate scraps from the ground. Darkness fell. The Maharwada was totally calm now. Ambarnak, Dhondnak, Bhimnak and Sidnak sat in front of the temple, chatting away. About the feast, the cooking. And about Mahars. The idle talk was like a balm—it eased their exhaustion. But all of a sudden, Dhondnak changed the topic.

'I must tell you before I forget. The East India Company is looking for people who can fire cannons. A Mahar from Rahimatpur has joined the army of the Company. The Company officers think that the Mahars can operate the cannon. Raynak Mahar's cannon kept firing even after he had been beheaded. This is why the British are looking for Mahars to be recruited in their army. We should join,' Dhondanak went on excitedly.

'Mahars are being taken into the army?' Ambarnak exclaimed.

'Yes! Yes!' said Dhondnak.

'They become polluted by our very shadows. How would they give us cannons?' Bhimnak questioned.

'Only Hindus think like that! Not the British! Mark my words! The British will hand us Mahars the cannons and ask us to shoot the Hindus. That is how they will reign over the Hindus,' Dhondanak went on wisely.

'Mahars eat the leftovers of the Hindus. How will they shoot them?' Sidnak was cynical.

'What Hindu! What British! Everyone will go with whoever gives two rotis!' Dhondnak said.

'Foreigners must rule!' Bhimnak was inspired to say.

'To take away the broom and hand a cannon to the Mahars is nothing short of a miracle. The upper castes have tortured us enough. If the untouchables get weapons, revenge will surely be taken!' Ambarnak's tone was acrimonious.

'Let's take the path near the temple. It's quite late,' suggested Dhondnak.

'Yes, Betal will come to meet Mari Ma at night! Ghosts will dance in front of the temple. Lick the blood off the ground. It is not safe to stay here any longer. Let's go!' said Ambarnak.

'Yes, let's go,' echoed Dhondnak.

They all got up swiftly. Dhondnak went to sleep in Ambarnak's house. They had planned to sleep in the yard. In the morning, Dhondnak was supposed to carry the hide of the buffalo with him. The Dhor would pay him for it. Masai had madc beds for both of them in the yard. They lay down. While closing the door, Masai said, 'I have heated the mutton. It is in the box. Take it with you when you go.'

Dhondnak promptly replied, 'No, no. I can't take it. My wife has strictly forbidden me to take home the mutton. She is very afraid of the ghosts in the field.' While Dhondnak was busy explaining why he couldn't take the mutton home, Masai had already closed the door. She had even fallen asleep. Only the rats were awake now.

The night sky was filled with stars, glittering brightly. The moon had risen too. A pleasantly cool breeze blew. White clouds were racing in the sky. One looked like a dog, another like a donkey. A line of clouds looked like piglets following their mother. Champi the dog was munching a bone. Ambarnak's and Dhondnak's snores seemed to be competing against one another.

Parbati was narrating the story of Betal. Bhootnak was sleepy; he tried to fill in a 'yes' here and there, but he soon began to snore. Parbati's ears started ringing with the sound of the bells of the Mari Ma temple. Parbati tried to wake Bhootnak up. 'I had told you not to sleep. Keep saying yes!' Bhootnak muttered 'yes' in his sleep. Silence reigned all around. Pin-drop silence.

* * *

Bhootnak was walking, his axe on his shoulder. Messages had repeatedly come from Devrao Patil's mansion—to cut some wood. Bhootnak reached the chawadi. A *behrupiya* was performing. Drums were being beaten. People had gathered to see the show. Bhootnak changed his path. He walked along the brink of the street, so that his shadow didn't fall on anyone. While crossing one of the streets he saw Babruvan Kharate. He sat on the ground. His shadow should not fall on Babruvan. Bhootnak would have to do this often. He would have to get out of the way whenever anyone came near him. Babruvan spoke to him. 'When are you coming to our house? Our wood is nearly over.'

'As soon as I am done with Patil's work.'

'How many days will it take?'

'Three days.'

'Pick up the stale rotis from our house when you return.'

'Yes, master.'

Bhootnak stood up only when Babruvan Kharate had passed. Bhootnak must have walked only a couple of steps when Sidram Kore's wife was seen approaching with her waterpot. She was out to fetch water. Bhootnak sat promptly. 'Evil omen! Crossed my way! Ominous!' she muttered in disgust as she went past him. She was evidently very angry.

The sound of the behrupiya's song came floating in the wind. Children were running towards it.

Bhootnak walked cautiously towards Devrao Patil's mansion. He was pondering over Babruvan's words. He thought, 'We do so much for the village and its people.' This thought filled him with pride. His physique was like an old fort! What is the job of a Mahar? Keep waiting for food for all the twelve months. And what are the wages for his work? Stale food! If he falls sick he must send a replacement. The village's work mustn't stop for a Mahar. This was the way things worked.

Bhootnak reached the threshold of Devrao Patil's mansion. 'Mahar is here!' he shouted. Sidram Kore came out of the Patil mansion. He showed Bhootnak some wood that needed to be chopped. Bhootnak looked at it. Sidram Kore was the Patils' servant. Bhootnak placed his axe between his legs for a moment, spat on his hands and held the axe again. He struck the wood with his axe. The strike ignited a spark. The wood was hard. He kept hitting it. The sun shone hard. The wood was hard. Bhootnak kept hitting the hard wood with his axe in the hard sunlight.

The behrupiyas had now reached the Patil mansion. A crowd accompanied them. Drums were beating. A behrupiya dressed as Hanuman was jumping around with a mace on his shoulder. He was making strange noises. The crowd was excited to see his antics. More people gathered. Patil's wife came out now. She looked at the crowd while Bhootnak looked at her. Her beauty made him restless.

Since the behrupiya's show had started, Sidram Kore asked Bhootnak to stop his work. 'Wait a while. A splinter may fly off and hurt someone!' Sidram began to watch the show. Bhootnak kept his axe down and sat with his back to the wall. Patil's wife was enjoying the spectacle. Looking at her, Bhootnak thought, 'She has never stepped out in the sun. That is why she is so fair.' Bhootnak cherished her beauty. He remembered Amritnak. He wiped his sweat and was lost in thought. 'Patil's wife should get lost someday and run into me in the fields.' He remembered the story narrated by his wife, Parbati. The story that Parbati's grandfather had told her. The story that Parbati had then told Bhootnak. He recalled the story heard by his wife . . .

Amritnak Mahar worked for Sultan Muhammad Shah in the Bahmani kingdom. He was in charge of the royal stables. He was responsible for looking after the royal horses. He would clean, bathe and feed them. He particularly loved the white and the red horses of the sultan. Those horses knew his touch. The red horse was a male, the white a female. They were in love. Amritnak knew both well!

The sultan had sent his wazir, Mahmud Gwan, on a campaign of the Konkan, and the wazir had been successful on that campaign. He had looted mounds of treasure. On returning, he presented the sultan with a sizeable reward. The king of Sangameshwar wanted to keep amicable relations with the sultan. He had sent his daughter Keertimati as a gift for him. The sultan was happy. He made Keertimati his darling wife. Her beauty mesmerized him. He loved her intensely. Soon, Keertimati was pregnant. The sultan was overjoyed. He wanted to please her and arranged a tour of the forest.

The sultan set up his den in the forest. Hunting, drinking, listening to music—the days passed by in great merriment. The sultan was very happy with Keertimati. One night, dacoits raided the sultan's den. The sultan was attacked. There was huge commotion. The dacoits escaped in the darkness. Rani Keertimati was missing. The soldiers searched everywhere, but the rani and her white horse were nowhere to be found. The sultan was anxious. The news spread. The common people were anxious too. Every effort was made to look for Rani Keertimati.

The sultan made an announcement: 'Anyone who can find the rani within fifteen days will get any reward he wants.' Everyone tried their luck. Anxious sultan! Anxious people! It was a matter of his honour. The sultan summoned his durbar. He challenged his courtiers to find the lost rani, but no one came forward. None had the courage. Amritnak Mahar asked permission to come to the durbar. The sultan was helpless. He wanted his rani back at any cost. He granted permission to the Mahar to attend the durbar. Amritnak Mahar was ready to take on the challenge. Everyone was surprised. Some were cynical. But the sultan agreed. Amritnak Mahar was given permission to find the rani.

Amritnak took the royal red horse on his search for the rani. He was sure that once he rode the red horse, he would reach the white one on which the rani had been taken. Riding the red horse, Amritnak went looking for the rani. The red horse galloped in the direction of the white horse. Amritnak let the horse gallop on. The horse stopped when it reached a certain spot and started neighing. Shortly, Amritnak saw the white horse and Rani Keertimati behind it. Amritnak felt as if he had touched the very skies. He bowed to the rani.

Rani Keertimati narrated her story. She had escaped so that the enemy would not be able to get her or her unborn baby, the royal heir. But she had lost her way in the jungle. She had since been wandering in the jungle.

Amritnak and Rani Keertimati now left for Bidar. On reaching the palace, Amritnak handed the rani over to the sultan. Everyone was happy that the rani was safe and sound. People celebrated her return.

Some were jealous that Amritnak would now be rewarded. They started gossiping. Some poisoned the ears of the sultan. 'People are doubting the Mahar. He may have polluted the rani, taken advantage of her in the forest when no one else was around. Inquiries must be made.' The sultan was sad. He wanted to dispel all doubts in his people and summoned the durbar. Amritnak Mahar was also called to attend, as was Rani Keertimati. People became increasingly restless.

Amritnak stood with folded hands. He thought he would be rewarded, but the sultan accused him in front of the entire court. The rani began to cry. It was as though the ground beneath her feet had disappeared. The court was silent. The accusation had no impact on Amritnak. He stood still. People awaited the sultan's judgement. The rani's modesty had been questioned. Blasted. The sultan wanted to hear Amritnak's defense. Amritnak spoke calmly and courageously. 'Oh, master! Your command is supreme. But I have done no evil. So I am not sad or upset. This gossip is the work of people with dirty minds. I pity them. The begum's honour is untouched, and I have proof of it. I shall present it to you right away.' The sultan was happy to hear this. The courtiers began whispering. The sultan commanded all to be quiet and asked for the evidence to be presented. The rani was scared.

Amritnak stood calmly. He was unperturbed. 'Oh, master! Before going on the mission to search for the begum, I had given you a small silver box. I want that box now. That is my evidence.' People began whispering again. The sultan was enraged. He commanded silence. 'You have accused our rani, and now, when the evidence is to be presented, you dare make a commotion! Don't you understand the gravity of the situation?' The sultan's voice was like a canon going off. All fell silent. The sultan ordered for the silver box to be brought.

Amritnak was happy. The rani stood fearful. The sultan, anxious.

Servants brought the silver box. The sultan asked, 'Isn't this the silver box you gave me? Do you want it now?' Amritnak smiled. He said, 'Master, I do not want it. You may open and see what's inside. Only then will you trust me.' The sultan promptly opened the box. He was shocked. He could not believe his eyes. Amritnak had cut off his penis and put it in the box.

The sultan asked Amritnak to come near. He stroked his back and thanked him heartily. The courtiers were stunned.

'Amritnak, ask for your reward. What do you want?' The sultan was emotional.

The rani's eyes were overflowing with tears. Amritnak said, 'Oh, master, I want nothing for myself. We are untouchables by caste. The Hindu religion gives us no rights. All I want is a charter of fifty-two rights for my community.' The sultan immediately granted the charter.

Bhootnak sat with one knee on the ground and his elbow on the other. He had dozed off. He dreamt: Khunya Pardhi had looted Patil's mansion and run off with his beautiful wife. Bhootnak rode a horse and followed Khunya Pardhi, and finally rescued the wife. He then rode off on his horse, with Patil's wife next to him. The horse galloped in the wind.

Bhootnak was snoring now, amid the sound of drumbeats. The behrupiyas were dancing in their various costumes—Ram, Lakshman, Sita. Singing. The Hanuman jumped here and there. Women brought atta and jowar flour from their houses. Sita was collecting them. The sound of drums. Patil's wife appreciated the deftness of the Sita behrupiya. The Hanuman behrupiya was busy performing silly antics in front of Bhootnak, who continued to snore.

* * *

Evening. Darkness began to descend. The women of the Padewar Mahars began to enter the village to beg for food. Masai, Satvai—they had a stick-with-bells and a basket in their hands. Masai walked on one street, Satvai on another. They had divided the village in half between themselves. They would stand before each threshold and rattle their stick-with-bells. 'Bring the Padewar roti, mother.' Wait! Watch the dogs! Move to the next door after collecting the roti! Thus the Padewars would patrol the village, and ask for stale rotis and leftovers in return.

The Mahars and their dogs were very watchful. They would not let a fly pass into the village. After the night's meal, the Mahars would take a short nap. Then they would start patrolling the village again, armed with mashals and their stick-with-bells. Ambarnak on one street, Bhootnak on another. They would meet at the chawadi. They were wonderful watchmen. Their calls would set anyone's chest thumping—it was like lightning during heavy rain. It was as though the Padewar Mahars were demons. Their voices sounded inhuman. The pigeons would fly away in fear hearing Ambarnak's thunderous voice, and Bhootnak's voice sent ripples in the water of the zamindar's well. His voice was bestial—it was like a sound emanating from a prehistoric cave. The villagers knew these voices well. Helpless during the day, the Mahar looked menacing at night. No one dared to look at them then.

Ambarnak was passing by the lane where the shepherd lived. The sleeping dogs had woken up and started barking. Teli's buffalo was chewing the cud. The sound of her grinding teeth was audible. A cat leapt out of the tailor's window. Ambarnak was surprised by its suddenness and took a few steps back. Frogs leapt in the Kasar lane. Bhootnak called out. His voice was like the neighing of a young horse. It was a strange shriek, like bubbles in water. Ambarnak had worked hard on his voice. With all the practice he'd had, his call sounded tense. There was terror in it. And a note of warning as well. It was a call that would make birds ruffle their feathers and fly away. Mysterious in the dark night.

Ambarnak and Bhootnak came near the chawadi. They turned towards the zamindar's well. Bhootnak could hear the sound of anklets. He felt goosebumps crawl over his body. So many had died by suicide here in this well. Near the well was a banyan tree. Ever so often a corpse would hang from it. People said that the well was a den for ghosts. Ambarnak and Bhootnak had never dealt with ghosts before, but the sound of the anklets so late at night scared them. Ambarnak made a loud noise, so loud that it scared even Bhootnak. A figure began to run. Weeping, shuddering, she ran towards the well. Bhootnak deftly caught hold of her. She tried to wriggle free, but Bhootnak held her tightly. It was Meenakshi. Ambarnak came running towards them. He wanted to help. They both held her tightly and took her to the banyan tree. She was very scared.

Meenakshi was Babruvan Kharate's daughter. Her voice was quivering. She wanted to jump into the well because Akbar Ali's son Haider had stopped her on the way when she was out to fetch water. This had become a matter of gossip in the village. Afraid of the slander and the infamy, she wanted to end her life. If not for these Padewar Mahars, who had stopped her, she would have ended her life.

'Leave me. Don't touch me.'

'We will leave you at your house.'

'They will beat me up if they come to know.'

'We will leave you near your house. We won't tell anyone.'

'Let go of my hand. You are untouchables.'

Babruvan Kharate's daughter walked ahead and the two Mahars followed her. Quietly. They stopped at a crossroads. She went towards her house and entered it. She did not turn back. Ambarnak burst out in laughter. His laughter awoke Arjun Khatal's wife. She began to listen keenly to the sound of the laughter. Why would a Mahar be laughing near our house? Bhootnak joined in the laughter. They had touched Meenakshi. Held her. She was polluted now. And she went into her house. Babruvan Kharate's house was polluted now. They felt a demonic pleasure at the thought. Arjun Khatal's wife was scared. Will the Mahars break into her house? She tightened her body. Someone had once told her a story: 'A woman became pregnant after she heard the Mahars' laughter. She aborted the foetus. The midwife rubbed oil on the womb, and the womb opened. The foetus fell out. It was a tortoise. It walked away and sat on the threshold.' Arjun Khatal's wife was trembling with fear. She thought, 'If I give birth to a tortoise, I will leave it in the zamindar's well.' She then fell into a deep sleep.

Ambarnak was sleeping next to his wife. Snoring. He shrieked in his sleep. Masai woke up. She shook her husband awake. He was still half asleep, muttering, 'Where is the anklet woman?' Masai was intrigued! 'What drama is this? Which ghost of a woman are you talking about in the dead of night?' Ambarnak turned on his side and began snoring again. But Masai's sleep was gone for good.

Bhootnak had not slept yet. Parbati had abdominal cramps. Her menses were sporadic. It had come after four months this time, causing a lot of pain. The late menses would always be painful—her head, waist, her whole body ached. There would be cramps in her legs and feet. She would have a fever.

Bhootnak lay beside her. He could not sleep. Meenakshi's touch was fresh on his body, and the sound of her anklets still rang in his ears. He narrated everything to Parbati truthfully. She heard everything but could not come up with a response. Sometimes Parbati narrated stories, sometimes Bhootnak. They were companions. Comrades. Not having any kids brought them very close to each other. Parbati said, 'Yes, go on, I'm listening. But I won't be able to respond.'

Bhootnak told her the story of Vithya Mahar. He had narrated this story to Parbati many times before. Bhootnak had heard this story from his grandfather.

'There was a drought in Mangalveda town. The Bahmanis were the rulers at the time. Paatshah used to look after the work. Damaji Pant was the registrar. People were dying due to the drought and famine. Birds and animals were dying too—there was neither food nor water. Crime increased. Robbery was common. Food grains were being looted. The Paatshah was scared. Worried and extremely perturbed, he pleaded to the sultan for help, but there was no response. The farmers were unable to pay taxes. Prices skyrocketed. Crop yields were uncertain.

'Vithya dacoit was infamous in Mangalveda. He was a Mahar. He had earned a lot from his dacoities. The Paatshah was also helpless in front of him. The people were harried and furious. Crimes were the order of the day. People were robbed in broad daylight. It was becoming impossible to maintain law and order. In this dire situation, Damaji Pant opened the gates of his granary. Many lives were saved. People gathered the courage to face the famine. They blessed Damaji Pant.

'The news reached the sultan of Bidar. Opening the granary to the general public would weaken the state's financial resources. The sultan sent for the Paatshah. The Paatshah reached the sultan's court. With him were Damaji Pant, the patil of Mangalveda, and other officials.

'"Who is responsible for the losses caused by opening the granary? Who will pay for the losses? The keepers of the granary are allowing it to be looted! Damaji Pant has caused great losses." The sultan was fuming. Damaji was in tears. The punishment was about to be announced. The court was all set to hear the sultan's judgement. Suddenly, Vithya Mahar asked for permission to come to the durbar. The sultan granted permission. In walked Vithya Mahar. People were scared. He began speaking, "Oh, master, I am Vithya Mahar. I am from Mangalveda. I will bear the losses. I have brought money. Take what you want. Damaji Pant has committed no crime. Don't punish him. I looted the granary. Punish me." The sultan was only interested in recovering his losses, and so he agreed to take the money from Vithya Mahar.

'The sultan was happy. He wanted to reward Vithya Mahar. Vithya Mahar pleaded, "Your majesty, all I want is the fifty-two-rights charter for our untouchable people. We Mahars have been subjected to a lot of injustice." The sultan granted Vithya Mahar's wish. Damaji Pant was not punished. Everyone sang praises of Damaji Pant, and he came to be known as Saint Damaji Pant. But no one remembered Vithya Mahar.'

Bhootnak would spice up the story in each retelling. It was as though Bhootnak was trying to shake history out of its slumber while Parbati was deep asleep. She was snoring, just as history itself was!

Bhootnak was drowsy too. At some unidentifiable moment, he dozed off.

The twittering of birds and Ambarnak's call awoke Bhootnak. He rubbed his eyes. They were heavy from sleep. He came out somehow and removed the basket at the door. Before him stood Ambarnak, Bhimnak, Sidnak. They were smiling. Bhootnak yawned. Sleep lingered heavy on his eyelids.

'I am joining the Company army,' said Sidnak.

'I came to bid you farewell,' added Bhimnak.

'I'm coming. I slept quite late last night,' Bhootnak said.

Bhimnak and Sidnak were bid farewell by Kera, Tuknak, Yesnak, Tukai, Satvai, Ambarnak, Bhootnak, Masai. They were all excited that the untouchables would now get weapons. Kondamay sat outside her hut, staring ahead. Bhimnak went away from her. The sun was rising. Bhimnak and Sidnak said goodbye, joyfully waving their hands. The rising sun was almost within reach now—the Mahars would be able to touch it very soon.

* * *

Bhimnak's departure left Kondamay distraught with grief. She stopped eating. She was completely devastated. Shattered. Day by day, she grew thin, skeletal almost. Ambarnak and Bhootnak sat close to her, trying to reason with her. Kera stood near her head. Ambarnak tried to make her drink a potion. But Kondamay did not open her eyes. Bhootnak tried to sound hopeful. 'Bhimnak will start tomorrow. He will reach in two days' time. Take a sip!' But Kondamay did not open her eyes. Her lifeforce was held within those closed eyes.

They gave up and sat in the shade of the tamarind tree. Ambarnak was seriously concerned. 'Kondamay is nearing her end. Maybe she will last another couple of days! The bird of life will take flight any moment. She is not ready to listen to anyone. How distressed must she be!'

Bhootnak spoke in a dismal voice. 'The old hag must go now. Kera has to do so much. She cleans her mother's shit. The girl has served her mother so well. In her next life, she will be born from the womb of a cow!'

New buds had filled the tamarind tree. It looked green, fresh and youthful. Biru the shepherd was walking down the road with his herd of sheep. Behind him walked his dog. A black dog, waist-high. The sheep were making a loud noise. Their bleating mixed with the dust rising from the road. A tornado swept across the road that led to the river. Tukai was out to fetch water; she stood quietly waiting for the tornado to pass.

'The tornado has crossed the burial ground on its path. It is very powerful,' said Ambarnak.

'Last night I was walking past the burial ground. Ten to fifteen ghosts were squatting there, their coffins on their heads. They were chatting away merrily. One of them called out to me. I didn't turn back!' said Bhootnak.

'You were saved. Had you turned back, the ghosts would have twisted your neck. Once a ghost had stopped me on my way. I stood chanting Mari Ma's name and kept my eyes averted. The ghost went on its way,' Ambarnak confided.

Wild pigeons were cooing. Navnath Jakikore's buffalo had run away from the village and made its way into the Maharwada. Navnath Jakikore and Babruvan Kharate were trying to catch it. But it was uncontrollable. Running helter-skelter. Ambarnak and Bhootnak stood firm in the buffalo's way. They caught hold of it. Navnath tightened the ropes! The buffalo was mad with rage and tried to escape with all its might. After a while, they somehow managed to control it and take it back with them.

'The buffalo should be fed poisoned grass. Its meat will be nice and tender!' Bhootnak said candidly. Seeing the buffalo made him yearn for its meat. An owl screeched on the neem tree nearby.

'The owl has been screeching for the last two days. It's a bad omen.'

'Kondamay will die soon. That's what it is.'

'Bhimnak won't be here to lend a shoulder to his mother's corpse.'

'Don't you know where he is?'

'Sidnak's father, too, looks tired.'

'Kondamay, Dhondamay, Tuknak . . . The older generation . . .'

Kera's loud cries could be heard from Bhimnak's house. 'Kondamay must have passed away,' said Bhootnak.

'We were with her in her last moments,' said Ambarnak sadly.

They stood up and started walking towards Bhimnak's house. Kera's cries grew louder. Stoves were extinguished. Someone had thrown water on them. There was no smoke to be seen in any of the houses. The Maharwada lay drowned in grief. The old woman had served many. Been a part of marriages. Deaths. Kera beat her breast. Her cries could be heard from afar. More and more Mahars gathered at Bhimnak's house. Women sat near the corpse.

Ambarnak sent a messenger to Jhol. Khoklayi was informed. Messages were also sent to Pitapur and Pipri villages. Everyone would not be able to make it by today. The corpse must be buried tomorrow. All relatives were informed. The villagers learnt of the news. The Mahars were getting ready for a funeral.

Bhootnak sat up all night, singing bhajans. No one had a proper sleep that night. Ambarnak went patrolling alone. Tuknak and Yesnak sat quietly in front of their huts. The night trembled with Kera's heart-wrenching cries. The silence of death hung all around. Two kittens cried helplessly. Masai drove them away. The darkness was ghostly. There was no wind, not a leaf moved. The corpse created a sinister atmosphere in the area. Everyone was waiting impatiently for dawn.

Morning came. No one went to work. Everyone spoke of Kondamay. Except for two elderly people in the Maharwada, everyone else had been born after her. The corpse had stiffened. It would soon start stinking. They thought of burying the corpse. Everyone was tired. At about noon, Khoklayi, Ramnak and Dhondnak came from Jhol. Kondamay's brother, Bhiknak, came from Pitapur. Her sister, Dagadu, from Pimpri. No one else was expected to come. Bhootnak began making arrangements for the burial with two others. Ambarnak and Dhondnak tied the corpse's neck carefully, so that the head would not shake. Women sitting near it were wailing. Flies swarmed over it. Kera tried to deflect them. Men were scattered here and there—some stood in the courtyard, some in the Mari Ma temple, some sat below the tamarind and neem trees, some were near the dargah of Peer Baba Dawal Malik. Children were not playing, and dogs were not barking. The wind was silent. The twigs were silent. This day was different from all other days.

Lahu Matang had brought a dafli, Yesnak a trumpet. The two instruments played a duet. Tensions rose. It was time to lift the corpse. The crowd thickened. Khoklayi was wailing as she recalled her memories with Kondamay. Masai consoled her. 'What use is crying? God wanted her close and called her.' But Khoklayi was inconsolable. She would break into loud lamentations every now and then: 'Why didn't god call for me? Why did god call for my mother? Where is that god? I want to see him! I'll cast thorns on his doors—calling my mother so soon. Who will I call Mother now? She was tender as a doe . . . Oh, dear Mother!'

The dafli–trumpet duet's tempo was rising. The corpse kept stiffening up. The rituals started. Money was to be looked for in the trumpet. Ambarnak whispered in Lahu Matang's ear, told him where the money was kept. The latter nodded. The trumpet man, Yesnak, was to search for the money when the dafli man signalled. Both of them played their instruments in full flow and with great energy—they were perspiring with the effort. Ambarnak threw the coin on the floor. The dafli man, Lahu Matang, knelt, and when he got up the coin stuck to his forehead—all the while he had been playing the dafli. He put the coin in his pocket.

It was now Yesnak's turn. He gestured to the east and west. Lahu Matang indicated with his beats that this was not right. Yesnak then signalled to the north. Lahu Matang played a 'yes' beat. The duet went on. Yesnak smiled. The Mari Ma temple was to the north. Tuknak was sitting there. Yesnak placed his hand in the direction of the temple. The dafli replied 'yes'. He went towards the temple. The dafli kept playing a 'yes' beat. Yesnak was standing in front of the temple. Yesnak glanced inside the temple. The dafli played a 'no'. Yesnak searched Tuknak. The dafli played a 'yes'. The money was hidden in his ear. He took the money and showed it to Lahu Matang. The dafli replied 'yes'. The game continued. The corpse was bathed. Women took turns to sprinkle water on it. The duet and the money game continued, with the money being hidden in a new place each time. Coins were also hidden in the iron container with kumkum water that was kept beside the corpse. The duo were experts in the money-finding game.

The *tati* was ready to be lifted. Kera and Khoklai performed the puja rituals. Kera was crying profusely. Dhondnak consoled her. 'Calm down. The old woman died peacefully on an auspicious day, the day of Devi Ma . . .' Ambarnak shouted, 'Lift it!' and the tati was lifted. The wailing and moaning of the women intensified. The funeral procession moved towards the burial ground. The trumpet and dafli were being played at the head of the procession. The men walked in front of the corpse, while the women walked behind it. Khoklayi flicked the flies flitting over the corpse.

Babruvan Kharate stopped the funeral procession. Arjun Khatal, Navnath Jakikore, Sidram Kore and Biru shepherd stood armed with lathis. 'The funeral procession will not go through the farmland. You people have made the farmland a burial site.' Babruvan Kharate was furious. Ambarnak came forward. He began pleading with folded hands. Arjun Khatal pushed him back with his lathi. Then Dhondnak came forward. 'We can't keep the corpse any longer. The old woman died yesterday. She will start stinking soon.' Navnath Jakikore fumed. Tuknak tried to say something. Babruvan was further incensed.

'Go away with your corpse!'

'Tell us, where should we go?'

'Take it where you want to, but we won't let you bury her in our fields.'

'You trespassed our burial ground. You captured it and cultivated it. Now where do we go?'

'I will not allow you Mahars.'

'She is Bhimnak's mother. There is no one in the house. Bhimnak has joined the army.'

'Don't try to scare us with all that. Get going from here. Get lost.'

Babruvan started hitting Dhondnak. The others, too, joined in—Arjun Khatal, Navnath Jakikore, Sidram Kore and Biru shepherd all began to beat the Mahars. The funeral procession scattered. The corpse was lying on the street now. Most of the Mahars ran away. Only Ambarnak, Bhootnak, Dhondnak and Ramnak stuck around, despite the beatings. Tuknak's head was injured, and he sat holding it. Kera and Khoklayi moaned. The dafli and trumpet had stopped. Ambarnak decided it was best to go back. The injured Mahars brought the corpse back home.

'Let's bury Mother in the house,' said Kera.

'Where are you, Bhimnak? Come with your gun! Your mother's corpse was not allowed to be buried!' screamed Khoklayi.

Dhondnak: 'Shall we bury her behind the house?'

Ambarnak: 'Let me go to the village and talk to Patil.'

Tuknak: 'Let's wait for Ambarnak.'

Ramnak: 'Let's take the corpse to the village.'

Ambarnak: 'Keep your cool!'

Ambarnak and Bhootnak went towards the village. The Mahars were worried. The corpse had begun to stink. A heavy curtain of sadness hung over the Maharwada. Everyone was perturbed. The Mahars live a life of pain and ignominy. But that is not all. Even death brings such helplessness!

Ambarnak and Bhootnak returned after a couple of hours. Akbar Ali had allowed the corpse to be buried in his field. The corpse was lifted, and the procession now went towards the field of Akbar Ali. Bhootnak had a spade. Ambarnak took a basket. The procession went silently. No music accompanied it this time. 'All need not come. Only a few will do.' Ambarnak chose who would go with them, and they soon reached Akbar Ali's field to bury the corpse. Stoves were lit and smoke rose from the huts. Champi stood in front of Bhimnak's hut. The Maharwada had coped with the loss.

* * *

Sidram Kore came to the Maharwada. Tensions rose on seeing Patil's messenger. He announced, 'Bhimnak and Sidnak have been summoned to the chawadi.' Devrao Patil began seething with anger when he heard the news about the Mahars being admitted to the Company army. He wanted to insult the two men somehow.

'The diwan of Jhol has asked that we should keep an eye on the two of you. You have to report here every day!'

The Sonai village was a part of the Jhol princely state, which in turn was a tributary to the nizam of Hyderabad. The princely state of Jhol was ruled by Bahmani, Adilshah and the nizam. Although the raja of Jhol, Jaysingh Maharaj, was a Hindu, it was the Muslims who ruled the roost in Sonai.

Devrao Patil felt threatened when he heard that two Mahars from Sonai had been recruited to the East India Company's army.

Sidnak and Bhimnak were back home on leave. Now they were aware of their rights and were filled with long-overdue self-respect. They understood that Patil was consciously trying to provoke them. The village had always undermined and insulted the Mahars. The upper castes always wanted to show the Mahars their 'rightful' place. Insulting the Mahars made the villagers feel proud of themselves. The sense of superiority ran in their veins. It was in their blood. It was what they were born with.

'We are citizens under the nizam's rule. The diwan of Jhol has called for you. But we are answerable to the nizam. I have told the diwan that they are Mahars from our village. Don't look at them in the same way that you would look at other Company soldiers. Look at them as Mahars. They dare not cross their limits.' Patil spoke smugly.

Meanwhile, Ambarnak had reached the spot. He stood with folded hands.

'What is to be told to the diwan?' Sidnak asked Patil.

A shadow of fear fell on Patil's face. 'Why do you want to create trouble? Go away quietly. Don't stay long. And keep low. Try not to be too visible. The Company government has recruited you, but that is going against Hindu scriptures. There can be a ruckus in the village. Who knows how people may think or react?'

Devrao Patil was trying his best to intimidate them.

'I came because my mother died. I took leave. Sidnak came with me. Can't we come to the village?' Bhimnak huffed.

Devrao changed his tactic. 'Lower your voice, you are in the village now. Who will carry the dead animals? What do the British know of our practices? But you know them well, don't you?' His tone was patronizing.

Bhimnak felt hurt, but he said, 'The Company army is not just filled with Mahars. There are Marathas, Muslims and Rajputs too.' He sounded dauntless.

Devrao Patil felt a silent terror. Bhimnak and Sidnak were speaking in a new voice. A new language. Their way of presenting themselves had changed too. But Devrao Patil was intent on hurting them. He taunted, 'You can change your religion if you want. We have no objection to that. But to be a Hindu you must follow the rules. If you go against the rules, you are going against the religion. I said what I had to. This has been our tradition for generations!' He sounded angry.

'We have joined the army, but we still live in the Maharwada. We haven't given up our caste. The two of us have joined the army. But the rest of us are still here. Which rules have they broken?

They are still very much in the service of the village,' Sidnak said earnestly.

Patil was in trouble now. He knew that Sidnak was speaking logically. He couldn't find a proper response. His malice poured out through his tongue. 'The Mahars have it easy. The moment they ask for a roti while patrolling they get it. Look at the farmers. They work year-round in the fields. After a lot of hard work, when the grain is in the granary, the freeloader Mahars reach for a share. Some want the grass, some want something else. The farmers perspire, and the Mahars just want their share! And the Mahars are so lazy. One has to ask so many times before any work gets done. Farmers wait patiently for the Mahars to come and do the job. What kind of work is this? Go away and take the rest with you. Go and clean the shit of the British. Wash their asses. Drink their piss. I have nothing to say. All Mahars will be polluted looking at your ways. Do you understand?' His voice carried traces of his helplessness.

Sidnak and Bhimnak left. They did not bother to ask Patil's permission to leave. Ambarnak turned to go too. But Patil stopped him. 'Wait. Let them go.' Ambarnak stood there, his head bowed.

Bhimnak's head was throbbing. 'He is the patil of the village, so we did not want to insult him.' Sidnak, too, was fuming. It enraged Bhimnak to think that he and his lot were so marginalized. His mother's corpse had been disrespected by these people. He seethed with anger, felt as if someone was grinding him in a machine. Who was to blame? Patil or the entire system they were born into? Bhimnak was raging like fire.

The Muslims had made it possible for the untouchables to change their religion. Not just the untouchables, even some upper-caste Hindus had become Muslims. The change of religion by the untouchables pricked upper-caste Hindus. If all untouchables became Muslims, whom would they rule over? Whom would they abuse? What would happen to the tradition of abuse? These thoughts were torturous. And now, the British had opened another route for the untouchables to change their religion.

Bhimnak was bewildered. It was as though the helplessness he felt, the helplessness of the untouchables, would break the dam and flow out. The dream of breaking free—perhaps that dream could be realized now, in this golden moment. Bhimnak and Sidnak walked towards the Maharwada, but they did not carry the Mahar's stick with them. They were not afraid of defiling anyone with their shadow.

Ambarnak walked towards the Maharwada too, carefully guarding his shadow.

* * *

An epidemic fell on Sonai. People were scared. The disease could not be controlled. Arjun Khatal's father died. Two of his grandsons died too. Sidram Kore's three sons died, one after the other. Krishna Javde lost his mother and younger brother. Babruvan Kharate's widowed younger sister passed away. Lahu Matang lost both his children, Navnath Jakikore his grandson. Biru shepherd's daughter, Akbar Ali's grandson, Bhimnak's sister Kera, Dhondamay—they all died. Every day there was news of someone or the other dying. Most of the dead were children. The village was terrorized.

The Maharwada was deserted. The village was facing the wrath of Mari Ma. Diarrhoea, vomiting and fever. Hands and legs went weak. The ailing would take to their bed. And then it was a matter of a week. A corpse would leave the house. The epidemic was as wrathful as the Tandava. People were scared to walk from one lane to the other. The moment people knew a house was infected, it would be isolated. No one would go near the infected house. Everyone was living some kind of a death. But the gods and goddesses were far from being content.

The sun was setting, and Arjun Khatal had come to the Maharwada. The Mahars of Pitapur had installed a chariot carrying the rock of Mari Ma on the border of his fields. He had come to ask the Mahars to carry it to the next village. 'Don't let Mari Ma stop here.' There was a strange softness in his voice. His face was lean, full of humility.

Ambarnak replied, 'Yes, yes.'

Khatal went back to the village.

It was a tradition that if an epidemic happened, the Mahars must carry the chariot to the next village. But this was a dangerous task. If the people of the other village found out, it would lead to a fight. To move the chariot would mean pushing the problems of their own village to the next. The Mahars gathered in front of the Mari Ma temple. They were unable to come to a consensus.

'We will put it there and come back before they find out. Mari Ma's chariot cannot be kept in one place. If it is removed, the scourge will end. Mari Ma's wrath will end. She would be pacified.' Ambarnak tried to convince them. But the question was: Who would shoulder the responsibility? Who would drag it to the border of the next village?

Two weeks passed. The chariot had not been carried away by the Mahars. Arjun Khatal hadn't gone to his fields those two weeks. When he went, he saw the chariot in the same place. No one had removed it. Arjun Khatal was scared. He was angry at the Mahars. He went to the Maharwada.

'You beg for food in the village. And you won't work for the village? Aren't you ashamed? Do I have to come here every day? Don't you understand? You must pull it tomorrow! Keep it in your own house if you have to.'

Ambarnak couldn't help but laugh at Arjun Khatal's misplaced anger.

Mari Ma's chariot had been left below a plant at the border of Arjun Khatal's fields. The Mahars performed a puja of the chariot.

Five stones had been kept there, all smeared with vermilion. Beside it were lemons, coconuts, green chillies and wooden dolls. The Mahars looked at the chariot. Some of them took vows, prayed. Now that the village was in dire straits, the Mahars were the saviours. Their prestige increased.

Next day Arjun Khatal came again. He stood with folded hands before Ambarnak. He was all humility. 'Ambarnak, I have helped you so much. Don't you dare forget my favours! Remove the chariot! I will give you half a sack of jowar. What else do you want? I won't say no to anything. But please help. No one wants to go to the fields. Everyone is scared of Mari Ma. I will give her a chicken. Will that do?' Arjun Khatal's voice was steeped in modesty.

Ambarnak assured him that they would remove the chariot the next day. 'Tomorrow is Devi Ma's day. Don't worry. We have seen it. Done a puja.'

Ambarnak's words brought a smile to Arjun Khatal's face. The news spread in the village.

The next day, the Mahars went out to lift the chariot of Mari Ma. Bhootnak took a basket, Ambarnak took an old blanket and the stick-with-bells. Yesnak and Tuknak joined them. They took things needed for the puja.

Ambarnak said, 'Arjun Khatal had come again! He said he would give us jowar and chicken. Let's see if he keeps his word.'

Bhootnak said with pride, 'Good that the villagers finally realized the power of Mari Ma.'

'But they will never understand the value of the Mahars. They will always treat us like dirt,' Yesnak said bitterly.

They went to Arjun Khatal's fields. Tearing off some twigs from the neem tree, they began to worship Mari Ma. The lemon, green chillies, coconut and all the other things were placed on the chariot. Bhootnak made a turban of the blanket and put it on his head. Ambarnak and Yesnak placed the basket carrying the chariot on his head. They chanted Mari Ma's name, asked for her blessings and began to lift the basket with the chariot.

The entire village was rife with speculation. When would the ominous thing be taken out of the village? People were deep in thought. So many had been victims of Mari Ma's wrath. The village was almost empty. But now that the Mahars were drawing the rock out, the villagers heaved a sigh of relief. They eagerly waited for it to be out of the village.

The Mahars were coming from the direction of Pitapur. Women closed the doors and windows of their houses, and called their children in. Everyone hid themselves from the eye of Mari Ma. The Mahars were walking on the narrow footpath between the fields.

The chariot was now brought to the Maharwada outside the village. It was kept in Mari Ma's temple. A puja was performed. Parbati poured water on the steps of the temple. Khatal had sent the chicken. The Mahars lifted the chariot. The chicken squawked.

The chariot was now out of the village. So was Mari Ma's wrath. Everyone was relieved. The Mahars left the chariot on the border of the Pimpri village. They paid their respects with folded hands and released the chicken. It was as though a cyclone had passed. The scourge had lifted.

The Mahars remembered how Kondamay's corpse had been disrespected. And during the epidemic the Mahars had to bury their dead in the garbage dump, because their burial ground had been usurped by Babruvan Kharate.

Yet the Mahars never complained. They never even looked the upper castes in the eye. They existed only in the past. They had no sense of the present or the future. They spoke of the sins of past life. They thought it was all a matter of fate. As a matter of fact, their fate was their prison. But they never realized this.

The leftovers, the meat of dead animals, the garbage heap—they found their joy in these.

Ambarnak laughed. Bhootnak was content. Yesnak and Tuknak were glad that they had served Mari Ma. The Maharwada was eagerly awaiting the return of the Mahars who had gone with the chariot. Dogs played hide and seek in front of the Mari Ma temple.

Two

The fight between Ram and Ravana was about to begin. The people of Devgadh were restless. They were eagerly waiting for evening to set in so that they could immerse themselves in devotion, as the holy text would be read out in the Vitthal temple. It was the Shravan month and the Ramayana was being read in the evenings. The month of Shravan lent a glow to the temple. Its smooth black stone walls were glistening, washed by the rain. Fresh green peepal saplings had sprouted in the cracks in the walls. The devoted were enraptured by the holy aura of the great epic. The ones present there would exaggerate the stories of the epic and narrate them to those who had not attended the evening readings. The Ramayana had taken a hold of the entire village.

The overcast sky trembled with the thunderous voice of the clouds—the sound of the bells tolling in the Vitthal temple had a similar effect on the people. Shrirang Barne was clanging the bell loudly. The readings were to start—the bell was the signal. The village surged towards the temple. It was on Mahipatirao Deshmukh's plea that Govind Bhatt had come to Devgadh to do the readings. Last year he had done this in Rahimatpur. His fame went far and wide. People spoke about him. This year, Govind Bhatt was in Devgadh, and his elder son, Moropant, was doing the reading in Rahimatpur. His younger son, Narsopant, was in Sultanpur. The two sons had learnt the Vedas in a Vedashram.

Govind Bhatt's rendering was so perfect that one would be transported to those ancient times. Today, the temple was even more crowded than on other days. Some praised Hanuman's devotion to Ram, while others spoke of Lakshmana's nobility. Everyone was immersed in the spirit of the Ramayana. People of all castes sat down to hear the story—each according to their caste, in their rightful place. The untouchables were barred from entering the temple, so they never came anywhere near it. The inner sanctum of the Vitthal temple resonated with the sound of the veena. People's faces glowed with pure devotion. Govind Bhatt's mesmerizing voice, his wisdom, the soft, molten hearts of the bhakts, water dripping from the holy pot, the holy text like a butterfly fluttering its wings, the setting sun on its way to a distant land through a landscape bathed in beauty . . . the evening descending like a meek cow's gentle mooing . . . the dim corner of the sky . . . and the sound of the arrows fired by Ram and Ravana resounding in the heart of the bhakts. In the fight between the gods and demons, the gods emerge stronger. Ravana attacks Ram with the Sarpastra, the snake weapon. Ram's retort is the Garudastra, the eagle weapon. The minds of the bhakts went numb in silence. They could clearly imagine the battlefield. Govind Bhatt's voice raged like the shrill call of a conch shell. His yogic body in a taut posture but without any restlessness in it. His face blazing like the holy *havan kund.*

Ram's Agnibaan, the arrow of fire, Ravana's Parjanyabaan, the arrow of rain, the fierce attack of the Rakshasas, the shriek of the Vanar Sena, Hanuman's aerial journey—the war is in its climactic moment. The sound of horses' hooves outside the temple. The temple is terrorized. Govind Bhatt's thunderous voice fell like an old wall in the heavy rain. The terror moved ahead. The Vanar Sena was once more displaying its bravery. The bhakts were once more immersed in the Ramayana. Govind Bhatt regained his voice. He was well versed in the Purana, as though it was dancing on the tip of his tongue! His rendering of the Ramayana touched hearts. Robust voice, clear enunciation, attractive demeanour, scholarly analysis! He was famous for bringing the ancient times alive! He seemed to have witnessed those glorious days of the past!

Govind Bhatt was describing the valiant Ravana. The war episode rolled ahead like the sound of firecrackers. Govind Bhatt was firing cannon balls. The bhakts were restless. Everyone could clearly see the end of Ravana coming. Govind Bhatt's voice now sounded like the unsheathing of a sword. And thus fell Ravana's huge, strong body to the ground, with a thud. Everyone chanted 'Jai Shri Ram'. The temple shook with the tremor of the heart-rending cry. Before anyone could sense what was happening, there were sounds of rocks falling, walls crumbling.

Mahipatirao Deshmukh's mansion had collapsed!

People screamed in shock and terror. The bhakts deserted the temple. They ran for their lives. Govind Bhatt stood rooted to the spot like a lone warrior on a battlefield. He wrapped his holy text and went towards the Brahmin alley, like a cloud of dust.

Hambirrao Deshmukh was the motbar sardar of the princely state of Rampur. His Kaala Wada was full of riches. The Wada was spread over 10 acres and made of black etched stones. Before it stood a wooden Arab horse. Astride the horse was the wooden sculpture of Khanderao, the *kuladevta*, personal deity of the Wada. The Wada was beautifully decorated with tiles. It had four courtyards, huge platforms, spacious rooms, glass windows and decorated walls.

To the right of the Kaala Wada were the women's quarters. Behind it were the dwellings of the officials. To the left were the servant quarters and next to it the stables—all this was protected by a moat and a heavy wall. And canons! The entrance had a tower. 381 stairs.

Hambirrao Deshmukh was proud of his tower. When it fell, six months after construction, he hung the masons on trees by their feet. They screamed, begged for mercy. But Hambirrao was unmoved. They hung there till death.

Hambirrao built the tower again. And it fell again. This time he sensed a bad omen. After Hambirrao Deshmukh, his adopted son, Mahipatirao, built the tower. Next to it were the entrance and the wall, which was three metres long. The entrance door was made of red stones by Rajasthani craftsmen. On either side were Mughal lattice artworks. With its own throne, its flag, its horsemen, its foot soldiers, the Kaala Wada inspired awe!

The king of Rampur, Shrimant Kalyanrao Kadambande, always sent Mahipatirao on military campaigns. Mahipatirao commanded fear in the princely state of Rampur. He had seven wives. He was so rich from the money he had looted during his campaigns that he had become uncontrollable. A summon from the Kaala Wada would send shivers down people's spines; no one had the courage to go against it. If anyone dared, they would lose their limbs. A dozen such people could be seen on crutches in Devgadh, having paid the price for their bravery.

Govind Bhatt spent a sleepless night. He was fearful. The collapse of both Ravana and the tower was a mere coincidence—and yet he was gripped by fear. He had recently done a puja for the tower, for which he had received good money. And now the tower had fallen. He was desolate. His wife, Malti, shivered in fever. Their daughters-in-law—Moropant's wife, Padma, and Narsopant's wife, Saraswati—sat beside their ailing mother-in-law the entire night. The Ramayana kept on the stool nearby seemed as though it was a part of the fallen tower's debris. The whole village was busy removing the debris. Eight people had died. The village was submerged in grief.

Mahipatirao's tower had lasted only a year and a half. But Govind Bhatt had prophesied that the tower would not fall!

Wild pigeons had made their nest in the tower. Cats roamed in it. A saffron flag was hoisted atop. Grasses grew. There were stairs leading to the top of the tower. One could get a panoramic view from up there. When the tower fell, Mahipatirao was holding the *khalita* sent by Shrimant Kadambande Maharaj. The tower crashed before the khalita could be read. Mahipatirao was baffled. The Kaala Wada was under a cloud of dust. Half the tower lay razed to the ground, the rest had cracks in it. The fallen bit looked like a crocodile with a gaping mouth.

Mahipatirao read the khalita, and it crushed him completely, left him broken, just like the tower! His official status as the sardar, the regional administrator, was lost! The princely state of Rampur was now a wingless bird. The Company government had rejected the adoption legislation and attached the princely state. The army occupied the palace. The maharaj would now get a pension. The sardars, chiefs of the regions of the princely states of Sultanpur, Rahimatpur, Devgadh, Saykheda, were now rendered powerless. The raja was a king in name only. All power was now in the hands of the Company.

Rampur was a small princely state. It was spread over an area of 498 miles and had a population of 56,523 people! Its capital, Rampur, had a population of 6366. Agent Henry Wilson of the East India Company had reached Rampur. The king was now a pensioner of the Company. The British had grabbed much of his treasury. His army was reduced in strength, and the Union Jack was hoisted on the palace. The collector of Nashik appointed George Thomas to the post of the tehsildar of Rampur. The Company would get a sum of Rs 26,563 annually as revenue tax from the princely state of Rampur. Out of this sum, the British government would get Rs 1000. So, in effect, the princely state of Rampur was now ruled by the Company.

Mahipatirao, once a powerful sardar, now felt as though he had gone blind. He had never been in combat; he never had the taste for it. All he knew was how to loot. Kidnapping attractive women, killing innocent people as though they were insects, plundering—this was all he was interested in. He had even stopped giving an account of his exploits to the king. He had become insolent.

A weak king gives rise to powerful sardars. This was how it was. Every sardar had his own army. They would make their own decisions. What had to happen to a weak king happened soon. The king was substituted. Power changed hands. Mahipatirao was helpless. He was mired in anxiety. He didn't have the strength to rebel. The thought of losing his treasury perturbed him. His rights would be severely curtailed now. He was in deep distress.

Hedonism is the soul of power; ambition is what sustains it, nurtures it; and what lies at its centre is a king or ruler. So what does it mean when the ruler changes?

Rani Pramila sat beside Mahipatirao. She remembered a moment from the past. Mahipatirao had beheaded her father and shoved a sword into her brother. She had tried to escape, but Mahipatirao held her hand. She was destitute at that moment. For her, a change of kings meant the dance of naked swords, bloodbath, screams . . . to fall victim to someone's evil eye . . . a stranger holding her hand . . . someone dragging her over streams of blood . . . feet painted with blood instead of the nuptial *mehendi* . . . and then the women's quarters . . . being disrobed . . . no garment . . . feeling someone's hand on her vagina . . . Pramila was scared! She began to hear the clashing of swords, the neighing of horses . . . She turned to look at Mahipatirao! He was sitting with the khalita! He looked so naked. Stripped. Exposed. He had been violated. Clawed. A whirlwind of thoughts stormed Pramila's mind. She had never seen a king. She had, many a time, expressed her wish to meet Shrimant Kalyanrao Kadambande, but Mahipatirao wanted to keep her safe from the eyes of the king.

She began to think about the king. Perhaps the king's feet were those of a horse and his body that of an elephant . . . Eyes like swords, tongue like a snake and his penis . . . perhaps that, too, was like a horse's . . . The king—the demonic force who ruled over thousands, made them weak, caused them suffering! Her mind was restless! She could not fathom how the British would make their way into the mansion. What would she do if someone held her hand? She felt countless funeral pyres burning all around her. She felt dizzy.

> Let the people be king!
> The king should be weak.
> The people must disrobe the king.
> The king must wash the feet of his people and drink the water.
> Power must be born of the rights of the people.
> The king's arms must be thrown in the garbage dump.
> Let people be king!

The bells of the Vitthal temple began to toll. It was the hour to read the holy text. Mahipatirao sat meekly as a cow in the Kaala Wada. Govind Bhatt took his seat. There were only a few people present for the reading. Two widows, four old men. Govind Bhatt began the recital. His voice had lost its force. The splendour was missing. People were still busy removing the debris. Three more corpses had been unearthed. The relatives of the dead had gathered at the site. The Kaala Wada was grief-stricken.

On the inside, Mahipatirao had collapsed just as much as the tower had. He was thinking, 'The palace will be but a place of tourist attraction now, an exhibit. The king's elephants will be seen at weddings . . . and the king in the theatre . . .' Meanwhile, Rani Pramila's thoughts were, 'Those in power are always guilty—that is why they speak of people's welfare . . .'

Govind Bhatt's reading ended earlier than usual.

Devgadh's Mahipatirao Deshmukh, Rahimatpur's Ibrahim Pathan, Sultanpur's Shripatrao Rathore, Saykheda's Mansingh Rao Chauhan—these were the powerful sardars. Among them, Devgadh enjoyed a special status. Devgadh, Rampur and Rahimatpur had thick bamboo forests. The mountains, valleys, deep forests and the Adivasis living in the forests—all these made the place unsafe.

The Adivasis were fierce people—they could not be controlled by anybody. Devgadh was surrounded on all sides by thick and high bamboo trees. There was a big lake near the mountain, and peacocks lived there; it came to be known as Peacock Lake. Attached to the lake was a field, and more than half of it was covered with grass. There were groundnut and jackfruit trees on the field, all planted by Hambirrao. The Tapi River ran through the mountain valleys—the river lent a charm to the landscape of Devgadh, made it delectable. Herds of deer and small animals, like rabbits, ran around merrily. Devgadh seemed to be abundantly blessed by nature. The king of Rampur came here twice a year to hunt. He would stay for a fortnight every time. A bungalow had been built on 5 acres of land for the king. There were ninety rooms in the palatial bungalow. The king was happy with Devgadh, so this region developed well.

Between Sultanpur and Rahimatpur lay the Satpuda mountain range. In the triangular area of Rahimatpur, Jhol and Saykheda were silk gardens. The British had their eyes on it. The Falguni River ran through Jhol, Sonai, Saykheda and Rampur. Jhol and Rampur were independent princely states, both ruled by Hindu kings. The kingdom of Jhol was under the nizam, while Rampur was independent. Although the Peshwa and Haider had attacked a few times, Rampur had remained independent. Natural barriers made it difficult to capture the state.

The king's Devgadh bungalow was named Parnakuti, and it was more magnificent than the Kaala Wada. The grandeur of its durbar hall dazed onlookers. People crowded to meet the king. Adivasi dances were arranged for his entertainment. Villagers would be given feasts. All expenses were borne by the Kaala Wada. The Tapi River, which rose from the mountains of Sultanpur, circled Rahimatpur, crossed the valleys and fields of Devgadh, and finally met the Falguni River near Saykheda. The water in Peacock Lake never dried, even when the rivers dried up. Every year, migratory birds would come from far-off lands. Hambirrao had planted palm and coconut trees beside the lake. Bigger animals also came here to drink water. The shadow of the sky fell on the water during the day, while the light of the stars sparkled on it during lazy nights. The breeze and the stunning views of nature . . . Devgadh became a hill station!

To the east of Devgadh was the Maharwada. It was around this Maharwada that the road to Saykheda and Jhol lay. Thick forests, roads winding through mountains and valleys, difficult turns, high peaks, deep valleys, jungles that spread over miles, animals, dacoits . . . the traveller through these parts had to encounter all of these and needed a guide. This work was done by the Mahars. Which road gets lost in the jungle, where the dacoits attack, which footpath leads where—the Mahars knew everything.

One reign passed and another came, but nothing really changed in the Purana readings of Govind Bhatt. His power was undiminished. The Yuddha Kanda battle episode was over. The Uttara Kanda, the resolution episode, had started. The bhakts had lessened in number, but the readings continued. Lakshmana had left Sita in the forest. The concluding session was on the last Monday of the Shravan month. People were talking about the change of power while Govind Bhatt was discussing Sanatan Dharma as revealed in his readings. Rani Pramila had come to do her puja. She mumbled, 'Religion loots the soul of human beings, and power loots their rights. Religion and power are evils that have eclipsed human life.'

Srirang Barne was playing the veena. The eyes of the bhakts were fixated on Rani Pramila. They were keenly, intently looking—to see whether the change in power had diminished the glamour of their queen.

'The British will surely preach their religion!' Govind Bhatt whispered in the ears of his veena player as he securely placed his holy text under his arms.

Tehsildar George Thomas had reached Devgadh. People were not allowed to congregate. There was an atmosphere of fear all around—people were scared of the British. If the Mahabali Kadambande Maharaj had been rendered helpless, what good were the common people! This thought was prominent in their minds. 'The tehsildar has come to the town,' announced Bhatnak Mahar, beating his drum. George Thomas and his officials were staying in Parnakuti, which the British had occupied. They put up a canopy for the soldiers in the field in front of the mansion. Govind Bhatt was reading his holy text.

Lord Ram ruled over Ayodhya. Govind Bhatt was praising the Ram Rajya. The bhakts were saying that Mahipatirao was to come for a puja. That was why more people had gathered today. Govind Bhatt was pouring his soul into his reading. The happiness of the people in Ram Rajya, the absence of any sin, any crime, the omnipresence of saintliness—the people heard it all. The veena played on, accompanying the reading. Suddenly, there arose a commotion. People thought it must be Mahipatirao, but it was the tehsildar, George Thomas, who had come. The sound of his boots drowned the music of the veena. Behind him were his soldiers, who carried guns on their shoulders. The locals were seeing such red faces for the first time. More than fear, it was a sense of surprise that gripped them.

None had the courage to stop George Thomas. He had come to inquire why there was such a crowd in spite of the ban on gatherings. He firmly believed that in Hindustan, people killed each other in the name of religion. George Thomas reprimanded the people for disobeying the law and threatened to take action, punish the guilty. Then he exited the temple. Govind Bhatt resumed his reading, but people were busy discussing the red-faced tehsildar. Govind Bhatt was bewildered!

'Mahipatirao is going to come tomorrow. All of you must come!' So saying, Govind Bhatt ended his reading. People went home. The story of Ram had taken a back seat; instead, people were curious about the tehsildar. The fact that he wore boots inside the temple, and no one had the courage to stop him . . . Govind

Bhatt losing his voice . . . These were intriguing occurrences for the people. There were many Hindu kings in Hindustan. Big and small. The Mughals had won over so many Hindu kings and confiscated their states. The Mughal Empire was born. The Hindustan that had been divided into small states became a united Hindustan. The British did the same. The people of Hindustan united and integrated during the British rule. The only barrier to that union was the existence of a plethora of regional languages and cultures.

A reindeer that had come to drink water in Peacock Lake fell prey to George Thomas's gunshot. The thunderous sound scared all the animals in the area. Birds fled their nests. The water in Peacock Lake itself seemed melancholy. Tears had deserted the reindeer's eyes. A cool breeze blew. The soldiers ran to the dead animal. Sidnak and Bhimnak carefully lifted the reindeer. They had the experience of lifting dead animals. George Thomas was happy. Birds resumed their chirping.

The ambience of Parnakuti, and the general attitudes, had changed by now. More people visited the place. Even the king's presence had never warranted such a crowd. The army was on strict guard. No one ventured near Peacock Lake. George Thomas was writing an inspection report on Devgadh. He was to send it to his seniors. The aroma of the reindeer's meat filled Parnakuti.

Mahipatirao had come to meet George Thomas. He wore a diamond-laden sherwani for the visit. He had brought Thomas a box full of jewels as a tribute. But Thomas made him wait. In the twenty-minute meeting, Thomas asked him a few questions: How is your relationship with the Adivasis? What is the size of the army? How many horses? How do you guard your treasury? When was Peacock Lake cleaned last? Why are the untouchables not allowed to fill water from Peacock Lake? These unexpected questions by George Thomas puzzled Mahipatirao. 'I will ask you to come again.' George Thomas had hung a sword on Mahipatirao's neck.

He had been asked to reduce his army, also to report his weapons and treasury. Mahipatirao was in trouble.

Mahipatirao left Parnakuti. At the gate he saw Sidnak and Bhimnak holding his black horse. The two were fighting with his bodyguards. Sidnak wanted the black horse. He stood there holding its reins. He pointed his gun at Mahipatirao. The servants informed the tehsildar. George Thomas reached the scene. He was upset. He shouted, 'Sidnak! Sidnak! Leave him! Nonsense!' Mahipatirao was scared.

Such a huge crowd had gathered at the Vitthal temple for the reading that there was no place to sit. Govind Bhatt was seated in his usual place. He looked at the holy text and chanted a hymn. He had just recited the first shloka when the crowd became restless. Mahipatirao was here. He paid obeisance to the idol and sat down to hear the scripture. His seat had been kept ready. No one paid attention to Govind Bhatt any more. All eyes were on Mahipatirao. Someone dared to ask, 'What is your opinion on the British rule? What should we do? Please give us some solutions.' Govind Bhatt stopped. Mahipatirao was in trouble. If there was a British spy in the crowd, he would end up in a difficult situation. He kept silent. Govind Bhatt muttered, 'Shanti, shanti,' and tried to quieten the crowd. But people refused to be silent!

Mahipatirao realized the delicacy of the situation. He began to measure his words carefully and started, 'The sun never sets on the British Empire. They have attached Rampur. We have become a part of the British Empire. We are now answerable to the East India Company rulers. Kings change, but the prevailing life of the common people doesn't change. Peacock Lake will remain where it is, just as the jackals will howl in the bamboo forests. The sun will rise. And set.' Mahipatirao was speaking guardedly. 'Don't worry. The Kaala Wada is a shield. Neither the sun nor the rain, nor even thunder, can have an effect on it.' People applauded.

Govind Bhatt resumed his reading. Many people left. Mahipatirao stayed seated. His grandeur had blurred. He had lost the appetite for power. No one felt scared to look at him now. But he still tried to maintain a show of splendour. He acted happy. People viewed his meekness with pity.

Govind Bhatt was freely praising Lord Ramchandra. He was chirping like the koel in spring, explaining every shloka. It seemed as though something was tickling him from within. 'There was a commotion in the court of Shri Ram. An ascetic had come to the court, carrying the corpse of his dead son, and stood before Ram. It felt ominous. Ramchandra was astonished. He got up from his throne and went close to the Brahmin.' Govind Bhatt's voice was raging. People were fascinated.

'The Brahmin began abusing Ram. He was infuriated. "Hey Ram, how did this sin happen in your kingdom? The places of pilgrimage are now infested with pigs. Jackals howl where one could earlier hear the songs of Ram? We are saddened," the Brahmin bemoaned. Shri Ram was saddened, too. He pacified the Brahmins. "Oh Brahmins! By your blessings I am the king of this earth, and my name is Ram."'

Govind Bhatt was displaying his wisdom. He was well-read in the Vedas. The Ramayana was the medium through which he conveyed the message of Sanatan Dharma. Mahipatirao's presence filled him with enthusiasm. 'Shri Ram was pleading, and the Brahmins complained. "Shri Ram! It is because of the sins in your kingdom that my son has died. Your kingdom will perish. The whole universe will deride you. Revive my son or I will give up my life too. You will be responsible for the death of a Brahmin."' Govind Bhatt spoke as if he himself was the Brahmin with the dead boy. Mahipatirao yawned. Govind Bhatt was preaching the king's dharma. Mahipatirao found it tedious.

'Shri Ram was perplexed that there was sin in his kingdom. He summoned Narad Muni, who arrived chanting, "Narayan-

Narayan." He was a visionary. He said, "My Lord, it is true that sins are increasing in your kingdom. The Brahmin's son would not have died otherwise. A Shudra is doing deep penance. The Puranas do not allow Shudras to do penance. This can endanger Sanatan Dharma. The king must protect the Dharma, destroy the *adharmi*s. You must fulfil the king's dharma, or else there will be danger." Saying so, Narad Muni disappeared.' Govind Bhatt's voice was feverish.

Govind Bhatt looked at Mahipatirao. His face was like the Falgu River ghat in Gaya, where people perform the *shradh*. Govind Bhatt was engrossed in his portrayal.

'Shri Ram went in search of the Shudra ascetic. He was hurt by the adharma in his kingdom. He was travelling through the skies, but his vision was fixed on the earth below. He was on the lookout for ascetics performing yagya and havan. He could hear the prayers, chants.

'He saw an ascetic deep in penance. He landed his Pushpak Viman. Shri Ram was shocked at what he saw. He went near the ascetic!' Govind Bhatt's voice was tense. People had become curious. But Mahipatirao was indifferent. He remembered George Thomas's question: How are your relations with the Adivasis of the bamboo forests? He had to reduce his army. He was in trouble.

The tale progressed. '"Oh hermit, what is the reason for such deep penance?" asked Shri Ram. "I have roamed the entire earth. I haven't seen a sterner ascetic than you. Of what clan are you, oh great hermit?" If the ascetic were to say "Brahmin", Ramchandra would have taken his blessings.' Govind Bhatt took a sip of water. Mahipatirao was lost in his thoughts. Govind Bhatt was building the suspense of his story. '"Oh Ram! I want to attain God! I will keep meditating till I reach my goal. I am a Shudra. My name is Shambuk." At that very moment, Ram drew his sword and beheaded Shambuk. Thirty-three crore gods applauded from the heavens! Rained flowers! Shri Ram was gratified. He had protected Sanatan Dharma. Shri Ram folded his hands and prayed to the gods: "Revive the Brahmin boy!" Lord Brahma said, "The moment you beheaded Shambuk, the boy was alive again. You have abided by the Varnasram. You are blessed. Ram Rajya will prosper. Its name and fame will spread everywhere on earth."'

Govind Bhatt's voice was trembling. The devoted bhakts chanted, 'Jai Shri Ram!' There were tears in Govind Bhatt's eyes. Mahipatirao stood up and went near Govind Bhatt. With folded hands he said, 'Make some time to come to the Wada. I need to talk to you.' Govind Bhatt nodded.

Mahipatirao left the temple. He had this newly developed disease of thinking. 'Did Shambuk's soul enter the dead body of the Brahmin boy?' Many of Govind Bhatt's counsels had gone against him. He thought that the Brahmins were cunningly causing him harm. He prayed that he would not see some maimed apparition, of those whom he had punished and wounded for disobedience. He heard the sound of a drum. These days, he would often hear such sounds.

Mahipatirao reached his Wada. He saw Sidnak and Bhimnak circling on horseback. He became angry. Seeing Company soldiers in his Wada distressed him. He smelt espionage. He realized that the Wada might not be safe any more. The falling of the tower had left a big gap at the entrance. Mahipatirao looked towards Parnakuti. He could see a crowd gathered there. His heart sank. People were sycophantic by nature. They fell in line with whoever was in power. The Kaala Wada never witnessed such crowds. What if people spoke to the British against him? His mind was tormented. Sidnak and Bhimnak went to the stables. Mahipatirao summoned Ratnak Mahar, who came running.

'Did the Company soldiers make inquiries?'

'Yes!'

'What did you say?'

'They asked how many horses we have. I said I don't know! They asked: How many queens? I said I don't know! They were angry because I did not say anything! They wanted to ride the black horse, but since you had it with you they went away!'

'They will return!'

'Do not worry. I know them. They are my caste—Mahars!'

Mahipatirao felt as if someone had thrown garbage on him! Lower castes! How they take advantage of the situation! He went towards the women's quarters. He thought, when power changes hands it is not just that the king changes, the change of power reaches the horse's reins. It exhumes garbage. The same people who begged at your feet when you had power turn their backs on you. People are scared to talk to one who has lost power. Mahipatirao was suffering from both insult and indifference. He was experiencing the pains of the loss of power. He began doubting his queens. He was afraid of the fallen tower. He was afraid of the people he had once tortured. He began to be afraid of his own shadow. Power is not merely political; there are many faces to it. He was living the reality of this idea. He was in deep distress. He lost appetite. Lost sleep. Lost weight. His eyes were enclosed in dark circles.

* * *

The Marathas had been badly defeated in the Battle of Panipat. They suffered heavy losses. The Mughals had won, but they were now in danger of losing power. The Battle of Panipat had weakened both the Marathas and the Mughals, and the British gained from this situation. The British adopted an attacking policy and gradually defeated the nawab of Bengal, the badshah of Delhi, the nawab of Ayodhya, the Rajputs, the Jats, the nizam, the Marathas, Tipu Sultan, and other big and small kings. The local power holders had no unity, and thus the British vanquished them one by one.

The losses at Panipat proved harmful to the Marathas as the British began making inroads. The Company sarkar began expanding its business. Power is never merely political; the power holder seeks to control culture and religion too. The people were dazed at what was happening around them. What all was going to change and how? Rumours made rounds. One must learn a new language . . . The currency will change, and the old currency will have no value . . . Everyone must pay taxes . . . worship a new god . . . have a new religion . . . clothes and food will be different . . . names will change . . . crops will change . . . Every day a new topic of discussion came up among the people.

Govind Bhatt had gone to the Kaala Wada. He entered easily. Silence reigned all around. There were fewer people there than before. Everything appeared worn out—the faces of people, animals, birds, even the Wada! Everything seemed lifeless. This atmosphere made Govind Bhatt tense. He felt like he had come to someone's funeral. Mahipatirao didn't know what to say. How to say anything? He was silent. Staring blankly. His face looked desolate. A *dasi* brought a glass of milk for Govind Bhatt. Mahipatirao looked like a frog as he sat on his throne. His silence sat coiled like a snake. Govind Bhatt drank the milk.

Govind Bhatt began speaking. He had to say something. His words were like pigeons fluttering. 'I heard that a church is being built!' Mahipatirao said nothing. Govind Bhatt felt helpless. During the Purana readings, his voice would soar. But who knew what came over him when he was before Mahipatirao! He wondered if he had said anything offensive. 'There is not a single Christian in the village . . . Then why do we need a church?' Govind Bhatt was speaking from his love of the Hindu religion.

Mahipatirao was irritated. 'Mahars, Matangs, Adivasis—they will convert. Christians won't come from outside, will they? Have you been to Vasai? Go and see. Our people have become Christians. The White Christians do not touch the Brown Christians. Our own people became Muslims earlier. The Muslims here, have they come from outside? Our people do not trust or love their own religion. They have no self-respect. No pride. They have no interest in their own religion, language or rule.' Mahipatirao was moaning. Govind Bhatt intervened. 'The Hindu religion will suffer.'

Mahipatirao fanned the fire. 'George Thomas has Mahar soldiers with him. They have given guns to the Mahars.' His pain was evident.

'Guns to Mahars! Shiv-Shiv! This is against the Hindu religion. Hindu kings would never do such a thing! But how can we expect sense from foreign rulers?' Govind Bhatt spoke helplessly.

'I must rebuild the tower immediately. Why does it fall every time? Change its location, change the workers. Get an exorcist from somewhere. Conduct a shanti yagya. Bring Brahmins from Pune for the puja and the *hom havan*. We must do a mahapuja. Standing on the tower one can see what is happening all around. It is the eye of the Wada.' Mahipatirao's tone was grave.

'I will find an auspicious time,' said Govind Bhatt.

'Yes . . . hurry!' said Mahipatirao.

'Earlier we could hear so many sounds when walking down the street—the sound of the aarti in the temple . . . the sound of the various animals . . . the bleating sheep . . . folk songs sung by homemakers . . . the sound of the bells around the necks of the cattle . . . babies crying . . . kitchen sounds . . . husband and wife arguing . . . so many domestic sounds . . . And now? All we hear is the sound of horses' hooves. Rumours, moans, disbanded soldiers and robberies.' Govind Bhatt was speaking his mind.

'I haven't slept for many nights!' Mahipatirao said.

'It is the same with everyone. The night is an enemy. How can one sleep?' replied Govind Bhatt.

'Let me know the mahurat once you fix it. I am not well! You can leave!'

Govind Bhatt walked down the stairs of the Wada. He was feeling better after talking to Mahipatirao. Chindya Bhil was walking up the stairs of the Wada. He would visit once in six months or so and would usually bring honey, Ayurvedic herbs, wild lizard and more. This time he had a rabbit with him.

The British had cleared the dense forests between Devgadh and Rahimatpur. They had usurped Adivasi lands. They had started building a road through the cleared forest space. Bridges were being constructed at places. Measurements were being taken. The Adivasis were rendered homeless because of this deforestation. Their security was at stake. Their very means of livelihood had been snatched from them. The Adivasis of the bamboo forest were driven to desperate measures. They attacked the labourers working on the roads, and the British responded with gunfire. But the Adivasis were determined. Chindya Bhil had come to the Wada to narrate the plight of his people. He wanted the support of the Wada.

'We are the kings of the forests. We won't allow this assault on the forests. We are not afraid of the British. The British never come before us. Our own people come before us, with guns in hand. Our people should not stand between the British and us . . .' Chindya Bhil was angry. There had been a tiff between the Adivasis and the local labourers. The labourers worked for the British because they got good money for it, and they knew the forest well.

Mahipatirao was guarded about what he said regarding the British. 'The British won't last long. The heat will drive them away. We won't need to kill them. I am with you people. The Wada has always stood by your side. We have never discriminated,' Mahipatirao assured Chindya Bhil.

Chindya Bhil was proud to receive Mahipatirao's support. 'The labourers are our people, so are the gun-trotters. We are fighting among ourselves, while the British are in hiding!' Chindya Bhil spoke his mind, and Mahipatirao was happy to hear him. It was certainly a good thing if the Adivasis were against the British.

'Chindya! Those who shake hands with the enemies, they are not our own. They are our enemies too. You must not think of them as our own!' Mahipatirao spoke firmly, and Chindya Bhil agreed. Today was a good day for Mahipatirao. The meetings with Govind Bhatt and Chindya Bhil had eased his mental burden.

The tehsildar had begun to gradually pay more and more attention to the business dealings in the town. He had ejected Mahipatirao from the town business. The Wada had lost its value. The British had a strange policy with Mahipatirao. They did not leave him alone, but they neither considered him an ally nor tried to develop close relations with him. Having once been at the height of power, this treatment was intolerable to Mahipatirao. The whole situation was like something stuck sorely in his throat, which he could neither swallow nor spit out. He had no clue about the doings of the sardars of Sultanpur, Rahimatpur, Saykheda. He had only vaguely heard that the people of Rampur had made some demonstrations in front of the Rampur palace.

The dasi announced: 'Ratnak Mahar has brought a message.' Mahipatirao thought that he must have some information about the British soldiers. Otherwise he never cared about the Mahars. He never gave any importance to the untouchables. But the situation had changed. He went downstairs. The Mahars did a pranam.

'What is it? What do you want?'

'My boy Jatnak is getting married. I have come with an invitation.' Ratnak placed the haldi-smeared rice on the stairs. He folded his hands. 'Please bless my boy,' he said.

'What does your boy do?'

'He wants to join the British Army. I wanted to give you the news,' Ratnak explained.

'Good. We have no army any more. So let him join the British. We will get information. You should go too. See if you can get a job there.'

'I am your devoted servant. I will die at your step. I will serve the horses even if you don't pay my salary!'

Mahipatirao began climbing up the stairs back to his Wada. Ratnak Mahar paid his obeisance to Mahipatirao's back.

Mahipatirao found it difficult to climb the stairs. His mind was like sour milk. He stopped for a moment. The British may well rule over the Hindus, but they should not have taken the Mahars into the army. They were making a mistake. The last step was the most painful for Mahipatirao.

The rice lay unattended where Ratnak had placed it.

* * *

Prataprao sat before Mahipatirao like an obedient child. He was the elder son. But he was still young! The dasi brought a glass of milk. Prataprao took the glass and handed it to Mahipatirao. The latter looked at his son lovingly as he brought the glass to his lips. He thought, 'My son is of marriageable age. He may not be able to say it out loud, but he must want to marry. Ratnak Mahar is getting his son married. I haven't paid attention to my son.' He felt guilty.

'The tehsildar had called for Patil, Deshpande, Deshmukh and Diwan. He has asked them to report to him every day. I met Diwan on the road but didn't speak much. Everyone seems to be dumbfounded,' said Prataprao.

'I know. This is what will happen from now on,' said Mahipatirao.

'I never thought people would change so much!' added Prataprao.

'People are helping the British!'

'They are afraid of the British, not of us!'

'How does it matter? Don't pay attention! There is nothing to worry about. Eleven pots filled with gold coins are kept near the tower—protected by the Mahars' ghosts. Below the wooden horse there are pots of gold bars and trunks filled with jewels. The rooms in the bungalow downstairs are filled with so much gold that seventy generations can live on it. Don't worry. If it gets difficult here, we can move to Pune,' said Mahipatirao.

Prataprao was happy to hear his father's words—they were an indication of his father's trust in him. The conversation between father and son was a secret one. Mahipatirao felt that his son's youthful face was no less than a treasure in itself. He remembered his own father. Prataprao sat for a while and left.

There was some commotion outside. Something untoward must have happened. The British must have tortured someone. The British were testing people's patience. Thinking so, Mahipatirao himself became restless.

Ratnak Mahar had come to the Wada, but the servants did not allow him in. His head was bleeding, and he had come with a complaint. The servants told him, 'Go to the tehsildar with your complaint. There's no use coming here. Mahipatirao has no power now. He doesn't meet anyone. He has given these instructions. Do you want to complain against the villagers?' Mahipatirao's servants asked him to be patient.

Ratnak was disappointed. He felt no one understood his urgency. No one was helping him. He returned to the Maharwada and saw the Mahars running helter-skelter. Running for their lives.

Ratnak Mahar had arranged for sweets for the wedding feast of his son, Jatnak. Ghee was also served. This had enraged the villagers. The upper castes of Devgadh had gathered together. 'The Mahars are becoming too proud. They must be taught a lesson.' So saying, they reached the Maharwada with their sticks and axes. The feast was on. The food was being served.

The goons entered the wedding hall and began beating up the servers. They threw mud in the food. They beat up the guests. Kicked the plates. Kicked the Mahars. They beat the bridegroom, Jatnak, heavily. They killed the brother of the bride. Ratnak Mahar was pleading and begging for mercy. But no one paid any heed to him. Ratnak's wife, Kersuni, became unconscious. Nagnak, Krishnanak, Ramnak, Khandnak were wounded. Raynak's wife, Kanhopatra, had taken the bride to her house. The bride, Yesubai, was very scared. Ratnak's house was a site of devastation. The wedding pavilion had collapsed.

Hearing the commotion from the Maharwada, Father Francis came running. 'Please stop! For God's sake!' he kept pleading. The goons were afraid now. They thought that Father Francis would be followed by the tehsildar. So they ran away. Father Francis stood firmly by Ratnak Mahar. He embraced Ratnak, who began to weep. The Mahars came back. Father Francis's presence comforted them. He was saddened by this inhuman behaviour. He was shaken to his very core.

* * *

The settlements in Devgadh were arranged according to the castes. The Brahmin alley, the cobbler alley, the tailor alley, the shepherd alley, the blacksmith alley, the Maratha alley, the Musalman Mohalla, the fishermen's area, the Chambharwada, Matangwada and Maharwada. Every caste was different, separate. The Maharwadas were always on the outskirts. The relationship between the castes was based on discrimination, not harmony. Hindu society was based on principles of high and low. Every village was proof of that. The upper castes hated the lower castes; they thought that the lower castes were dirt—not to be kept relations with. The lower castes thought that they were lowly and should respect the upper castes. They all belonged to the same religion, but their minds were divided, compartmentalized by caste.

The Maharwada of Devgadh was quite large. Many Mahars worked in the Kaala Wada. Thus most of them were well off. They looked after all the needs of the horses—right from birthing to feeding, clothing and training them. Some of the Mahars worked as masons and were building the church. They had to work to keep the stoves burning.

The first converts in Devgadh were Ratnak and Jatnak. Father Francis baptized them. They now began to work on building the church. Ratnak Mahar left his job at the Kaala Wada. They got new names. Ratnak became Stephan, and Jatnak became Harry! Ratnak's wife, Kersuni, became Rebecca. Jatnak's wife, Yesubai, became Serena. Christian families began living in the Maharwada. It was fun trying to pronounce the new Christian names. Stephan threw away the idols of Hindu gods and goddesses in the rubbish heap. The atmosphere in the village was tense. Stephan had the support of the church, so hurting him would mean trouble.

Father Francis would visit Stephan's house. He would hold prayer meetings there. Devgadh began to take notice of the father. 'All are children of God,' Father Francis would say. This surprised the Mahars. The Mahars believed that they were born as Mahars because of the sins of their previous lives. Now they knew that they, too, were the children of God. There was no difference between them and others. Govind Bhatt, however, used to preach differently. He would say that those who were born from the mouth of Brahma were the finest, the supreme among men. And the ones born from the feet of Brahma were the lower ones. But Father said something else, and hence the entire Brahmin alley was furious.

After the Sunday prayer was over, Father went towards the Maharwada. Bhimnak and Sidnak were with him. Father stopped them and said, 'People have seen guns on your shoulders. The gun is a weapon of fire, not of love. People will love you only if you pray for them. The two of you must get baptized. Then come with me. I am giving you time to think.' Father patted them affectionately. The Mahars now knew the meaning of words like 'baptism', 'church', 'father', 'Bible', 'cross'; even words such as 'English', 'good morning', 'good evening', 'good night', 'thank you', 'sorry'. They began using these words.

Every year, Govind Bhatt would reinforce the idea that every man was born into a certain caste and religion. It could not be changed.

This life is the fruit of a previous life. Sinners are born into lower castes, and those who were pious in their previous lives are born into the upper castes. Birth is a matter of fate. When there is too much sin in the world, God is born in human form, and he destroys the sinners. This made people attach more importance to the next life than to the present one. Heaven was more attractive than earth. Because of the Muslims, people had already come to know that religion could be changed and caste destroyed. The lower castes had begun to take this route. And now the British had come! So people were well aware that birth was not dependent on karma and sin.

Sidnak and Bhimnak were deep in thought. Father had asked them to get baptized. Sidnak was in a dilemma. Bhimnak was sure that one must not give up the Hindu dharma. If our parents treat us badly, do we disclaim and dishonour them? The Hindu dharma had treated him badly, but he was not ready to give it up. Sidnak was thinking of converting. He said, 'The Hindu dharma is not for us. There is no well-being for us in it. We have no rights. The Hindu dharma has made us slaves. Made us untouchables. Cursed us. It has been thrust on us forcefully. We must give it up.' He had begun to like Christianity.

Father Francis was of the opinion that 'the caste system is a destructive tradition of the Hindu dharma. To give rights of development only to the upper castes—this is discrimination. Depriving the lower castes of any rights is a shrewd strategy of the Hindu dharma. A caste cannot thrive only on the basis of economic development. The only way forward is conversion. Conversion will free the lower castes from slavery.' Father Francis also visited the bamboo forests. He would live for weeks among the Adivasis and serve them. The Brahmins were now worried that if the untouchables and the Adivasis all changed their religion, the Hindu dharma would be in danger.

The Brahmins had arranged for a meeting at the Vishnu temple. Many were in attendance. Brahmins from Pune had come to offer guidance. Govind Bhatt was addressed the meeting.

'The Hindu dharma will become mute if the Brahmins remain silent. More than in its temples and places of pilgrimage, the Hindu dharma lives on the tongues of the Brahmins. Our ancestors have built this religion. Islam and Christianity are out to destroy it. People are being converted either by coaxing or coercion. We must stop this. We are the gods here—the gods on earth. If God does not descend on earth to save the religion and annihilate evil, then we must do that job!' Govind Bhatt was shouting. 'We must annihilate the evildoers! Hindus will take revenge on the converted! Torture them! People should be scared! The Hindu dharma is safe as long as there is fear in the minds of the lower castes. People must be afraid of the gods! Afraid of sin! We can win over people by scaring them. If you cannot induce fear, you cannot protect your tradition! We must build idols that incarnate destruction! People must be made to fear hell! Only the Brahmins can do it!' Some applauded him, some ridiculed him.

Sidnak was baptized. He got a new religion, a new identity. Father had christened him Philip. Philip Bush. Christian.

Bhimnak stayed away from conversion. 'Conversion takes one away from his own people, society and relations. I won't be a traitor to my religion,' Bhimnak told Sidnak.

The Company sent an army of a hundred soldiers to Devgadh. Dealing with the dacoits, controlling the Adivasis of the bamboo forests, stopping the agitation of the disbanded soldiers—these were the objectives of the army. The existing soldiers were to be transferred. Bhimnak was transferred to Bombay. He was separated from Sidnak now. They hugged and cried as they bade farewell to each other.

* * *

Govind Bhatt's grandchildren sat before him as they sang 'Deep Jyoti Namostute'. Moropant was wearing the *janave* as he performed the puja. The children touched their eyes with holy water. Govind Bhatt's face glowed like the hom havan. Narsopant's daughter was gathering flowers. Moropant's puja was over. He sprinkled the holy water of the puja on the tulsi plant in the yard. His upper body was bare. The tuft of his hair that was woven into a braid swung to and fro at the back of his head. 'You haven't even taken a bath or done your puja! Where are you off to?' said Malti to Padma. Padma was giving alms to a man at the door.

Malti stood before the puja room. The omens were good, the gods would be pleased. 'I have vowed to Mahadev that Padma will go to the temple every day.' Govind Bhatt rose. He wore the *rudraksha* beads. His feet were large. He put on his slippers, and remembered that both he and Mahipatirao wore the same size-12 shoe. Shekappa Chambhar made shoes for them both.

Govind Bhatt came to the yard. Flowers of Parijatak lay scattered on the ground. The neighbour Dayashankar's voice could be heard. He was arguing loudly with a Brahmin. 'Are you Brahmin? Tell me, can you recite the whole Purusha Sukta?' He had a very loud voice. His wife would always ask him to speak softly. She was worried that people would hear him and know about their domestic matters. But his wife's words had no effect on Dayashankar. 'I will throw away my janave and my loincloth.' Dayashankar was fully enmeshed in the argument.

Govind Bhatt returned home. The chants of the Gayatri Mantra could be heard coming from the ashram. Padma and Saraswati were in the kitchen, preparing food.

Govind Bhatt was taking rest. Dayashankar came hurriedly to meet him. His gestures signalled that something serious had happened.

'Do you know what happened?' Dayashankar asked.

Govind Bhatt expressed his interest.

'I am telling you what is floating around. I do not know what is true and what is not. They say that the British took away all the powers of Mahipatirao. His army was disbanded. He wanted to save his treasure and began dividing it among his queens. But he was partial to the youngest queen, Pramila. The other queens rebelled. Pratap's mother, Queen Sumitra, threatened to tell the tehsildar. Dissent has been bubbling for quite a few days in the Kaala Wada. Some say Mahipatirao died in his sleep. Others say that Pratap strangled him. All the queens are with Prataprao. Pramila is isolated. She is a young girl. Barely sixteen! They will put her on the funeral pyre.' Dayashankar spoke breathlessly.

Govind Bhatt was dazed. He barely muttered, 'Shiv! Shiv!'

Dayashankar was still babbling away. 'Mahipatirao has been brought to his knees by the British. But this was all done by the king of Rampur. Mahipatirao didn't obey the king, and this is how he got his revenge.'

'May I join in?' asked Umashankar as he walked towards the two. 'Mahipati is gone,' he said and sat beside Govind Bhatt.

Govind Bhatt sounded worried. 'It was bad. He was an oldie. He knew so much. Now the British will have their way with the young Pratap. What does he know?'

Umashankar was heady with excitement. 'I saw the Mahars with axes on their backs. They must be gathering wood for the funeral pyre.'

A messenger had come to Govind Bhatt's house from the Kaala Wada. 'Mahipatirao is no more. Please prepare for the funeral service!'

Govind Bhatt did not reply. That was an old tradition with the Kaala Wada—to only send out messages and not pay heed to the replies. 'A message has come from the Wada. We must inform Ramnarayan and Bishwanath. Let me know when we should start. I am ready,' Govind Bhatt told Dayashankar and Umashankar.

People were running helter-skelter on the streets. The young and the old moaned alike. 'Our ruler is no more,' they wailed in distress. The roads were busy with people and horsemen. The British had stepped up their security measures.

* * *

Prataprao was married to Sanyogita, the daughter of Mansinghrao, the sardar of Saykheda. Devgadh and Saykheda were now bound by kinship ties. These relations between the two regions had existed in the past as well, through marriages of daughters. In the old days, the people of Devgadh would visit the Wada on special occasions; Prataprao would make arrangements for the programme. But the Wada had now lost much of its earlier splendour. Only a few people visited these days.

The British had divided Rampur into five revenue divisions. Company officials collected taxes. The Christian missionaries preached their religion. Dacoits, Bhils, thugs, disbanded soldiers—they were all kept in check using force. Criminals were imprisoned in the stables of Parnakuti. The thumbs of the weavers of Rahimatpur had been cut off to prevent them from working. The tax evaders were punished with severity. British terror had spread.

Prataprao was looking towards Peacock Lake from the Wada. He had picked up this habit from his father. Mahipatirao would look at the lake with his hands on his waist. He called Pramila as soon as he sighted an animal that had come to drink water. Prataprao had his own manner, but he wanted to imitate his father.

Christian dwellings had spread all around Peacock Lake. The sound of cannons had driven the deer and rabbits away. Animals did not come to the lake any more. Soldiers had set up camps around it. The church building was ready. The tehsildar, George Thomas, had been transferred. In his place came George Stewart. Converting to Christianity allowed one to drink water from Peacock Lake, and so nine Mahar families had been baptized.

Prataprao was looking at the march of the British soldiers. He was surprised by the sudden noise of wailing. He leant forward. The handicapped people who had been maimed during the days of Mahipatirao were hurling curses at the haveli: 'It will be razed to the ground! People will come here to drink and gamble and commit adultery! You will all will perish!' The voices were portentous. Their bodies looked like tortoises crawling on the ground. Prataprao felt a sense of dread.

The servants of the haveli ran. They caught hold of the handicapped people, who dragged and grovelled on the ground, trying to wriggle free. The handicapped were driven away from the Wada. Then the guards were called back.

Sumitra was scared. There was no security guard at the gate. The guards had all been removed. Prataprao was shaken. Sanyogita's face looked worn. The Brahmins were summoned. Sumitra, Prataprao, Sanyogita and the Brahmins were deep in thought. Sumitra egged them on to do something immediately. 'A new member is going to arrive in the family. We must complete the tower at the earliest. There will be a feast. Please fix a mahurat for the bhoomi puja.' Govind Bhatt, Dayashankar, Umashankar, Ramnarayan, Bishwanath—they all sat down with the almanack. A dasi served the guests. Sanyogita's body looked like a ripe cob of corn. She glowed like the rich golden champa flowers.

Govind Bhatt said, 'The month of Ashada will be over in fifteen days. There are good auspicious days in the Shravan month. Let us do the mahapuja on the first Monday of Shravan. There will be hom havan. We can do the bhumi puja on the day after that—the day of the *narli-punam*.'

Prataprao interrupted, 'It's okay. Do not worry about your remuneration. The programme must be perfect.' Govind Bhatt was happy to hear that.

Sumitra was pleased that the mahurat had been decided. The Brahmins stood up, looking satisfied. The church bell could be heard. The Wada's usual crowd had thinned.

At night, the Wada did not seem safe enough. Sumitra often thought of moving somewhere else. Prataprao agreed with her: 'It's no use staying here.' Sanyogita would often have nightmares. The Wada was crumbling. It was absolutely essential to revamp it and rebuild the tower. Some of the queens had left with their share of the wealth. Sumitra was sure that the Wada must be strengthened.

The only way to end the hopelessness was to shake off the lethargy. The Wada was in a sorry state because the soldiers and servants had been removed. Something must be done. Prataprao began paying attention to cleaning—the gardens, the stables—and decorative activities. He also began paying attention to security measures.

The month of Shravan arrived. The Purana readings resumed in the Vitthal temple. These days, Govind Bhatt would tire easily. He was short of breath and panted when he read the holy Puranas. There were long bouts of coughing. He would take sips of water now and then. Sometimes, Moropant attended the readings. People didn't like to listen to Moropant. Still, scriptural readings started in the Mahadev temple as well. The responsibility for this lay with Dayashankar. The Bhagavata Purana was read at the Mahadev temple, while at the Vitthal temple it was the Mahabharata.

Chokha Mahar came to hear the readings, with a saffron flag on his shoulders. He would sit far from the temple, near the villagers' chappals. It was difficult to say how much he heard or understood. But he would come and sit there, if only to proclaim his stained existence. His face looked like the arid sand along the Chandrabhaga River. His body was a storehouse of enormous sin! He would have to be very careful that his shadow didn't fall on anyone. He looked like a sepulchre. His name was Bapnak Mahar, but he came to be known as Chokha Mahar. He pretended to be a humble devotee and chanted the name of Saint Vitthal. He had taken on the garb of Chokha Mahar well, chanting 'Vithhal-Vitthal, Hari-Hari' all the time.

Chokha Mahar's wife, Rahi, had no child, and so other women jeered at her. He was meek and did not protest. People had evil intentions towards her. She had to tread very carefully. Once, Chokha Mahar's elder brother, Sonnak, came into the house and grabbed Rahi from behind. She said, 'Please leave me alone. I am having my menses now.' Sonnak was not ready to believe her and lifted her sari. He saw a piece of cloth tied to her waist. He left in a huff. Rahi knew anyone could try to get hold of her. So she had contrived this clever trick.

Chokha Mahar was telling Rahi the story of Saint Chokha Mahar. She was listening eagerly. 'Saint Chokha Mahar's parents were devotees of Lord Vitthal. They had no children. Vithhal came to know of their misery. Vitthal took the form of the Brahmin. He ate half a mango and gave the other half to Chokha Mahar's wife. She went home and ate half the mango tasted by Vitthal and became pregnant. This was how Chokha Mahar was born.'

Rahi laughed. 'Bring me such a mango too.' She kept laughing.

Chokha Mahar played a harp and sang hymns. He would sing hymns late into the night so that people would think he was a great devotee of Vitthal.

The mahapuja commenced, and people thronged the Kaala Wada. Brahmins were being fed. Their leftovers would be thrown away into a ditch, and the Mahars were eager to eat those and purify themselves. The Mahars, crows and dogs attacked the ditch.

Brahmins were seen in large numbers everywhere. The people of Devgadh were happy that they got to see Brahmins every day. They smeared their foreheads with the dust from the Brahmins' feet. Carpets were spread out for the Brahmins to walk on. People prostrated before them. The Brahmins were great. The caste system had been invented to maintain their glory and greatness. The Mahars were prohibited to come before nine in the morning and after three in the afternoon, so that their shadow would not pollute the upper castes. This was an age-old custom.

Chokha Mahar was playing his harp. Sleep eluded him. Rahi, too, was awake. She smiled as she looked at Chokha.

'Why are you smiling?'

'Is it forbidden to smile?'

'Your smile is different today.'

'Do you notice my smiles every day?'

'Who else will?'

'No one, but all your attention goes to Lord Vitthal.'

'Tell me what happened.'

'Vitthal is about to come to our house.'

'Really?'

Rahi was pregnant. Luck had smiled on them.

Stones were being carved for the repair of the Kaala Wada. The sound of the carving could be heard from afar. It was the Mahars who had built the Kaala Wada and the Vitthal temple. They had carved the idol of Vitthal from black stone. They had carved the Shivalinga, built the houses in Devgadh, dug wells. The Mahars would be needed whenever there was work. At other times they were untouchables. Day and night, stones were being carved in the Kaala Wada. Many were wounded in the act—some lost their eyes, some their ears—but the work did not stop.

Nagnak, Krishnanak and Khandnak were returning home with hammers on their shoulders. They had finished early today. They saw that Chokha Mahar's door was open and called out to him. Chokha could normally come out at once, but he did not do so. He wore tulsi beads around his neck, hung the holy ash pouch on his waist, put his saffron flag on his shoulders. Only then did he come out. He smeared the tika on the foreheads of all who had come. Everyone touched his feet. Nagnak, Krishnanak, Khandnak—they all stood looking grave, while Chokha Mahar had a smile on his face.

'The foundation of the tower was about to be laid, but Prataprao was waiting for an exorcist. They could not get one for a long time, but now one has been found. He will come from Konkan,' said Krishnanak.

'They will sacrifice Mahars in the foundation,' said Nagnak.

'We will have to go once we get the call from the Wada. Who knows whom they will call for?' said Khandnak.

'I am thinking of leaving the village,' said Nagnak.

Chokha Mahar became serious now. He said, 'Hari-Hari.' The ominous sound of the cutting of rocks could be heard coming from the Wada. Nagnak, Krishnanak, Khandnak had left. Chokha Mahar felt helpless. He could not sleep. 'Whom to sacrifice at the tower's foundation? Whose name will I say if I am asked?' He was deep in thought. Rahi was asleep. Late at night, he dozed off for a bit but saw flocks of vultures in his sleep. He tried to understand the meaning of his strange dream but could not think of anything. He tried to sleep again.

Rahi was surprised when she woke up in the morning. Chokha Mahar was still deep asleep. He always woke up before her. But today was different. Chokha Mahar had missed the morning aarti.

Rahi went to work as Chokha Mahar sat alone at home. He did none of his usual activities, did not wear his beads or chant 'Hari-Hari'. He did not touch his saffron flag or his harp. Evening fell. Bells began to toll in the Vitthal temple. It was time to read the Puranas. He now wore his tulsi beads, took the pouch of holy ash and his saffron flag, and left home. The Mahar children playing on the streets saw him and bowed, and he smeared holy ash on their foreheads. He said, 'Hari-Hari.' He met Rebecca and Serena. The mother-in-law and daughter-in-law were coming from the church. They were Christians now but had not given up their old customs. They bowed to Chokha Mahar, and he smeared holy ash on their forehead as a blessing. He said, 'Hari-Hari.'

Chokha Mahar began walking towards the Vitthal temple. He was near the Marwari building, which was deserted now. Beyond the building lay the open fields. Patil's cattle pen was there. A road stretched from the Marwari building to the Vitthal temple. Chokha Mahar took this road to the temple because people did not use it. He walked for a bit and sat at some distance from the temple. This ensured that he would not touch anyone by mistake. People felt good when they saw the helpless Chokha Mahar. 'Mahars must be full of humility, like Chokha Mahar. He knows his limits. Other Mahars should follow him!' people thought and pretended not to notice him. They found Chokha Mahar to be wretched, an unholy figure. He was the ideal Mahar for other Mahars.

Govind Bhatt came out as soon as he saw Chokha Mahar. It was not yet time to read the Puranas. People were still arriving. Shrirang Warren had taken up his veena. Chokha Mahar folded his hands and stared at Govind Bhatt. The passers-by were surprised.

Govind Bhatt said, 'Take this as the message of Sumitra Rani. As a message from the Kaala Wada. She asked me to tell you this because you come to the temple every day. Listen carefully!' Govind Bhatt's voice choked. Chokha Mahar was tense. Govind Bhatt began narrating the tale of Saint Chokha Mahar.

'A Mahar named Chokha Mela lived in the village of Mangalaveda. A tower was being built in the town. The tower would fall every time. Chokha was working in it with his wife. The tower fell, and Chokha was buried in the debris. When people removed the debris they found his bones, and the chant of 'Hari-Hari' was heard from the bones. This is called bhakti—Vitthal bhakti! You have taken the flag of Chokha Mela on your shoulders. Sumitra Rani wants to honour you. Do a baby shower for Rahi. The exorcist has told her that a Mahar must be honoured before the work on the tower starts. A religious-minded Mahar is the best choice for the honour. I have suggested your name,' Govind Bhatt said vigorously.

It was now time to read the Puranas. People were waiting eagerly. Govind Bhatt said, 'It is okay if you do not listen to the reading today. Fulfil your responsibilities.' Govind Bhatt went inside the temple. Chokha Mahar remembered Vitthal. He said, 'If all are equal for you, why am I standing outside the temple?'

Chokha started walking towards the Maharwada. He walked along the outskirts of the village. He wondered why he had been summoned to the Wada. He was bewildered.

Rahi was in front of the stove. She was kneading dough. The fire of the stove filled the house with smoke. Rahi perspired heavily. Chokha came in. Neither was he chanting Hari-Hari, as he usually did, nor was he singing hymns. He was solemn, almost numb. Rahi understood something was wrong.

'What is it?' she asked.

He replied helplessly, 'The Wada has sent a call.'

Rahi was delighted. 'So let's go.'

Chokha Mahar was angry now. 'They want a baby shower for you!'

Rahi smiled. 'What? Why?'

He coldly replied, 'You are going to be a mother, that's why.'

Rahi was surprised, 'How do they know?'

Chokha Mahar replied nervously, 'The Kaala Wada knows everything! It has eyes! It has ears!'

Chokha Mahar was angry again. 'We must go. You have to come with me.'

Rahi assured him, 'I will come.'

Chokha Mahar fell silent.

The stone cutters were doing their job. Splinters flew in the air. Sometimes, sparks flew. Chokha Mahar felt that the blows on the stones were blows falling on his head. He bore them with great fortitude. His face looked like a broken stone.

The exorcist circled the Kaala Wada. He stopped near the tower and listened carefully with his ears glued to its walls. He looked at the cracks and crevices, pursed his lips. Then he remarked, 'It's a dangerous place.' He took a few steps forward and backwards. He placed his hands on the walls. The Wada servants were with him. They were staring at him and his strange antics. The exorcist looked towards Peacock Lake. He looked at the bamboo forest. 'There is a ghost in the tower. It's a male ghost. He wants a companion.'

The Maharwada was in deep sleep. Moonlight flooded the place. It would be full moon in a few days. The breeze made a wailing sound like the sea. Chokha Mahar's head was bursting. The past rushed by—how he became Chokha Mahar from Bapnak, his marriage with Rahi. She was so young then, and they had seen such bad days together—those who helped them contributed whatever they could. Rahi suffered so much. Should I go to the

Wada? What will happen? What if I don't go? What will happen? What if they bury me in the tower? What if I go away forever? Questions danced in a frenzy in his mind.

Chokha Mahar left his house. Behind him was Rahi. The dark night was drowsy. The sound of the cutting of stones had stopped now. Frogs croaked. The dogs were asleep. The wind snored. All doors were tightly shut. Chokha Mahar held a saffron flag on his shoulder. The two shadows walked on in the moonlight. The moon, the stars and the crickets kept them company. Rahi walked with heavy steps.

Chokha Mahar dropped the saffron flag on the road to Saykheda. He threw away the tulsi beads and the packet of holy ash. He was afraid to cast off his habitual costume. He turned towards the bamboo forest. He knew the ins and outs of the forest. Even if someone would look for him, he could just disappear among the trees. He trod on his fears as he walked ahead. With courage. With his back to his past. Rahi, scared, confused, too shocked to speak, followed her husband silently.

The trees in the bamboo forest looked silvery. Jackals howled. The water of the Tapi River was exultant. Thud. Something had fallen into the water. Rahi followed him like his own shadow. Their footsteps woke the jungle. Their footsteps had rejected the supremacy of the Wada.

Chokha Mahar was not present in the temple for the daily ritual. Govind Bhat thought he must have gone to the Wada. The Maharwada was also rife with rumours—Chokha Mahar had been called to the Wada. Krishnanak, Nagnak, Raynak, they were all anxious. What could have happened? The sight of Chokha's empty hut made Sonnak sad. Whom should they ask? And how? No one had the courage. They kept mum. Hushed voices in the town spoke of the disappearance of Chokha Mahar.

Govind Bhatt was going through the Puranas. Moropant and Narsopant were helping him wrap up the Puranas. Govind Bhatt thought aloud, 'From now on I will be reading only from the Ramayana!' He was overwhelmed with emotion.

'These Puranas were given to me by my father, Sridharpant. He was a great kirtan singer. He was given these texts by his father. The texts carry the touch of our ancestors. They are our invaluable wealth.'

Govind Bhatt continued ardently, 'My work is now complete. It is up to you now to carry it forward. These are difficult times. A grave crisis is before us. People are converting to become Muslims, Christians. No one is converting to become Hindu. Even if someone did, which caste would he be taken into? If the conversions are not checked, Hindu dharma will be in danger!' Govind Bhat finished in a passionate frenzy.

The Christian missionaries had reached places that could perhaps not be reached even by the rays of the sun—the deepest recesses of the jungles. They had gained the trust of the Adivasis, understood their way of living, their language. Father D'Souza had introduced them to a whole new world. Baptized them. Given them new names. Given them the cross. The Bible, new woollen clothes, medicinal help. But some of the Adivasis did not consent—they were forced to convert. The missionaries wanted to 'civilize' the Adivasis and make them good Christians.

Chokha Mahar and Rahi were wandering in the forest. The Adivasis caught hold of them and beat them up! Chokha was afraid. Would he be sent off to the Kaala Wada now? He was shivering with fear. Rahi grew restless. She started weeping. Chokha was unable to answer the Adivasis' questions. Father D'Souza arrived at the scene. He had answers to every question. He said, 'This is my darling son, John, and this is his wife, Zoya. They had lost their way for a bit. They will return home now. Jesus worries for each of us.' Father D'Souza embraced Chokha and Rahi lovingly. They were overwhelmed by such affection.

Chokha became a myth for the people of Devgadh. Some said he was buried in the tower. Some said he was eaten by a tiger. Some said he was killed by dacoits. Some said he had run away, never to return. Others said he was seen begging as a madman on the streets of Rampur, that he had gone insane.

Chokha Mahar's responsibilities now fell on Raynak Mahar. He wore tulsi beads around his neck, bore the saffron flag on his shoulder, gave up eating meat. He became Chokha Mahar.

The work at the Kaala Wada was on in full swing. People were now used to the sound of stones being cut. The monsoon season was about to end. The readings had come to an end. No one went near the temple now. Dogs had begun to sleep there.

Noon. The Wada workers had sat down to lunch. There was nothing new in the Maharwada. Someone or the other would come begging. Sometimes the Mahars fought among themselves. Sometimes there was a domestic brawl between man and wife. Dead animals were often seen being dragged along. The daily grind of life . . . rain . . . sun . . . storm . . . full moon. Chigurs came to the tamarind tree, vultures sat on the neem, the water level was high in the river, someone died in the village. These were the things that people talked about! The Maharwada was like a stagnant pool. There was no way to throw a pebble into it. 'Did you eat?' 'Did you sleep?' 'What did you cook?' 'Will you go to fetch water?' 'Will you go to defecate?' There were no other questions. These days there were talks of conversion and talks about the Kaala Wada.

Children playing on the streets began to scream, 'Chokha Mahar is coming!' Raynak ran out. Krishnanak, Nagnak came too. Rebecca came. Their eyes were fixed on the way to Saykheda. Someone was approaching with a saffron flag on his shoulder. Everyone knitted their brows. Raynak felt worried. Krishnak said, 'He must be from some other village.'

He was not Chokha Mahar. He did not say 'Hari-Hari'. He carried the saffron flag of Chokha Mahar. Krishnak began to make inquiries. The visitor began to display strange antics. Rebecca brought him some water. He drank the water and sat down clutching his head. Nagnak asked him to sit comfortably, and he did so. He looked at all the curious faces around him and said, 'I am Bhootnak Mahar from Sonai village. I have come for Sidnak.

He is from our Maharwada. I want to meet him. He is a soldier in the British Army. I have some work with him. Do you know him?'

Rebecca answered quickly, 'Yes, we know him.'

Bhootnak's face brightened. Raynak brought some food on a plate. Bhootnak devoured it hungrily. A crowd had gathered. But he was not looking at anyone any more.

Harry arrived. He took Bhootnak to the Christian dwellings. Bhootnak walked slowly. Harry held him by the hand and led him on. The sun was on its way down. Seeing Bhootnak walking with the saffron flag on his shoulder, Narsopant was vexed. 'You bastard! Converting to Christianity!' Harry introduced Bhootnak to Philip. Philip recognized Bhootnak immediately and embraced him. Bhootnak, however, could not recognize Philip so easily.

Bhootnak was in tears now. Philip's eyes welled up too. Harry left. Philip was lost in nostalgic memories. Bhootnak began to narrate his story. He was eager to say everything quickly. After all, that was why he had come here, having walked day and night.

'Parbati had gone to work. Kachra went with her. She was kidnapped. Kachra said, "They took her towards Saykheda." Whom do I have but you? Tell the British. Ask them for help to free her. I haven't slept since that day. I have walked day and night on foot to come here. Only you can help me.' Bhootnak was full of humility.

Philip felt restless. He thought that this could only be the work of the sardar of Saykheda. Prataprao's wife was the daughter of the sardar of Saykheda. Maybe Parbati was sacrificed at the foundation of the tower. Philip got goosebumps thinking about this. He held Bhootnak's hand and helped him stand up. The two of them left for the Kaala Wada.

Philip and Bhootnak climbed the stairs of the Kaala Wada. The workers had started arriving. Others were also coming and going. The two of them mingled in the crowd. Birds were flying back to their nests. The sun was setting. Bhootnak was tired climbing the stairs. He stopped intermittently to catch his breath.

Philip had earlier said to him, 'We don't know where Parbati is. But let us go to the Wada. Workers gather there from many places. Perhaps they will know something. But you must be careful. We must go very quietly. If anyone doubts us, we will be in trouble.' Bhootnak nodded. Philip was in civilian clothes. They climbed the stairs one at a time.

The two of them reached the Wada. The construction work on the tower was on in full swing. The masons had rebuilt quite a bit of the tower. The workers were passing stones. Lime was being ground. There were heaps of sand. Stones were being sculpted. The workers spoke loudly. The tower was about 4 feet tall now. Bhootnak spotted Parbati's slippers near a heap of sand. He screamed, 'Parbati's sandals! I had mended the toe strap with some rope. See! Parbati is here.' Philip held his hand tightly.

Philip knew exactly what had transpired. A Mahar woman, Parbati, had been sacrificed at the foundation of the tower. He tried to calm Bhootnak down.

'How shall I leave Parbati behind? Let me at least see her!' Philip began to drag Bhootnak away, but the latter was in a whirlwind of emotional upheaval. Bhootnak could barely stand on his feet. The servants of the Wada had noticed that something was wrong. They stopped the two. Philip, realizing the delicacy of the situation, made an excuse. 'I have come to take him away. He is a suspect. I have to take him to the tehsildar.'

The servants recognized Philip. They had seen him many times wearing the soldier's uniform. They believed him. 'Let them go.' The two came out of the Wada.

Bhootnak was in a state of shock and agitation. Philip could gauge his pain but could do nothing about it. Bhootnak's very soul seemed to be popping out of his body, through his tears. He was looking towards the Wada. The setting sun was just above the Wada. The horizon was a play of colours. Philip looked at Bhootnak, at the seas churning in his eyes. Bhootnak was looking beyond the colours of the horizon. Beyond the clouds. Perhaps he could see his Parbati in one of the rays of the setting sun. The sky had descended in his eyes. He was lost in the horizon. He was conversing with the silence of the infinite skies. Philip felt shaken.

The spirit should possess Parbati. She should scream like thunder. Dance as if the earth was sinking. Flash on the Kaala Wada like lightning. The Kaala Wada must be obliterated. Mari Ma should possess Parbati once more. She must hurl the tower off and walk out of it . . . Philip was bewildered. He thought of Bhimnak. The stars were out now. Twinkling, just like Parbati's bindi used to twinkle when she was possessed. Philip's mind was distressed. Crows cawed. The darkness gradually deepened. Bhootnak looked as lifeless and inert as a useless piece of stone.

Three

A treaty had been signed between the British and the Peshwa. Because of this treaty, a subsidiary force entered the court of the Peshwa. Philip was transferred to Pune and arrived at the court of the Peshwa as a British soldier. Bands of experienced soldiers from Devgadh, Saykheda, Rahimatpur, Sultanpur and Rampur had been sent to Pune. Most of the soldiers were from northern India. The subsidiary force was employed under the Peshwa, but its loyalty lay fully with the British.

Srimant Peshwa Bajirao II had gone to the Parvati Hill with his queen. The soldiers kept a vigil around him. The Parvati Hill in Pune has a special significance. Philip and Imran were going towards Parvati from Gultekdi. They saw a terrible sight in Gultekdi and stopped. They felt immobilized and helpless with fear. Anyone from the Matang or Mahar caste crossing the pool would have their head chopped off. The severed head, cut with a sword, was tossed like a ball to the ground. It was a game, with spectators who enjoyed it. Philip and Imran were a bit relieved to remember that they were converts, no longer Hindus, no longer untouchables.

'The untouchables have to suffer everywhere, but here in the Peshwai, all limits have been crossed,' said Imran.

'What justice is this? A pot hangs around the neck of the Mahars so that they don't spit on the roads, and a broom hangs from their backs so that their footsteps are wiped away,' said Philip.

'It is a dreadful situation,' Imran said with a sigh.

Philip continued, 'A Maratha soldier once told me a true story. Ganpat Mahar was a gatekeeper. The Peshwa's queen had left Shaniwarwada on her palanquin. Ganpat Mahar looked at the queen. And the queen happened to notice this. The Peshwa was infuriated that a Mahar had the audacity to look at the queen. He passed a sentence on Ganpat Mahar. But a sentence on Ganpat Mahar meant a sentence on the whole caste. They would have to carry a pot around their necks to spit into and a broom on their backs to sweep away their footprints!'

Philip's throat was dry, but he continued. 'Ganpat Mahar died and became a ghost. He continued to haunt the queen! The Peshwa tried many cures, but nothing worked. He finally decided to build a temple of Ganpati in the south of Shaniwarwada to punish the ghost. But the restrictions put on the Mahars were never lifted.'

'Muslims did not face such torture,' said Imran.

'Our village was part of the Bahmani kingdom. Then came the nizam! The Muslims held sway in the village, and we never had pots around our necks,' answered Philip.

'The persecuted always take revenge,' huffed Imran.

Philip introspected. He remembered his wife, Ruby. His son, Warren. The village floated before his eyes: Sonai village! He remembered the stick-with-bells. The British came and took the stick-with-bells away, and gave them guns instead! And so, the village was left behind! As were the Mahars. And the menial work. He thought of Bhimnak.

Bhimnak had been transferred to Bombay. He had then been sent to London. Across the seven seas! And he never came back. Ships were filled with labourers, being sent to work on sugarcane plantations. Bhimnak was sent with those labourers. Where would he be now? How was he? So many untouchables were being sent out of the country. To far-off lands, colonies. Are there any records?

How many died? In the fields, while doing construction work, while digging? How many died in India? In the Maharwadas, fields and dams? How many were killed in the fields of Gultekdi? How many eyes had been gouged out? How many hands, feet or tongues had been cut off? How many were hanged? How many huts were burned? How many were raped? In how many places? Are there any records? At least the gods in heaven must have the record? Or does no one want to keep any record of these things? When will the thousands of years of persecution against the untouchables be written down?

Philip was keeping a watch on two things at once—the Peshwa's street and the past of the Mahars. Imran was lost in the distant past! The two kept quiet for a long time. At last, Imran spoke, as though he was thinking aloud. 'I cannot even go to the masjid because there's so much work. Tomorrow is Jumma. I will go to the masjid. I will sit for a couple of hours in the dargah. Read the namaz. I will have food there!'

The Muslims who had come from Arabia, Iran and Central Asia thought themselves superior. They looked down on the Muslims who were converts. They discriminated against the converted Muslims at masjids and graveyards.

Changing their religion did not solve the problems of the untouchables but rather complicated them further. If on the one hand conversion caused the untouchables to shrink in numbers, on the other hand, their caste identity remained stuck to those who were converted. They could not really get rid of it. The untouchables left their villages, their birthplace, but wherever they went their identity was determined by their caste and never by their art, craftsmanship, talents and qualities. They still had to bear injustices, dishonour, discrimination, torture and persecution. Philip Bush and Imran Nat were not the only victims of this torture. Wherever the untouchables went, they put up a brave fight. They were so used to poverty and discrimination that they could cast their roots even on a cliff. They remained alive in the most challenging environments. They were never obliterated. They knew that it was useless to complain about torture and injustice, and bore their sorrows with laughter. They never lost hope. Every day brought with it new hope. They could do any work for a handful of bread. They did not know how to say 'no'. Perhaps non-violence was born of the untouchables' resilience to centuries of torture and pain. This system was built on a foundation laid by the untouchables, and that was why it never tottered.

Businesses in London established the Company of Merchants of London Trading into the East Indies, for trade with East Asian countries, and especially India. The queen of Britain, Queen Elizabeth, granted trading rights to this company on 31 December 1600. This company was engaged in trading operations in India for a period of ninety-eight years, from 1601 to 1698. Godowns were constructed in Surat, Bombay, Calcutta and Madras. They got rights of trade from the local kings. The company also provided military training to its employees. Seeing the beneficial trade prospects in India, more traders reached India in 1698. They established a new company. This new company had more rights than the previous one. Thus, the two companies clashed. To end this clash, the two companies were merged in 1708, to form the United Company of Merchants of England trading to the East Indies. This company later came to be known as the East India Company.

Many nations, such as the English, the French, the Dutch, etc., were keen to set up their empire on the eastern front of India. These foreign powers fought among themselves as well as with Indians who held power. At that time, northern India was ruled by the Mughals and the south by the Marathas. The foreigners realized that unless they defeated the Mughals and the Marathas, they could not win over India. In the Battle of Plassey in 1757, the British defeated the nawab of Bengal and laid the foundation for the British Empire in India. Although the British had defeated the nawab, they kept him on the throne. He was a nawab in name only; the actual power lay with the British. Through this dual government system, the British looted the people of Bengal, but the nawab was blamed for it and not the British. In 1758, the Company enlisted huge numbers of soldiers, most of whom were people from the various backward castes.

The British had modern technological knowledge and arms, and the Indian kings and rulers were no match for them. The Indian power-holders had no unity either; they fought among themselves. The caste system had caused much unhappiness among the lower castes. The British took advantage of the situation and looted the defeated kingdoms heavily. The Company officials began to behave like kings themselves and amassed illicit wealth. Complaints about their behaviour were sent to the British parliament, but no steps were taken against them. The Company officials would retire and return to England with huge wealth, and lead the rest of their lives in great luxury. Their lifestyle and wealth gave rise to jealousy among their friends and relations. The wealth gathered by these officials in unlawful ways was such that they began to exert influence on the British parliamentary elections. For these reasons there was widespread discontent with Company officials.

The colonies in America had gained their independence, and the British Empire had considerably weakened there. The British were in a financial crisis. They had but one option now: to fleece India. Thus the British parliament passed the Regulating Act in 1773, in a bid to gain control of the East India Company. In accordance with this, Warren Hastings was appointed the first governor-general of India. But this act caused some problems in the operations of the East India Company. So in 1784, Pitt's India Act was passed. With this act, the British government acquired greater powers over the Company.

The British, the nizam of Hyderabad and Tipu Sultan were all waiting for the Maratha power to come to an end. The last

Peshwa of the Marathas, Bajirao II, and the British were engaged in a struggle. The reins of the Maratha Empire were handed over to Bajirao II, Daulatrao Shinde and Yashwantrao Holkar. Bajirao II and Daulatrao Shinde wanted to get rid of Yashwantrao Holkar, and hence they put Kashirao on the throne of Indore. This enraged Yashwantrao Holkar and his brothers, Malharrao Holkar and Vithojirao Holkar. They created a furore. In all this excitement, Daulatrao Shinde attacked Malharrao Holkar's camp and killed him. Infuriated at the death of their brother, Yashwantrao Holkar and Vithojirao Holkar started a rebellion against the Peshwa. The Peshwa's valiant sardar, Bapurao Gokhale, attacked Vithojirao Holkar and arrested him. Then they brought him to Pune. He was later put to death—under the feet of an elephant. Yashwantrao Holkar now wanted to withdraw and sign a treaty with the Peshwa, but the Peshwa declared war. In the battle fought on 25 October 1802, Yashwantrao Holkar defeated the Peshwa. The defeated Peshwa called on the British for help. The British were waiting for an opportunity like this. The British Army entered Pune. Yashwantrao Holkar stopped fighting and left Pune. Thus the British won without a fight. In return for this help, the British made the Peshwa sign the Treaty of Vasai. According to it, the Peshwa kingdom was under British protection and the Peshwa could not fight anyone without British permission. Nor could he independently forge relations with any other king. If the Peshwa had any disagreements with any other kingdom, they would have to be resolved only through British intervention. All these conditions infringed on the rights of the Peshwa. It was due to the Treaty of Vasai that the Maratha Empire was now in the grip of the British, who had put up a subsidiary army to keep things under their control.

It was the job of Philip Bush and Imran Nat to keep the resident of Pune informed. They were lowly people whom no one doubted. They were walking from the Shani temple towards the Nagnath Par when they saw a poor Kunbeen woman wailing on the street. A Brahmin had kicked her out of his house, accusing her of theft. She was begging for forgiveness. The Brahmin was out of control. Philip went and stood before the Brahmin, who raged, 'Take her away! I don't want her in my house!'

The woman was scared when she saw Philip and Imran, who took her away.

Imran said, 'Let's keep her.'

Philip said, 'Let's hand her over to the British.'

The Kunbeen woman said, 'I will stay only with a Brahmin, or I will go back home!'

Finally, Philip handed her over to the British official Willsman. He made the woman sit beside him and asked Philip to leave. Imran, who was standing nearby, jeered. The two of them started to walk along the Mutha riverbank. A Brahmin *batu* was playing with his tuft of hair in front of the Omkareshwar temple. The Kunbeen's touch had aroused Philip.

In those days, the Brahmins kept Kunbeens in their houses. They would do household chores. They were sometimes given away as gifts or were bought. Men used them for their pleasure. A Kunbeen passed by the Omkareshwar temple. Brahmin batus were talking among themselves in front of the temple.

'There should be no battle between the Peshwa and the British. If the Peshwai is lost, we Brahmins will be in danger. We will go to the dogs. The British came to India and saved the Hindus. These Mughals had all but destroyed the Hindu religion.'

'The peshwas put a pot around the Mahars' neck, and the British gave them guns. Now the Peshwas will be fired at not by the British but by the Mahars. I can give it in writing.'

'The British should be killed in broad daylight.'

'That is bound to happen in the days to come.'

'The Brahmins hate the Mahars. They curse them, but they sit beside the British with love and respect. How strange!

According to the shastras, the Mahars are closer to us than the British!'

'We accept a converted Christian Mahar but not a Hindu Mahar. This is our attitude and religion.'

The Brahmins were thus engaged in voicing their opinions. They looked at Philip and Imran and jeered. Philip and Imran ignored the Brahmins and went on their way towards the Jogeshwari temple of Budhvar Peth.

'We are lucky that we are in the Company army. There are untouchables in the Maratha Army too, but only as foot soldiers in the infantry. A foot soldier has to groom the horses, take care of them and clean their dirt. What sort of work is that? What value does a foot soldier have? He just runs behind the horseman.'

'There is more. Carry the wounded soldiers from the battlefield. Carry the wood and other goods. Or sit beside the horses. Is this what it means to be a soldier? The Maratha Army has always kept the untouchables away from real work.'

Imran and Philip had reached the Lal Mahal by now. They did a darshan of Ganeshji of Shaniwarwada in memory of Ganpat Mahar. They had both converted, but in their minds they were still Hindus.

> Give me the vision of Ganpat Mahar.
> May the queen appear before me.
> I am ready to wear the pot around my neck if I get to see the queen but once.

Imran and Philip put a muzzle on the horse's mouth. Imran patted the horse, which was shivering. Philip scratched its ears. Ganpati was being worshipped in the temple. It seemed as if the stone walls of Shaniwarwada were staring at them.

An air of terror hung all around. The dreaded mantras were dripping sentiments of caste superiority and purity of lineage, crossing all limits. The prayers before the all-merciful god resonated with the conch-shell sound of powerful Sanatan:

Dear god . . . let our hands do the heinous sin
Let our lives be a mountain of sins
May we see a thousand hells in this very life
Dear god, make me a Mahar in every life
Let me be polluted
Oh! Heaven! Thirty-three crore gods!
Let me tie the pot as a *mangalsutra* on the neck of your queen
Let me bathe in the places of pilgrimage
Let the holy rivers be polluted
Let their streams carry my broom

The Brahmins returning after the Ganesh aarti were praising the Peshwai. They were also saying that the Peshwai would get its own army. This was a great piece of news for Imran and Philip. They carried the news to the residency. The resident responded with, 'Good.' They felt joyous. The horse, opening its foot-long penis, peed on the Sangam bridge. People looked at the horse's penis covertly. The stench of urine filled the air. Imran and Philip were laughing. They had unearthed news like the horse's penis. They were proud of themselves.

The sardars of the Peshwas had their own armies because they would have to go on expeditions, but the Peshwas themselves had none. Bajirao Peshwa II was under the protection of a subsidiary of the Company army, but he didn't trust them. The Peshwas had annexed the estates of the sardars. This enraged the sardars, who had served the Maratha Empire for generations. They now looked after their businesses independently. They had begun to ignore orders sent by the Peshwas. Cases of theft had gone up. The Peshwa wanted to put an end to all this, and so he wanted his own army. To keep the British appeased, the Peshwa handed over to them the job of training his army. Captain Ford accepted the responsibility.

A crowd of Brahmins had gathered in front of Shaniwarwada, as donations were being given out. Preparations had been made for feeding a thousand people. Hom havan and other rituals were in full swing. The lure of getting good donations had brought Brahmins from far-off places. Shaniwarwada's entrance was glowing with the festive spirit. The Brahmins were excited and joyous; they heaped blessings on the Peshwas.

Philip and Imran were walking towards the Ganesh temple. Matang women were ferrying cow dung. 'Cow dung! Cow dung!' they shouted at the top of their voices. The Brahmin crowd swelled. In a Brahmin house, a Kunbeen woman was pregnant, and the Brahmin was denying his responsibility in this matter. He tried to put the blame on her, but she was very clever. She had asked for his janave as a gift. She was a courageous woman. When the Brahmin tried to throw her out of the house, she remained strong. Other Brahmins gathered there and started abusing the Kunbeen. The Kunbeen now brought out the janave and shouted, 'Whose janave is this? Ask him if he did not give it to me as a gift!'

The Brahmin bowed his head, and the Kunbeen was beside herself with excitement. The Kunbeen shouted, 'I have a bunch of janave. Whoever wants to blame me can come forward.'

Seeing her rage, all the Brahmins began to slip away. The Kunbeen went inside the Brahmin's house. Seeing Philip and Imran approach, all the Brahmins went into their homes and locked their doors. The Kunbeens in every Brahmin house were happy, while the faces of Brahmins were downcast.

Though the Peshwa had given his army to the British for training purposes, the army belonged to the Peshwa; and while he paid their salaries, the army was in the grips of the British. The Peshwa had begun to realize his mistake now. As a security measure, he prepared an army of the Gusaiyas of the north. The

British were alarmed to see this new army of the Peshwa. This was the starting point of the clash between the Peshwa and British that was about to happen.

In 1804, the Peshwa had given the Ahmedabad region to Gaikwad, of Baroda, on an annual rent of Rs 4.5 lakh. This arrangement was to end in 1814. Gaikwad wanted to increase the tenure, but the Peshwa wasn't ready. They clashed. According to the Treaty of Vasai, the conflict ought to have been resolved by the British, but the Peshwa was too excited. Gangadhar Shastri had brought the power of attorney from Baroda, and the Peshwa was responsible for his security. But Trimbak Dengle murdered Gangadhar Shastri. This worsened the tensions. The British ruled over Anandrao Gaikwad's Baroda. He sought British help and gave them Surat as a gift in return. The British took Gaikwad's side, and the British resident of Pune issued a fatwa on the Peshwa: 'Hand over Trimbak Dengle, who is responsible for the murder of Gangadhar Shastri, or be prepared for war.' The Peshwa had no choice but to hand over Trimbak Dengle to the British. The British put Dengle in jail in Thane, but he escaped and rebelled with the support of the Peshwa. Furious, the British captured the forts of Raigadh, Purandar, Singhad and Trimbak. The Peshwa was also vexed by this gesture of the British. He began to communicate with the sardars, asking them to rebel against the British. The British learnt of this and began to take measures to reduce the Peshwa's powers. They tried to end his relations with those from whom he had sought help. They exercised their right over the Peshwa's army.

The Peshwa began to prepare to fight the British, with the help of his brave sardar Bapu Gokhale. He kept 50,000 soldiers ready in Pune. The British resident ordered that this army must be kept outside Pune, but the Peshwa refused to give in. A battle ensued. It started on 5 November 1817 in Khadki. Bapu Gokhale fought bravely, but his army was defeated. Though the British won this battle, they could not take possession of the Peshwai.

After the one-day battle of Khadki, nothing much transpired for the next eight days.

General Smith entered Yerwada with his army from Bombay. The army of the Peshwa, trained by Captain Ford, was in Khadki. It was now under the British. Colonel Burr's army was also in Khadki. The British gathered all their armies in Yerwada and attacked the Peshwa on 17 November 1817. The Peshwas were defeated in this battle. Bajirao II escaped. Shaniwarwada was captured by the British. They made Balajipant Natu unfurl the Union Jack over Shaniwarwada.

The British wanted to obliterate the very name of the Peshwas. General Smith went in pursuit of the Peshwa with his army. But they were unable to find the Peshwa in spite of General Smith's best efforts. The Peshwa began to gather soldiers from his sardars. He wanted his Pune throne back. General Smith was still in pursuit. Smith wasn't able to find the Peshwa, who was planning an attack on Pune.

Colonel Burr was now in charge of the affairs in Pune. He got the news that the Peshwa had advanced as far as Chakan near Pune. He did not have a big army and was worried. He didn't know where General Smith's army, which had gone in pursuit of the Peshwa, was. He sent a soldier to get help from the British Army in Shirur. On getting Colonel Burr's message, Lieutenant Colonel Philsman began to prepare to send an army to Pune, and so he handed over the responsibility to Captain Francis Staunton.

Captain Staunton chose the Bombay Native Infantry to take with him to Pune. In this army were Mahar, Maratha and Muslim soldiers, though most were Mahars. They started on 31 December 1817 at 8 p.m. On 1 January 1818, they reached Bhima Koregaon at 10 a.m. There was a huge army of the Peshwa at Bhima Koregaon. Staunton could neither advance nor retreat. The Maratha army of the Peshwa had surrounded the British Army from all sides. There was no option but to fight. The British Army fired cannons on the Peshwa's army, and the battle began.

The British had two cannons. It was a violent, gory scene. Bapu Gokhale and Trimbak Dengle led the front. The Arab soldiers of the Peshwa attacked the British soldiers. Many British soldiers perished, and one of the cannons of the British was captured by the Peshwa's side. The British soldiers were demoralized, but Captain Staunton gave them courage. They began to fight desperately, not caring for their own lives. Mahar soldiers fought bravely with the Maratha army and were able to take the cannon back in their possession. Bajirao II watched the battle from his palanquin on the other side of the Bhima River. He was restless when he saw weapons in the hands of the Mahars. He thought it was an ominous sign. The Peshwai had put pots around the Mahar's necks and brooms on their backs. And now, those very Mahars were fighting against them! He had never imagined such a thing even in his wildest dreams. He felt this was sinful. He desperately wanted the Mahars to lose, so that the Peshwas would go back to hang pots around the Mahars' necks. His blood boiled at seeing the Mahars fighting for the British.

British cannons were raining fire. Mahar soldiers were fighting bravely, without a care in the world. Horses neighed. Swords clashed. Cannons. The sound of firing. Fountains of blood. Heaps of dead bodies. Mad soldiers. Screams. The lust to win. Dead horses. Corpses holding weapons. Blood-red water of the Bhima River. Soldiers fleeing for their lives. The Peshwas could see their defeat. The Mahars had valiantly fought to devastate the Peshwa army, to devastate the Sanatani tradition of dominance.

The Mahar soldiers won the Bhima Koregaon war, and the Maratha army retreated towards Pulgaon. The Peshwa fled with his defeated army to Karnataka, crossing the Ghataprabha River. The British Army pursued them. The resounding victory of the Mahars echoed everywhere. Bhima Koregaon became a site of Mahar valour.

British activity increased in Shaniwarwada. Philip and Imran embraced in joy when they heard the news that the Peshwai had been vanquished. The water of the Mutha River flowed at great pace. A Mahar was walking nearby with his rattle stick. Philip ran to him. The Mahar was afraid. Philip broke the pot around his neck. The Mahar begged for pity. Philip broke the broom hanging from his waist. Imran lifted the Mahar on his shoulders. Philip fired a shot in the air. The British Army was celebrating. They were buoyant.

Four

After his retirement, Philip settled down in Jhol. There was neither a Christian community in Sonai nor a church. Had he settled in the Maharwada of Sonai, he would have become a Mahar again, and he did not want that. Neither would the Mahars have accepted him. The Mahars looked at him as a renegade who had given up his religion. But the truth was that although his body was Christian, his mind was still that of a Mahar, of a Hindu.

Philip lived in the Christian colony in the foothills of Jhol. Imran had also retired. He did not go back to his village in Kanpur and had chosen to settle in Pune. Imran had once come to meet Philip in Jhol.

Father D'Souza had returned from his trip to London. He was now in charge of the church in Jhol. He had worked hard for the Adivasis. His deeds were celebrated in London. When Bhimnak heard that Father D'Souza had come from India, he had gone to meet him. Bhimnak had also retired. He now lived in Southall in London. He had been baptized. He was married—to a girl from an Indo–Caribbean family from Haiti. They had met at a construction site of the Southall railway station. She could speak Hindi. Her name was Mary. They had a son, Peter. Peter had married a Black girl, a Nigerian, named Barbara. She worked in a brickyard. She was pregnant.

Bhimnak had met Father D'Souza with his entire family. They took his blessings. Bhimnak was in tears when he heard that

Father D'Souza was from Jhol, and Father felt happy to know that Bhimnak had links to Jhol. Father inquired about their well-being.

Father D'Souza was happy to hear Bhimnak's name from Philip. He told Bhimnak's story to Philip, who got emotional.

'Just see how we have scattered. Our families have been uprooted. Fate has played a cruel joke on us, Father . . .' He was reflective. He asked Father many questions. Does Bhimnak speak English? How is his wife? How old is his son? What does his daughter-in-law do? What are their names? Father answered all the questions patiently. Philip was as happy as he would have been if he had met Bhimnak himself.

The town of Jhol was divided into three parts. Lal Dongar, Biruba Plateau and Chambhar Tekadi. There was a fort on Lal Dongar. Shrimant Vikram Singh Mudholkar's son, Digvijay Mudholkar, lived in the palace within the fort. The British paid him a pension. Bamboo forests lay to the north, west and south of the fort. The town stretched to the east. The Falguni River ran through Jhol. The church was on the foothills of Lal Dongar. The agent, collector and judge of Jhol lived in this area. This was also where the Christian missionary office was. New recruits were trained here. Philip worked here as a peon. He had got this job on a reference from Father D'Souza. The dwellings of the converts lay here. And they grew bigger every day.

Jhol sat on Biruba Plateau. It had a population of 17,852. There was an old Mahadev temple on Biruba Plateau. A lake lay adjacent to the temple. The lake added to the beauty of the plateau. Below the plateau lived the Diwan, Patil, Deshpande, Kulkarni, etc. A big market would be set up here. The speciality was horses. It was known far and wide. The nizam himself bought a hundred horses from the market every year.

There were only a few Muslims in Jhol, but they were well established and prosperous. There was also a chawadi, the Rani

Channamma Baag and well-stocked shops. A lot of the people were shepherds, and the Biruba temple was in their lane. The shepherds sang hymns every night. Each shepherd had a flock of sheep which would graze on the plateau. Near the plateau were the gardens and cotton fields. The landlords of Jhol had forcefully taken away the land of the Adivasis, who now worked here as tenants.

Next to the plateau was the Chambhar Tekadi. The untouchables lived here. The Mahars to the east, the Dhors to the north and the Matangs to the west. On the south was a deep chasm. Dead animals would be thrown into it, which was why vultures, eagles and crows always hovered over it. There were a large number of stray dogs, too. A terrible stench rose from the chasm. No one ever went near it. Sometimes, human corpses would be thrown into it, after a murder. People were afraid of this chasm. Mothers would quieten their children by talking of this deadly chasm. To the east of the Chambhar Tekadi, barren lands stretched for miles. Horses and other animals of the village grazed on this land.

Many days into his retirement, Philip went to visit his native village, Sonai. No one could recognize him. He had to tell people who he was. The older generation had aged. So many had died. The younger generation knew his name, but they didn't know him in person. Boys stared at him in surprise. 'This Mahar from our Maharwada joined the army . . . he looks different from a Mahar . . . speaks differently . . . his face . . . his clothes . . . way of talking . . .' Everyone wanted to imitate him. The older people inquired about him persistently. The vision of some had become hazy, while some had impaired hearing, weak knees.

Philip asked about Bhootnak. They said Bhootnak had gone insane, that one day he jumped into the flooded Falguni River and floated away somewhere . . . His body was never recovered. Philip asked about Ambarnak. They said that he had converted to Islam and gone to Bidar. Philip realized that he had no one in this village any more. Bhootnak's hut lay shattered. Yesnak's son, Lingnak, lived with his family in Ambarnak's hut. The Maharwada was in tatters. The tamarind and neem trees had become old. The front wall of the Mari Ma temple had collapsed due to the heavy rains. Sonai village looked desolate and deserted. It was the same Maharwada as before, but there was nothing within. There were more dogs and more children now. Many huts lay broken. Philip felt sad. The river had gone dry. The trees on the riverbank had been cut. The village was the same as before. Only a couple of new houses had come up.

Philip was lost in the past. 'What if I had not left the village? I would still have been living on the leftovers of the upper castes. Tolerated insults, disregard and torture. I would be sitting with these old skeletons. Would I have seen the world? I would have died without any of this. This village is but the graveyard of my fate.'

The village seemed alien to him as he roamed the bylanes of his past, sometimes falling and then getting up. Memories flocked like sheep. He met Biru shepherd. He was old now.

'Who are you?' Biru asked.

'I'm Philip Bush.'

'Why such a strange name?'

'I'm the same Sidnak Mahar.'

'Oh, you have changed your religion, haven't you?'

'Yes, I became a Christian.'

'Do you get money to become a Christian?'

'No.'

'Then? What do you get?'

'We get humanity.'

'True. We treated you like dirt! You should all leave!'

'That will happen in the days to come.'

'It will be good . . . Hinduism will get rid of its dirt.'

Biru shepherd went after his sheep. Stray dogs moved around him. Philip had become a Christian, joined the army, but his real identity was that of a Mahar. Young boys from the Maharwada were roaming around with Philip. They felt inspired by him. They asked a lot of questions.

'Will the British take us in the army?' asked Mahadev.

'What weight must one be? How wide should the chest be?' asked Lakshman.

'When do they recruit?' asked Balbhim.

'Must one fight?' asked Keshav.

The questions entertained Philip. He liked the curiosity of the young minds. He answered him sincerely. The boys' eyes sparkled. Philip felt good. The boys walked with him for as long as they could as he left for Jhol.

'I will inform you about the recruitment time. Then you must come. I live in the Christian colony on the foothills of Lal Dongar. Anyone will give you directions to my house. In front of my house is a son-chafa tree,' he told them.

Philip really liked this new generation. He had spent so many years in this Maharwada. He could not get that time back. He was returning empty-handed.

The boys could not go any further. Philip was walking alone now. He may have once wielded a gun, but right now he felt scared. Of ghosts! He kept looking ahead and looking back. The approaching storm scared him. He felt a sense of shock every time he passed under a banyan tree.

The place seemed desolate. Not a single human being could be seen. He felt that the ghosts would come from behind and hold him by the waist . . . or they would come from the front and stop him on the way . . . The ghosts might attack him from behind and entangle his feet, sit on his chest . . . The ghosts might spring on his shoulders from the trees, wring his neck . . . Philip walked as fast as he could. When he came near the peepal tree in Burhanpur, he panicked.

By the time he reached home it was night. Everyone was asleep. He woke them all. Ruby brought him water and served him food. She then gave him a packet that had come from the Christian missionary office and said, 'This packet must be delivered to Devgadh tomorrow. Give it to the church father. They said it's urgent.'

'I will start for Devgadh as soon as I wake up,' Philip thought and went to sleep. He fell asleep very quickly.

Philip began to snore and dream. He saw that he was in Devgadh. He was wearing the white gown of the father. He went to the church. People stood up. He opened the Bible, but it turned out to be the Ramayana. He began reading. People laughed.

'The Brahmin is speaking in the voice of a Mahar.'

He was unable to read like a Brahmin. He went to the Vitthal temple. He sat in the Brahmin's place. Govind Bhatt sat before him with folded hands.

'Panditji! Please speak in the voice of a Brahmin!' People were jeering at him.

He was incapable of speaking in a Brahmin's voice. But even then he laughed.

Ruby woke him up. 'What happened? Why were you laughing?' she asked.

'I was a Brahmin in my dream,' Philip answered innocently.

* * *

Philip went to the church as soon as he reached Devgadh. If he had reached even a little later, Father Edmund would have left. Philip handed him the envelope. Father Edmund was a robust, classy young man. He lovingly inquired about Philip's well-being. He was in a hurry, as he was going for a baptism in the countryside near Saykheda. The untouchables of Kalvan village were going to be converted en masse. Father Edmund took Philip's leave. Philip came out of the church.

The church had become old. There were cracks on the walls. The gulmohar tree had grown big. Some renovation work was going on in Father's quarters, so he was sleeping in the church these days. Philip saw Harry in front of the church. Harry's father, Stephan, had died. Harry had two sons and three daughters. Philip went to Harry's house and had his meal there.

'Last night I dreamt of Govind Bhatt,' said Philip.

'He is long dead. His elder son, Moropant, now does the readings in the Vitthal temple. The elder son is good, but the younger one is a rogue. He threatened Father Francis. Father didn't pay much attention. But Father is not here any more. He went away to London. This new father is enthusiastic, but he doesn't know the people well. They are two-faced,' said Harry.

'Let us do our work honestly, that's all,' said Philip.

'People are angry at the Christians,' said Harry.

Prataprao had left the Kaala Wada for good and settled in Pune. The Wada was now desolate. No one lived there. There were cobwebs all over. The windows were broken. Wild grass. The tower had collapsed. Wild pigeons had built nests in its ruins. The bamboo forests could be seen from the Kaala Wada. An earthen road now connected Devgadh and Rampur. People used this road now. Peacock Lake was full of moss. There were so many waterfowls that the entire lake was covered with them. The water level in the Tapi River had fallen.

Philip had come to Devgadh after a long time. He went around to take a look at the place. He then bade farewell to Harry, and to Devgadh. He had to cross the bamboo forests before it got dark. It was this same road that Chokha Mahar had taken, never to return, as Philip recalled.

The road from Devgadh to Jhol was not a straight one. One could go through Saykheda, but that was a longer route. A path also led through the bamboo forest. This was a shortcut, and one could get lost. It was also frequented by thieves. There was a bullock-cart road from Devgadh to Jhol. This road touched the borders of Rahimatpur, but it, too, was a longer route. Bhimnak and Sidnak had often walked on this path, so Philip knew it well. It followed the banks of the Tapi River. There was a chance of getting lost near the Kala Dongar area, and this was where the dacoits were waiting to attack.

The dacoits stopped Philip. They had axes on their shoulders. But Philip was not scared. He was an experienced soldier. He laughed loudly when he saw the dacoits, who were surprised at this response.

'I am a Mahar. I have nothing on me. Come and see!'

The chief said, 'Let him go, or we will become polluted.' The dacoits let him go. He went on his way, relaxed.

Deep forests and valleys. The path was difficult but beautiful. Waterfalls, fountains, chirping birds, cool breeze, deep shadows, Adivasis, cavorting monkeys, worms, wild-scented flowers, the blue sky peeping through the green leaves, solitude, the greenery, spellbinding views . . . one could not feel tired on this journey! Philip was walking fast. He remembered his home amid the sounds of the waterfall and the birds, amid the green trees and the breeze and the song of the shepherd.

When he reached home it was late at night. Ruby was awake. Warren was also awake, awaiting his return. Philip narrated to them the incident with the dacoits. Ruby heard it with all seriousness. Philip burst out laughing.

'What did the thieves do?' Ruby demanded.

'Stopped me,' said Philip.

'Then?'

'I told them I am a Mahar.'

'Then?'

'They let me go for fear of getting polluted.'

'That's good.'

'The benefit of being a Mahar.'

'Today was a bad day. You were stopped by dacoits there, and here, in the town, the Hindu Vahini stopped Warren. They told him that Christianity is a foreign religion, that by becoming Christians we are helping the foreigners. We must become Hindus again!' Ruby said.

Warren said, 'What will be my caste if I become a Hindu?'

'Then?' asked Philip.

'They were quiet. They walked off in anger. I did not want to engage any more with those goons,' Warren said.

'Do you know them? Show me tomorrow!' demanded Philip.

'Eat your food now,' Ruby insisted.

'They will threaten us if we are Mahars. They will threaten us if we become Christians. Same with Muslims. We should become goons like them!' Warren was agitated.

'Show me who they are tomorrow. Now let's eat and go to sleep,' Philip said.

The Sanatani Hindus were opposing the missionaries. The church had increased its activities. People from the Scottish Church in Pune had come over to help. They would come every six months or so. There was a lot of talk about Christianity. The backward castes did not listen to the arguments of the Sanatanis. 'We will go where we are treated with humanity,' they would say, showing signs of a new awakening.

Warren was of a marriageable age. But no one was ready to marry their daughter to him. People would come to the church every Sunday. They would meet and talk. But the moment it came to marriage, they would start thinking about caste. Philip was a Mahar, in spite of being a Christian. He would go to the Maharwada in Jhol. He had more connections with the Mahars than with the Christians. But then, he was distanced from the Mahars as well. He was neither here nor there. Upper-caste Christians did not marry their children to lower-caste Christians. White Christians had nothing to do with Brown Christians. The missionaries spread their religion, but they did not do anything to demolish caste. They would talk about caste discrimination in the Hindu religion but kept quiet about caste discrimination among Christians. The converted untouchables felt that they had been tricked. The British needed a Christian community in India so that they could feel secure about the empire. The growing Christian population made them feel secure. They built dams, bridges, opened medical units, schools. What lay behind all of this was not the desire to develop the country but to lay the foundations of a colonial culture.

Hindustan was never a nation; it was an amalgamation of small states. A small king under the aegis of a bigger king. In the development of power, certain things in a king's reign were inevitable. Violence, looting, persecution, the kidnapping of women—all of this was a show of power. Who benefits from states expanding their boundaries, the increase in revenue, the death of thousands in war? When weapons speak, the common people must become mum. Before the foreigners came, the kings of Hindustan were looting their own people. They looted by fighting others. Kingship meant uncontrolled looting. Then, imperialism was born. The British Empire sailed through by looting its colonies. To do so it had to kill people's political and moral rights. Looting is never really a financial thing; it has to do with the theft of identity. Philip was the devastated symbol of the proletariat that had lost everything. The caste system was a battlefield conducive to looting. Every upper-caste person in India looted the identity of the untouchables. Upper castes of all religions kept the lower castes at a distance.

Philip had to go to the Maharwada in search of a daughter-in-law. The Hindu religion divided its people into castes, created discrimination of high and low. The victims of this conspiracy were the lower castes.

Philip was sitting under a son-chafa tree. He was thinking about the Kunbeen woman. Ruby was threshing the jowar. Warren was reading the Bible. Philip was lost in thought, lost in his memories. He had undressed the Kunbeen woman and lifted her legs. Ruby picked out the gravel from the jowar. Worms crawled here and there on the ground. Philip took out his old gun. He wanted to fire it.

Ruby shouted, 'Get up! There's a crow above your head.'

Philip felt the crow droppings on his head. 'This is a good omen,' he said and laughed.

'People are going towards the church,' said Warren, looking up from his Bible.

'So many are going towards the Church, something must be wrong,' said Philip, getting up to leave.

Ruby was upset at what Philip had said. 'Look to your own home first.'

Philip was angry too. He said, 'We must go, or they will doubt if we are really Christians.'

Ruby said with agitation, 'What will you eat if the stove isn't lit?'

Warren got up now. Running out, he said, 'The church is our stove.'

The carriage arrived. The diwan of Jhol alighted. He had converted to Christianity. Everyone stood in the churchyard. The agent, Mark, the collector, Victor, and the tehsildar, Michael, also arrived. Everyone now went inside the church.

Father D'Souza was speaking in a grave voice. 'The murderers killed our Lord Jesus by nailing him to the cross. And when he was being killed, Jesus looked to the heavens and prayed for the killers, "Oh Lord, have mercy on the murderers!" We all are children of Jesus. We must pray for those murderers.'

Philip looked at the diwan's wife, who stood beside the diwan. He remembered the story of Ganpat Mahar. He looked away from her. He could smell the horse's piss. He felt distressed. 'What are people doing? What am I doing?' He remembered Parbati. She would dance crazily when she was possessed. People were paying their respects. He felt funny. He began to curse himself.

Father Edmund had been murdered. He remembered Father Edmund's robust appearance. He looked at the agent's wife. The agent had come with his family. If Father Edmund can be killed, what security do we have? He felt scared. The Sanatanis had also stopped Warren on his way.

Everyone came out of the church. Philip walked quickly, clutching his abdomen. Warren came up to him and asked what was wrong. Philip told Warren that he should stop the Adivasi woman selling firewood. Warren did as Philip said.

'We must be cautious,' thought Philip.

Warren noticed that Philip was deep in thought and said, 'What are you always thinking? No one will kill us. Important people are killed. We are not important.'

Philip tried to explain his worries to Warren, but Warren was too agitated to pay attention.

'Why do you think yourself to be so important? This is why you can't find a girl for me to marry!'

Philip lost his temper now. 'I am a soldier. What is your problem? Why don't you try to find a girl yourself?'

Warren cooled down. 'I should try?'

Philip was incensed. 'Do I have to teach you these things at my age? I looked at diwan's wife. I looked at the agent's wife. Have you inherited nothing from me? Why do you have eyes? Look! You will get someone. Did you look at that Adivasi woman?'

Warren once again felt a surge of anger. 'I don't want to talk to you.'

Philip was furious. 'Do you think you can speak to your father like this? Do you think I am retired and so I have no value? Remember, even at this age I work at the missionary office.'

Warren went away. The gatekeeper of the church was looking at them astounded.

Warren went home with the bundle of firewood. Philip, too, left for home. He met Khoklayee on the way. She had grown old. She did odd jobs.

'Did you find any girl?' asked Philip.

'There is one. Her marriage failed. See if you like her,' Khoklayee said.

'Broken marriage?'

'It is difficult to get a girl. You are polluted. People don't want to give their girls to you. All this trouble is because you have changed your religion. Your religion is coming in your way.'

'Is the girl beautiful?'

'I have spoken to the girl's family. They are ready. Go and take a look. The girl is good.'

Khoklayee was Bhimnak's elder sister. Dhondnak was dead now. If he were alive, he would have arranged for hundreds of girls to be seen. He knew a lot of people.

Philip reached home. The stove was burning. Ruby was making rotis. Warren was reading the Bible.

Philip sat in the yard. Some boys had come from Sonai: Mahadev, Balbhim, Lakhsman, Keshav. Philip asked them to sit. He was quietly itching his ear.

One of the boys gathered the courage to say, 'We want to become Christians!'

Warren came out. He had brought water for everyone.

'Why?' asked Philip.

'I want to marry a Christian girl,' said Lakshman.

Philip was livid. 'You don't change religion for getting girls or money. Mahars are changing their religion to get rid of their disgrace. I think of the insult, the disregard I have borne. I don't care for any religion. I have no use for gods and religions. You all must meet Father. Warren will take you to him.'

Ruby came out as she heard Philip's voice. Philip told her, 'These boys are from Sonai. They have come from far away. They want to become Christian so that they can marry Christian girls.'

Ruby laughed. 'Our boy is not getting a girl. How will you get one?'

'We don't know anything. We just came to ask,' Keshav responded.

'It's good that you thought to make inquiries,' Philip said appreciatively.

'I think people should change their religion every ten years. They should be Hindu, Christian and Muslim. Why stay in the same religion till death?' said Balbhim.

Philip was surprised at Balbhim's words. The new generation is so advanced! They have such foresight! Philip was lost in thought. The Hindus don't help anyone, nor do they let others help anyone. What was this outlook? It was supposed to be a religion that preached love. How did it become a religion that taught discrimination?

'Come, boys. Have your meal,' Ruby asked the visitors.

* * *

The skirmish that had started off in the bamboo forest showed no signs of coming to an end. The British and the Adivasis had clashed in a tremendous fight. The British had taken control of the forests and the landlords. Many Adivasis were tricked into selling their land at throwaway prices. Their lives had been impacted. They had been cut off from others, living independent, self-sufficient lives. But that was now at stake. The zamindars' goons began to torture them. The Adivasis now had to pay taxes on their own land. They were tenants on their own land. The goons forced them to pay taxes to fill the coffers of the British. Various kinds of taxes were imposed. Trees were being felled. Roads were being laid through the forest. Various machines were brought to do the work. Now that outsiders frequented the forest, the Adivasis had lost their rights to their *jal-jungle-zameen*. Those who opposed this incursion were shot down mercilessly. The Bhils were being heckled by the British. They were put in prisons as dacoits. When Chindya Bhil rebelled he was shot dead.

Chindya Bhil's sons, Siddhu and Bhujang, had grown up and were now the leaders of the Adivasis. The Adivasi population was scattered through the bamboo forest. They felt that the outsiders were fierce and cruel. The outsiders regarded them as uncivilized, savage thieves. Insulted them. Doubted them. Hurt them.

There was a rumour that a dam would be built on the Tapi River. This flickered discontent among the Adivasis. The dam would mean that the Adivasi settlements on the riverbanks would go under water. The forest, land, corpses of their ancestors, their ghost temples—everything would be flooded. They would have to make their living as labourers. The Adivasis were worried. They were going to be expelled from the forest and banished from the life they knew. Their customs, their traditions were mocked. Their plant-based cures, their rites, their magic—everything was declared obsolete. Their language was polluted. Their children were forcefully sent to schools and the adults to church! The Adivasis were in deep trouble.

They held a Jat panchayat. Clans of Chindya Bhil, Pistulya, Sanday, Patal Pardhan, Dubla Korku, Tantya Pawra, Kanhu Warli, Umaji Maveshi, Mahadev Koli, Katkari had all gathered. The Adivasis of the Rampur–Jhol area had also assembled. It was the first time that such a big Jat panchayat had been arranged. The Jat panchayat met and discussed their agenda the whole day. Even then, the work seemed unfinished at the end of day. The Adivasis felt unredeemed.

'Adivasi lives have no meaning any more. We are put down in every way. How much more do we have to tolerate?'

'The zamindars' goons, the British sepoys, the thekedars, the missionaries—they have all come together to make our lives miserable. Workers' groups . . . deforestation . . . the levelling of land . . . no one asks for our opinions.'

'There was a time when no one dared come to the forests. And now, our homes are in the way of the roads they have made. Even the village dogs have started coming here. If we do not oppose now, we will end up like the untouchables. We are the kings of the jungle . . .'

'The doctor comes into our houses and examines our women! The Father comes and says, "Pray!" The teacher comes and says, "Go to school." The zamindars' goons come and say, "Pay taxes!" The thekedar comes and wants us to work in construction. The police come and tell us we are thieves . . . How many people shall we answer to?'

Everyone was excited. Everyone spoke at the same time. It was as though the jungle was talking in myriad voices . . . animals . . . trees . . . rocks . . . waterfalls . . . wind. The water had caught fire. The jungle had broken its silence. After years of deep quiet, every voice was now speaking.

'They come to loot us. There is no communication between us. They say and we have to listen. We are not allowed to speak. No one wants to listen to us . . .'

'Our women are violated. We can only helplessly listen to their wailing. They think we don't understand anything. They cannot comprehend that we might also have something to say . . .'

'We do not oppose them. We tolerate. That is why they think we are garbage . . .'

The rustling of the leaves in the jungle had gained momentum. Drums were being beaten, Adivasi instruments played. Women sang community songs.

Siddhu Bhil spoke like thundering rain. 'We are being attacked. They call us Asuras, Rakhshas . . . Remember that Ram and Lakshmana went to the forest through this very way. Sita bathed in Peacock Lake of Devgadh. When the Pandavas came to the forest they stopped at the hill of Patal Bhil. There is a hot-water fountain there to this day. Draupadi needed hot water for her washing, and so Bhim struck his mace on the earth, creating a fountain of hot water. Rakshasas lived here, and we are their descendants. Kansa played here in his childhood. Mahishasura is our hero. There are other heroes too—Ravan, Keshi, Hiranyakashyap, Dundubhi, Jarasandh—so many.' Sidhu Bhil's voice was full of emotion.

'Are you ready to attack Rampur the day after Dussehra and loot the treasury? We will teach the British a lesson.'

The Adivasis roared in approval. The Jat panchayat went on for three days. Every voice was heard.

'No one should know of our plans. Let's get to work. Whoever opposes us will be excommunicated,' Siddhu Bhil thundered. Adivasi tongues were on fire. Their blood was boiling. It was the call of the earth.

The Jat panchayat went for a darshan of Patal Bhairav. Winds of change had begun to blow. People began to speak sharply. Rebellion had been induced. It was quickly catching on. At night, the Panch drank their local drink, tadi. Two deer were cut for the meal. The Adivasis danced before Patal Bhairav.

* * *

The sun rose, and there was a stir all around. There were doubts and fears. Rumours flew in the air. Vultures hovered overhead. Panic spread. Everyone asked, 'How did this happen? No one could have imagined this even in their dreams!'

But it did happen! It was impossible to escape that occurrence. The British were furious.

Father Edmund was returning late at night after finishing a baptism. He had been sleeping in the church for a week now. His living quarters were being painted. Every day, something new came up, and the renovation work got extended.

The cool breeze from Peacock Lake helped him get proper sleep. When he would go to the Adivasis' huts, he would sleep in a bed in their yard. Edmund was well versed in sociology and anthropology. He knew Sanskrit. He had studied the caste system in detail. He had read many Hindu scriptures and texts. As soon as he came to Devgadh, he visited the Brahmin alley.

The Brahmins looked at him with suspicion. Narsopant said, 'This father will read our texts and misinterpret them. We must be careful around him. He knows Sanskrit.'

Narsopant began to spread falsehoods about Father Edmund. Everyone in the Brahmin alley hated Father Edmund, but he was not one to give up easily. Father Edmund went to Jhol and began to live in the missionary office. He became friends with the diwan of Jhol, who converted to Christianity. Father Edmund knew that the Hindu religion had many castes. There was discrimination among the castes. There was no affinity between them. That was why there was no unity. They were opposed to each other. The untouchables were huge in numbers. These people always had to tolerate insults and disgrace. They were in dire need of love. Father Edmund knew that if the untouchables were accepted lovingly, they would convert en masse.

Armed with the Bhagavad Gita, Narsopant reached Edmund's residence. With him were Vishwanath, Dayashankar and Umashankar. Father Edmund welcomed them heartily. Edmund, too, had a Bhagavad Gita with him. He was well acquainted with it. These people, to whom the Gita had been handed down by their forefathers and who knew it by heart, found it difficult to answer Edmund's questions, which made it clear to everyone that he had studied the holy books in detail, and with much thought and depth. Edmund's perspective was different. He was a foreigner. He thought differently about the Hindu religion and society. Narsopant was convinced by his intelligence. Father Edmund walked them to the road.

'He is a good man. Studious.' Vishwanath was genuinely appreciative.

But Narsopant was upset. He thundered, 'Hindu Puranas must be read only by Brahmins. If other people read these texts, they can be misled. And then Edmund is a church father. He would always spread falsehoods about the Hindu religion. His questions clearly showed his intent.'

The others listened quietly. He went on, 'He wants to understand the caste system. Why? Because he has to provoke the Mahars and Matangs? Abuse the Brahmins? Our God had reserved all knowledge for Brahmins at the time of the creation of the universe. We don't want anyone else. The ruling power is for the Kshatriyas, business for the Vaishyas, and these three varnas must be served by the Shudras. This has been the tradition for years. And this is how it shall go on. This is God's will. Mortals cannot alter it.'

Narsopant went on, his voice getting louder. 'Whoever wants to study the Hindu religion must understand the concepts of the doctrines about karma and rebirth, the philosophies of Dwaita and Adwaita. Understand the divinity of the Vedas and Yoga. Understand the Hindu concept of God and avatars. Understand the greatness of the concepts of *paap*, *punya*, *swarga*, moksha, *narak*, *vairagya*. Read the Bhagavad Gita. Ignoring all these, why is he hell-bent on understanding the caste system?'

Narsopant's voice was choking now. He started coughing.

Vishwanath got a chance to speak. 'Our religious texts were written by Brahmins, and Brahmins are at their centre. Thus, they mean well for the Brahmins. We wrote them. We interpreted them. Non-Brahmins were not allowed access to them. They weren't even allowed to learn Sanskrit. That is why no one complained against the Brahmins. But we should go beyond Brahminism, and understand religion and society. We never did that till now. We cannot play any role in social welfare unless we bury the untouchability and Brahminism of the Hindu religion.'

'But if we get rid of untouchability and Brahminism, what else will remain in the Hindu religion?' Narsopant snapped. 'These two things are its very spine.'

Umashankar said with vehemence, 'I find great pleasure in reading Hindu scriptures because they talk about the greatness of the Brahmins. Brahmins have been regarded as the greatest progeny of the earth. I feel proud to read that Brahmins are the very foundation, the facilitators of all creation.'

'If we are to preserve the purity of the Hindu religion, then Vedas must only be read by the Brahmins,' Narsopant said, sounding arrogant and feverish with emotion. 'We must accept this fact. Sanskrit is the language of the gods. It is the key to understanding Hindu philosophical texts. That key should only hang by the waist of the Brahmins. Hindu texts were only meant to be read by the Brahmins. If the untouchables read them, they will be baffled. There will be tension in society. That is why our ancestors have written that if lower-caste people read these texts, their tongues should be cut off. If they hear them, their ears should be rammed with lead.'

There swept through the Brahmin alley a tide of hatred against Father Edmund. The hearsay was that Father Edmund would hand out the holy texts to his butler, who would, in turn, hand them out to the lower castes to pollute the texts. This was supposed to be Father Edmund's conspiracy to taint the holy texts.

The Brahmins of Pune had sent a local pistol. Prataprao Deshmukh had helped in the matter. Narsopant left with the pistol. He felt scared, but his brain was fired with thoughts of revenge. His hands and feet trembled, but he went on walking. He had made up his mind. It was past midnight. Silence reigned. He reached Father Edmund's quarters. The door was locked. He turned towards the church. A cool breeze came in from Peacock Lake.

Father Edmund was sleeping in front of the church. Narsopant felt giddy as soon as he saw him. He listened keenly in the darkness. Devgadh was sleeping peacefully. His hands trembled. What if he missed his target? The thought frightened him. He went closer to

Edmund. The Bible lay near his head. He was sleeping peacefully. His bright red face shone even in the darkness. Narsopant looked around him. There was no one. How could someone who had rattled Hinduism sleep so peacefully, so boldly, all by himself? Without delaying any further, he shot into Edmund's chest.

Edmund sat up clutching his chest and shrieked. 'Please stop! Stop! Help me!'

Narsopant fled with trembling steps. Father Edmund fell to the ground. Darkness descended on his body. He closed his eyes. His lips trembled. Pages of the Bible fluttered open on his lips.

Narsopant kept running. His hands and feet were swollen. He cast off his chappals; they were obstructing his running. Now he ran fast. He was afraid of being seen, being pursued and caught. The darkness creaked with the sounds of his footsteps. He entered the Brahmin alley, reached his house and went inside. Moropant was awake.

'The job is done!' Narsopant said and closed the door. He was shaking terribly. He was delighted that no one had seen him. He began to babble. 'Father would have been so pleased!'

Moropant was worried. 'Are you sure he died?'

Narsopant said excitedly, 'I shot him in the chest from very close. He took two stumbling steps and fell. The end.'

There was an air of carelessness about him as he spoke. His elderly mother, Malti, stood nearby, balancing unsteadily on a cane. Moropant's wife, Padma, and Narsopant's wife, Saraswati, were awake too. Padma was childless. Saraswati's children, Vedant and Yamu, were sleeping on her lap.

This was the first time a pistol had come from Pune; it was usually books and scriptures. The pistol frightened everyone. What if the British sepoys come? What if they search the house? What if they find the pistol? They had discussed possible answers.

Narsopant explained, 'Who will search the house of Brahmins? We are supposed to be cowards . . .'

Moropant asked everyone to go back to sleep, and they all went to bed.

Narsopant wrapped a scarf around himself and said to Saraswati, 'For so long I have protected the Hindu religion with my puja-paath. This time I did it with a weapon.'

His voice wavered. Devgadh was in deep sleep.

Rebecca came to the church in the morning for her regular cleaning duties and saw the dead body of Father Edmund. She ran to the road, shrieking. People gathered hearing her scream. The news of the father's murder spread like wildfire. There was a flurry in the Christian dwellings. People began to run to the church. The news soon reached the British camp. Slowly, the whole of Devgadh descended on the church. All Christians were wailing loudly. They called it a cowardly attack on their religion. Murdering Father Edmund was an attempt to spread terror. The murder was a kind of statement: 'If you go about converting people, you won't be spared.'

Christians were scared that there would be more attacks on them in the future. The Christians realized that conversion had another, deadly face. To convert would be to face the ire of the majority Hindus. This was not just a religious matter; it was related to the issue of population as well. And population is related to power. The power-holders had woken up. The ground beneath their feet had begun to slip away. Their stability was at stake. It had been challenged. It was important for them to safeguard their power over the minorities. This was what they had indicated by killing Father Edmund: 'If you challenge us, this is the fate that you will suffer.'

Search began for the father's murderer. British officials were raging. The army had set up blockades all around. Roads were patrolled. People were scared of the army's conduct. A soldier found a pair of chappals lying on the road and handed them over to Captain Lindlay, who began investigations. The intelligence service was put to work. Two soldiers were sent to the shoemakers' dwellings. All the shoemakers were brought in. The Padewar Mahars were summoned too. There were rumours that the doubt had now shifted to the shoemakers and Mahars. Speculations were rife. Silence descended on Devgadh.

Father Edmund's dead body was kept for viewing. Crowds of spectators thronged the church. Everyone spoke of Father's lively nature, his generosity, his affection for everyone. People crowded the crossroads. Arguments were on in full swing. There was a debate on whether the Adivasis were behind the murder. Devgadh was tense. The dead body was kept under strict security.

The British officials had sent reports to their seniors. All the Europeans in Devgadh had assembled. Speculations were rife. Captain Lindlay was still looking for the culprit. The sepoys brought the Mahars. Chokha Mahar came with the head of the Padewars. The panch of the Mahars, too, were here. Captain Lindlay spoke to them tenderly. 'Can you recognize these chappals?'

Chokha Mahar spoke instantly and with humility. 'I know. They belong to Narsopant Brahmin. I sit near the chappals at the temple. I know.'

The Mahars had not understood the gravity of that question. They were amused by it. Chokha Mahar was delighted that he knew the answer to a question asked by the British! The captain asked them to sit outside. They sat under the banyan tree.

Next, eight or ten shoemakers assembled, and the captain asked them the same question.

Shekappa Chambhar answered this time. 'These belong to Narsopant Brahmin. I make his chappals. I know the number of his feet. It is twelve.'

Shekappa Chambhar was also surprised that the British should ask about chappals. The captain asked them to wait outside too. They went and sat beneath another tree. They had to avoid getting too close to the Mahars!

About eight or ten sepoys reached the Brahmin alley. They knocked on Govind Bhatt's door. Narsopant realized that the sepoys had come. He was scared. No one had ever knocked on these doors so loudly. Moropant opened the door. He was shocked to see so many soldiers together. All eyes in the Brahmin alley were straining to see what was going on. Moropant stood guard at the door. His face was beaded with sweat.

'Where is Narsopant?'

'He is asleep.'

'Wake him up. We have come to take him.'

'Tell me the place. He will go after his bath and rituals.'

'No, we can't allow that. The captain has ordered that he must be taken along.'

'Ask the captain to come here and meet him.'

'We cannot go back without him.'

'Why do they want him?'

'We don't know. We can't ask our seniors.'

Realizing that the sepoys would not leave without him, Narsopant came out himself. Seeing him, the sepoys were in a fix. They paid him the customary obeisance.

'Captain Lindlay has called for you. He wants your guidance on some matters. Maybe it is about Father Edmund's funeral.' The sepoy was trying to be as polite as possible.

'Okay, I am coming,' Narsopant said and swaggered out with the sepoys.

The sepoys walked behind him. A crowd followed them. On the way, many people bowed to him. Narsopant noticed the crowd at several points on the road. He felt restless. He realized the seriousness of the situation. He knew that a quick investigation had been made. Gradually, his face fell. His pace slowed. His heart began to beat faster.

Narsopant was nurtured in the lap of Hindu scriptures. He could not think beyond them. Right now, he was thinking, 'Just as Vishnu is the foremost of all gods, Chudamani the best of all ornaments, thunder the most powerful weapon, mind the premium sense, the Brahmin is the best of all humans. The one with whom a Brahmin is happy and satisfied, Vishnu himself is satisfied with that person. The one who serves a Brahmin gains knowledge of the Parabrahma-Paramatma. Vishnu dwells permanently in the Brahmin's body. The household which satisfies a Brahmin is free of all sins and gets everlasting access to the heavens. They who worship Brahmins never fall sick or suffer from poverty. If a Brahmin's feet touch the threshold of a house, that place should be regarded as pious. The Vidhata has placed the Vedas in the Brahmin's mouth. All donations, charity, offerings, sacrifices are meaningless without the Brahmin. Where the Brahmin is not fed, there the Asuras, Bhutas, Rakshasas feed. Whenever a non-Brahmin sees a Brahmin, he must pay obeisance to the Brahmin. The Brahmin's blessings increase his lifespan. The one who does not respect a Brahmin or opposes him suffers and loses his life. He is destroyed. And then he finds himself in a Chandal womb. He is then born into a life of poverty, sickness and hunger. If one speaks roughly to a hungry Brahmin, eight kinds of sickness descend on his body. Such a man should be avoided. If one accidentally sees or meets such a man, one must take a bath to cleanse oneself. No poison is as dangerous as a Brahmin's curse. Poison kills a man. A Brahmin's curse destroys seventy generations. No one is as pure as the Brahmin. He is the enlightened guru of all . . .' These thoughts kept Narsopant occupied as he walked with the sepoys.

'If the king were a Hindu, the Brahmin would have felt protected. The Hindu king would have bowed down and smeared the dust from the Brahmin's feet on his kingly head. The British know nothing of this. What do they understand of a Brahmin's value, his glory? How shall one make them understand?'

Narsopant had a sombre look on his face. The sepoys walking behind him felt proud that they were walking behind a Brahmin.

This had a happened for the first time in the history of Devgadh: a Brahmin had been arrested. The British had crushed the Hindu religion under their feet. Moropant came out on the street. He was yelling at the top of his voice. His voice was so loud that all the Brahmins came out of their houses. Vishwanath was out of his house to cast the Nirmalya in the stream, but when he heard Moropant's voice, he got curious and went towards Moropant with the Nirmalya. The chanting of the Gayatri Mantra stopped in the ashrams. Even the Brahmin women peered outside. Something was surely wrong.

Moropant was shouting. 'How dare you arrest a Brahmin? Your tongue will fall off! There will be famine! You will die from a handicap! You will rot in hell! The Brahmin is the prime being. He can do no wrong. Whatever he does is piety. He can never sin. You will suffer! If you touch a Brahmin, you will burn to ashes! Try it if you have courage!' Moropant mouthed the choicest of curses.

Dayashankar went closer to Moropant. He whispered, 'Don't say Brahmin. Say Hindu.'

All the Brahmins in the Brahmin alley came near Moropant in an act of solidarity. An owl hooted on the peepal tree. Women wailed.

Dayashankar mumbled, 'Ominous! Shiv-Shiv! Something bad is about to befall.'

The Brahmins shuddered.

'The British are out to destroy the Hindu religion. They are building churches in every village,' Dayashankar said loudly, for all to hear.

'If people don't take care of their gods, their religion, the cow and the Brahmins, we shall stop all religious activities. If people want the British, then let them get their worship and their rituals done by the church father,' Umashankar said.

'Narsopant must be released. The British must apologize,' said Moropant.

'The Hindu kings have bowed their heads before the British. They could not prove their valour. They are all cowards. The British are now interfering in our religion. Doing whatever they like. Handing out weapons to the untouchables. Insulting the Kshatriyas, who are the only caste with a right to weapons. They are educating women and untouchables. No one questions them. All are weaklings, cowards,' Vishwanath thundered.

'The Hindus cannot survive without us. But now that we are in danger, no one raises a voice! They cannot keep their traditions alive without our blessings,' said Dayashankar.

'If the Hindus do not come out to support the Brahmins, I shall go and live in the Maharwada. Lift dead animals. Piss in places of pilgrimage. If God remains blind even then, I shall cast off my janave. Cut off my tuft of hair,' said Moropant, mad with rage.

The Brahmins were speaking over each other. They were infuriated. Slogans of 'Har Har Mahadev!' rent the air. Devgadh was shaken. The Brahmin group left for Parnakuti. They yelled when they saw the Kaala Wada. The soldiers were baffled. The passion of the Brahmins inflamed the local people's sentiments. They, too, began to speak against the British. The British allowed Umashankar, Dayashankar and Vishwanath to come inside to meet Captain Lindlay. Moropant was stopped by the sepoys. He felt affronted, and there was a scuffle. The sepoys pushed him. They asked all the Brahmins to go away.

'You cannot wait here. Your representatives have gone inside for the meeting. They will talk and tell you what you need to know. Go home. Move!'

Seeing the demeanour of the soldiers, the Brahmins began to disperse and return to their houses.

The agent, Henry Men, had come from Rampur. The meeting with the British officials was on. Captain Lindlay spoke to the Brahmins. There was no court of justice in Devgadh. The final decision would be taken by the army.

Vishwanath told the captain their side of the argument. 'According to the Hindu religion, you cannot punish a Brahmin. No matter what the crime, a Brahmin cannot be given the death penalty. If you want to rule Hindustan, you must understand the Hindu religion. Please do not interfere in our religion. Hindu people will come out on the streets. Revolt. If you have to hang someone, hang a Mahar.'

Vishwanath had spoken calmly, trying to reason with the British. Captain Lindlay, however, was not influenced at all.

The Brahmins were agitated now. The captain paid no heed to them. A European soldier came in and stood quietly. Lindlay looked at the soldier.

'What shall I do with the dead body?'

'Hand it over to the Brahmins!'

'What if they don't accept it?'

'Do the final rites according to Hindu customs.'

The sepoys said, 'Yes, sir!' and left.

Lindlay stood up and left. Umashankar, Dayashankar and Vishwanath were befuddled. They came out of the room, but there was no one there. A large number of soldiers had been assembled in front of Parnakuti. Lindlay left for the church for Father Edmund's funeral. Father Edmund had been his classmate. Dayashankar began to weep.

The British had declared a curfew. People vanished from the streets. Soldiers fired shots near the Vitthal temple. The roads were completely deserted. Narsopant's dead body was brought to the Brahmin alley. The soldiers were cautious. They had never fought with unarmed people. This was a distressing event for the Brahmins. People wailed. Raged. They began to endorse Father Edmund's murder and stood in support of the Brahmins.

* * *

The news of Father Edmund's murder reached the Adivasis. It inspired them. If an untrained Brahmin who does puja-paath all day can go and kill a Britisher, why not us? We are the kings of the jungle. We shall drive the British away. A wave of valour swept through the Adivasi hutment. Everyone was waiting for Dussehra.

If you are a Brahmin, you will die writing . . .

If you are an Adivasi you will die fighting . . .

Khwaja Bhil's *pada* was known as the Ghost Alley. There were said to be ninety-seven ghosts in the bamboo forest in all, of whom seventeen were in Khwaja Bhil's pada. Khwaja Bhil was engaged in occult practices. He would appease the angry ghosts, make them do this or that by either threatening or bribing them. He could make a ghost do as he pleased. Many Adivasis came to him to get rid of a ghost. He charged heavily from the people in distress who came to him for help. A cock, a coconut, rice or a cat . . . People complied. They gave him what he wanted. No one dared to upset him. There was a ghost temple in Khwaja's pada. Ghosts crowded there on days of the new moon and full moon.

One could say that the entire bamboo forest was full of ghost temples. The Adivasis worshipped the ghosts and played loud instruments during the rituals—so loud that the noise could burst eardrums. They sang songs of ghosts. The Adivasis were afraid of them, and this was a way to appease them. The new-moon and full-moon days were important. Women who were possessed by ghosts would come there to get them off, with the assistance of the ghost pujari. The pujari with the most expertise was Khwaja—he was well known for his skills. He could see the ghost, talk to them. He had learnt it as part of a family tradition that went back generations. He worshipped Brahmarakhas. His pada was full of dangerous, murderous places. Possessed trees. Abodes of the ghosts.

There were numerous palm trees in Khwaja's pada. Some had dried up, because all the liquid had been drained from them. Some were oozing in plenty, with clay pots tied around them. The clay pots were attached to bamboo frames and left to hang on the trees overnight. Sometimes they would overfill, and the liquid would spill on the ground. The Adivasis came to take the clay pots in the morning. The liquid, tadi, was delicious. The Adivasis drank a lot of tadi—it was their main drink.

A brook and a waterfall ran through Khwaja's pada; they went on to meet the water of the Falguni River. There were strange trees around them. Chennayya had been buried somewhere along the banks of the waterfall. He became a ghost. He had nabbed many. A temple was now being built for Chennayya. He had to be appeased. Christian missionaries tried their best to liberate the Adivasis from their superstitions.

'Don't worship a thousand ghosts.'

'Worship the one God.'

'God will take care of the ghosts.'

'Worshipping ghosts is going against God.'

'You will go to hell.'

But it all came to nothing.

* * *

A dam was being built on the Tapi River. There was a shortage of workers for the job. The thekedars were concerned. One thekedar sent his goons to Khwaja Bhil's pada. They brought along two elephants. The elephants had been hired from the palace of Jhol. The thekedar's men provoked the elephants, who began to run helter-skelter, trampling whatever came their way. Bhil huts were destroyed. The elephants went on the rampage. Women and children came under their feet. The Bhils began to run where they could, but the thekedar's men began to attack them. Some of them could run away deeper into the forest, but many wounded Bhils were taken captive. The cries of women and children rent the air as the captured Bhils were tied up. The thekedar's goons returned on the elephants, with captive Bhils walking behind them. Stray dogs completed the procession.

The Bhils who had run away came back at night and were horrified to see the condition of their huts. Khwaja was sleeping soundly, but it was a gloomy night for those who had lost their family members. What could they do but drink themselves to sleep. No lamp was lit that night. No song was heard, no drumbeat. The dam construction on the Tapi River was in full swing now. But the Adivasis did not want to help the British.

The East India Company had been facing a lot of trouble in recent times. Its days seemed numbered. People in all regions came out in opposition to it. There were frequent clashes between the British and the locals, who no longer gave in to threats. They wanted to be free, even though they had no leader or weapon or direction. They did not know when or where or how to revolt, but they protested all the same.

Khwaja's pada gradually restored its routine life. The Adivasis who had been driven away did not return. The only one to come back was Pinya Pawra's wife, Margi. The Adivasis remade their huts. They put the tragedy behind them and started again. Drums started to beat once again. The ghosts resumed their dancing.

It was evening. The Adivasis had returned from the forest. They came back with what they had gathered that day—some had chopped wood, some had hunted animals, some had gathered honey or flowers or roots, some had collected bundles of grass, while some had simply come back after drinking their fill of tadi. The sun had set. It was a desolate evening as usual. The zamindar's goons had come to the pada. The Adivasis tried to run away, but the goons caught hold of them. Bhairav Pawra was beaten black and blue.

'You borrow money and then don't return it? We have come to get the interest. Unless you pay up, we won't go back. Or maybe we can take your wives and children with us. Pay the money and bring them back.'

The goons had villainous motives. By beating up Bhairav Pawra, they wanted to appear menacing. The Adivasis watched silently. Being quiet was the only way of self-preservation they had learnt. They knew that whoever spoke up would become the target of the goons, and thus they decided to keep mum. If anyone interfered, the goon caught him and asked him to pay the installment of the loan.

One of the goons held Bhairav Pawra's wife Chamukhi's hand. She sank her teeth into him. He was enraged by this and kicked her. She fell to the ground. Children were screaming. Pinya Pawra's wife, Margi, brought water for Chamukhi. She tried to comfort her by fanning her. Bhairav Pawra began pleading with the goons. Chamukhi sat up, fearful. A goon came near her again and held her hand a second time. Margi became violent. She attacked him. Inspired by her courage, the other women, too, attacked the goon. They struck him with their sickles and tied him up against a tree. They smeared cow dung on his face as children played the drums and danced. The other goon had run away. The captive was now pleading for mercy. Thus, the Adivasis learnt the concept of retribution.

* * *

Many British officials in Devgadh had sought transfers citing security reasons. New officials had come to Devgadh. Captain Lindlay was transferred to Bombay. Father D'Souza of Jhol had come to Devgadh. Warren was training to be a father. After his training he would be sent to the church in Saykheda. The Christian missionaries were working in full capacity. Father Albert had come to the church in Jhol.

The Brahmin alley in Devgadh was gloomy, dejected. Moropant had left Devgadh and settled in Jhol. The Kaala Wada and Moropant's house were permanently locked. A litter of pups now lived in Chokha Mahar's hut.

Vishwanath came out on the street as soon as he woke up. The day was yet to break. A cool breeze blew. The night-blooming jasmine gave out a sweet scent. Vishwanath went near Moropant's house, and the sight of it filled him with dread. He promptly turned around. He was shaking with fear. He ran home, and once inside, he closed all the doors and windows. He lay on his bed but could not sleep. He kept gazing at the ceiling. He did not wake Yamu. Moropant had asked Vishwanath to look after his house when he was away. He was going to get possession of that big house someday.

The sight of Narsopant's dead body had driven his mother Malti insane. She had given up food and drink. She closed her eyes and kept them shut, and passed away within a month.

Moropant locked his house and left Devgadh forever. His wife, Padma, gave him strength. Narsopant's wife started living with them along with her son, Vedant. Moropant took on their responsibility. Narsopant's daughter, Yamu, had been married to Vishwanath, who was fifty-five years old. His first wife having died, Vishwanath had asked for Yamu's hand in marriage. Yamu was fourteen years old. Vishwanath had been waiting hopefully to take possession of this house. But when he went there, he got the fright of his life, because he saw Father Edmund sitting on the stairs, Bible in hand. The British ghost scared him.

The sound of utensils emanated from Dayashankar's house. Vishwanath felt relieved. He started chanting the Gayatri Mantra. Outside, it was daybreak. The cock was crowing to announce the same. Today was Dussehra.

* * *

The Adivasis encircled Rampur before the sun rose. The soldiers were sleeping when the Adivasis attacked. The army was reduced to corpses. Thousands of Adivasis entered Rampur. They killed eleven British officials and dumped their bodies in the Falguni River. The Adivasis began to kill whoever came in their way. Some civilians were killed too. Streets were streaming with blood. There was a heap of dead bodies at the Palace Square. The air was rife with arrows. The king of Rampur ran away to Rahimatpur.

The streets were full of half-naked, dark-skinned, bow-and-arrow-yielding Adivasis. People were terrified to see them in this warlike state. The Adivasis thronged the palace. All soldiers had run away. A big wooden statue of Mahishasura was set up at the palace square. All British flags and insignia were pulled down. The people of Rampur sat terrified in their houses, with doors and windows tightly shut. Many houses were razed to the ground. Granaries were looted. Whoever came in sight was shot. The Adivasis reigned over Rampur for three days. Someone was injured in every house. The Adivasis left Rampur on the fourth day.

The streets of Rampur were lined with corpses. A stench filled the air. The bodies had started to decay. Arrows lay scattered all over. The bodies were burnt in heaps in communal pyres in the fields outside Rampur. The Adivasis had shown their cruelty. Locals were traumatized. They could not leave their houses. The British Army was left embarrassed. The Company government had lost its sleep.

Given the Adivasi rebellion, the fretfulness of the disbanded soldiers, and the air of discontent among the general public, the Company government had to do something. It decided to increase its strength by enlisting new recruits. The Maharwada of Sonai heard the news. People in Devgadh were opposed to the decision of recruiting Mahars in the army. The Brahmins, too, opposed the idea tooth and nail, but their opposition counted for nothing. Dayashankar's son, Gangadhar, and Umashankar's son, Sripad, both joined the army. All the Brahmins were incensed at this. But the two boys did not change their mind.

'Are we to fight the British or to strengthen them?'

'If the Brahmins begin to fight, who will do the puja-paath?'

'The British, the English language, the church—everything must be opposed.'

'The British want to destroy the Hindu religion.'

Preparations were being made to excommunicate Dayashankar and Umashankar. Squabbles and altercations were common. Those who had been so vocal in opposing the British were shocked that their own sons were crossing over to the British side.

Those who could not take care of their own children, what leadership would they provide to the community? The matter was openly discussed among the Brahmins. Umashankar and Dayashakar had failed miserably. It was a cautionary tale for everyone. Hindustan and the Hindu religion were in grave danger. Hindus would be destroyed, overpowered by the British. People were rebelling against British rule. They began to realize that they had ill-treated the lower castes. Thus, an unrest formed against the British and the Sanatanis.

In 1848, Mahatma Jyotiba Phule opened a school for girls in Pune. The second girls' school came up in 1851 in Chiplunkar Kothi. Some Brahmins were generous enough to donate their houses to Mahatma Phule so they could be used as school buildings. In 1852, Mahatma Phule opened a school for the children of the untouchables in Vetal Peth. The Hindu religion had prohibited education to women and the lower castes, but the British did away with these restrictions. This did not go down well with many Brahmins.

Gangadhar and Sridhar enlisted in the army. About the same time, two Mahars from the Sonai village, Balbheem and Lakshman, also enlisted. Gangadhar and Sridhar were sent to Pune, Balbheem went to Bombay, and Laksham was sent to Madras. The East India Company needed the army to consolidate its power, but the army itself was filled with discontent. The wages of the soldiers were low and were not being revised. The demand for a dearness allowance was rejected. This had been an issue for a long time now. This was the very reason that a British regiment had joined Mir Quasim in the Battle of Buxar. There was another reason for the resentment the soldiers felt: the British were interfering in their daily routines and rituals.

The British were relentless in this regard. Their high-handedness knew no limits. Their contempt and disregard for

Indian social traditions did not sit well with the people. Sepoys had revolted against the British in Ballore and hoisted the flag of the maharaja of Mysore. There were sepoys of many castes and religions in the British Army. They were divided on many grounds. The presence of untouchables in the army caused much bitterness among the upper-caste sepoys. They found it disgraceful to stand in line with the untouchables. Many soldiers were sent overseas, which was another reason for resentment, because in Hindu religion overseas travel was forbidden. Nor did those soldiers get any special allowance. The sepoys had expressed their discontent on many occasions and refused to fight.

March 1, 1857. A spark flew in the British Army. There was a cartridge factory in Barrackpore in Bengal. The untouchables made up a large number of the workers in this factory. Cartridges were made here for the new Enfield rifle. These cartridges were oiled with the fat from pigs and cows. One of the soldiers in the regiment was thirsty. He asked his colleague, who was drinking water, for a sip. The soldier gave him the water. The one who had asked for water was Mangal Pandey, and the one who had given it was Matadin Bhangi.

Havaldar Ishwar Prasad came near Mangal Pandey and said, 'Don't drink water from a Bhangi! This man is a lower caste!'

Mangal Pandey threw the water away, and began cursing and insulting Matadin. But Matadin was not one to take the insult lying down. He reverted angrily, 'Oh, Brahmin! You are polluted when you drink the water I give you but not when you bite the cartridge oiled with the grease from cow and pig fat! Do you find that all right? What kind of a Brahmin are you?'

The words of Matadin Bhangi befuddled Mangal Pandey. He did not know how to respond. Mangal Pandey was angry at Bhangi, yet he was also grateful. Bhangi had revealed the truth and saved the Hindus!

Mangal Pandey gathered all the soldiers and went to Bhangi. He challenged him to repeat what he had just said.

Matadin was fearless. He said, 'I am not afraid to speak the truth! I can say it a thousand times. You bite cartridges lined with the grease of cow and pig fat! And that does not pollute you? And how does our touch pollute you?'

Every word spoken by Matadin exploded like a volcano. The cow was holy for the Hindus, and the pig was impious for the Muslims. Both the Hindus and the Muslims felt betrayed. Their religious sentiments had been disregarded, played with.

Mangal Pandey was a proud Brahmin. He felt insulted and could not do away with this hurt. The next day, he refused to bite the cartridge on the parade ground. There was a stir. Lieutenant Henry Baugh was informed of the stir in his regiment. He immediately armed himself and galloped on his horse to the parade ground. Mangal Pandey fired at Baugh but missed. Pandey then attacked with a sword. James Hewson confronted Pandey as the latter fought Baugh. Tension spread. General John Hayers reached the spot. Mangal Pandey was standing there with his rifle. General Hayers ordered that Mangal Pandey be arrested. Havaldar Ishwari Prasad ignored the order. The European soldiers arrested both Mangal Pandey and Ishwari Prasad. They were court-martialled. Mangal Pandey was hanged on 8 April 1857 and Ishwari Prasad on 21 April 1857. The incident dampened the morale of the Indian soldiers. Matadin Bhangi was also hanged as the one responsible for sparking the incident.

At first, all soldiers had the freedom to pursue their rituals, but with time this became more and more difficult. The Company was expanding all over India and even elsewhere across the globe. It had come to Hindustan to trade. It cared nothing for the people and their traditions. It took the decisions that benefitted it commercially and were profitable. The Company did not encourage discrimination in the army because it felt that it would affect the unity of the soldiers. The Company did not care about the feelings of Brahmin soldiers. Most Brahmin soldiers were in the Bengal region; elsewhere, there were hardly any. Thus, those who refused to bite the cartridge were removed. Those who were rebellious were also done away with. The Company handled the matters in a rough manner, and this only led to a rough response from the soldiers.

May 10, 1857. Meerut. The army revolted against the Company. The rebels included both Hindu and Muslim soldiers. They burnt down the toll. Many British officials were killed. They captured Meerut. This rebellious group had no leader, which was their weakness, but they still managed to attack and capture Delhi on 11 May 1857 from the East India Company.

The rebel group entered the Red Fort and requested Bahadur Shah Zafar to sit on the emperor's throne. He declined because he had been paid by the British ever since they had dethroned him. Still, the soldiers forced him to take the throne and declared him the emperor of Hindustan. The news was greeted with great enthusiasm by many, with the exception of the Sikhs. The reason was that Sikhs had been treated very badly by the Muslims, and Bahadur Shah was a Muslim. However, Nana Saheb Peshwa had accepted the leadership of Bahadur Shah Zafar.

Bajirao II was also given a pension by the British. After his death, his adopted son, Nana Saheb Peshwa, demanded the title of Peshwa and a pension from the British. The British refused to give Nana Saheb the title and declined his demand for a pension. This turned Nana Saheb against the British. He played an important role in the 1857 rebellion. He did not want to irk the British, and hence he wrote a letter to them on 5 June 1857 informing that a rebellion may erupt in Kanpur against the Company. The rebellion broke out in Kanpur on 6 June 1857. The Company's army was in Kanpur, headed by garrison. A fight broke out between the rebels and the Company's soldiers. On 23 June, Nana Saheb Peshwa and his rebellious soldiers entered Kanpur. On 24 June, Nana Saheb Peshwa asked the Company's army to surrender, but Lieutenant

Wheeler was unwilling. The rebellious soldiers intensified their attack, and on 25 June, Nana Saheb Peshwa repeated his request to the Company to surrender. Finally, on 27 June, the Company's army surrendered in return for a promise of safe passage to Allahabad by the river. Three big steamers were arranged to carry the Company officials and their families. But the rebels were ruthless. They killed the Europeans in the boats and dumped the corpses into the river. Their families, women and children, were kept in Bibighar for two weeks and were murdered cruelly after that. Nana Saheb Peshwa captured Kanpur.

In order to defeat the rebels, the British called their troops from different places. Balbhim, who was a Mahar from Sonai, was among the troop that had come from Bombay. The British recaptured Delhi. Along with the British officers, the rebels had killed their families as well. The British response was cruel. They killed civilians. They spread terror among the people. On 20 September 1857, British agent William Hudson imprisoned Bahadur Shah Zafar, whose children were gunned down. After wiping out his entire family, the British sent the eighty-year-old Bahadur Shah off to Burma in an old vehicle.

The British did not sit quietly even after that. They sent Henry Havelock and James Neil to tackle the rebels in Kanpur and Lucknow. They seized Kanpur once again. They avenged the Bibighar massacre. Nana Saheb Peshwa saw his imminent defeat and disappeared, never to be found by the British again. On the other hand, Tatya Tope fought the British to the last.

The British were suspicious that the Rani of Jhansi had helped the rebels. And so they tried to keep her in check.

Lord Dalhousie had rejected the adoption papers of Jhansi's husband, King Gangadhar Nevalkar, and annexed the kingdom. In 1854, they had offered to pay the Rani Rs 60,000 annually in exchange for leaving the fort. The Rani of Jhansi assembled an army of women whom she named Durga Dal. The chief of this army was Jhalkari Bai, a courageous woman who commanded great respect. She had been given the honour of a leader in spite of the fact that she belonged to the Kori caste. In appearance she equalled the Rani.

Rani Laksmi Bai arranged a programme of 'Haldi-Kumkum', wherein she clearly stated her stance against the British. She said, 'The British are cowards. We need not fear them.'

Many women attended this programme. The British wanted to teach her a lesson. They sent Hugh Rose to Jhansi. On 23 March 1958, Jhansi was surrounded by British forces. There were signs that the British Army would defeat Lakshmi Bai. Jhalkari Bai disguised herself as the Rani, wearing the latter's clothes, and bravely fought the British. The Rani herself escaped to safety with her adopted son.

The Rani of Jhansi and Jhalkari Bai were both great women. One was a queen, the other her servant. One a Brahmin, the other a Kori. Both were valiant warriors. Rani Lakshmi Bai did not see Jhalkari Bai's lower caste, but history did. History saw only the caste.

Balbhim stood with a rifle in hand in front of the palace. The British Army was suspicious of the palace. Balbhim witnessed the valour of Jhalkari Bai.

From 10 May 1857 to 4 July 1859, for two years and two months, the rebellious soldiers kept fighting the British. Meerut, Delhi, Kanpur, Agra, Barelli, Lucknow, Allahabad, Ambala, Jagdishpur, Jhansi, Aligarh, Faizabad were all up in rebellion. Hindus and Muslims fought together against the British. But the British cruelly crushed the rebellion everywhere.

Five

The impact of the revolt of 1857 would be felt far into the future. The army began to believe that an organized rebellion could work, and the British began to view the army with suspicion. British officials realized that if the army, the native kings and the local people came together in an organized manner, their own power would be jeopardized. They did not want their empire to lose a rich country like Hindustan. Thus the British parliament revoked the East India Company's powers and took over the rule of India. The reign of the East India Company ended. The rule of the Mughals and the Marathas ended. India came directly under British rule, under the rule of Queen Victoria.

If the revolt of 1857 had been successful, the power would have gone back to the native kings, the Mughals and the Marathas. It was because of the failure of the revolt that India remained in the grip of the English people, the English language and the English church. British rule incited waves of discontent among people all across India, thereby creating a national consciousness.

To please the upper castes, the queen of England issued a proclamation to Indians, clearly stating that henceforth the British would not meddle in matters of religion in India. To keep this promise, the British stopped recruiting the untouchables and Muslims in the army. Discrimination was at the very foundation of the Hindu religion. The British had now understood that this religion had no regard for equality. To take political advantage of this situation, they began to follow the policy of 'divide and rule'.

After being ousted from the army, Balbhim and Lakshman came to Sonai, but they were still restless. They knew that their life would not get better if they remained in the village. They moved to Jhol, where they were once again smeared with the stain of being untouchables. They had realized the value of weapons. But now their weapons had been taken away from them. They knew that until they took up weapons the predicament of the untouchables would not end.

They went to the Christian colony to meet Philip Bush. They also met Warren Bush. He had been transferred from Saykheda to Jhol. Philip Bush had died of old age. The Christian colony were the same. Nothing had changed, except the roads had become worse. The colony showed signs of dilapidation. People's faces seemed worn out. Warren's hair had greyed. He was old now. He had not married.

The lives of the untouchables had not improved after conversion. They were still very poor. They did not have jobs. The White Christians looked at the coloured Christians with pity. The caste system of the Hindu religion had made its way into the Indian Christian community. Caste was a reality for the converted Christians. The upper-caste converts and the Church fathers and nuns did not look upon the lower-caste converts as equals.

Warren Bush did not recognize Balbhim and Lakshman. Balbhim spoke to Warren about his past and shared old memories.

'You must be baptized,' Warren said.

'Will they take us back in the army after baptism?' Balbhim asked.

'How can I say that?'

'We must convert so that we don't face any more injustice,' Lakhsman concluded.

'You won't be an untouchable if you become Christian,' Warren said.

'Whether we become Christians or Muslims, we never get rid of our caste. Why should we become Christian then?' Balbhim countered.

'I won't force you to become Christian. If you think it right, you are welcome to convert,' Warren said.

'We were removed from the army because of our caste. What should we do now? We have come with great hope. Please suggest something. We need your advice.'

'I am writing an application. Send this petition to the governor–general,' said Warren.

'This means more to us than baptism,' said Lakshman.

'Both of you must sign the petition. Get more people to sign it if you can.'

'For so long we have fought for others. We shall fight for ourselves now. We know the path to freedom,' Balbhim declared.

'Christian missionaries from Pune came here last Sunday. One of them was our man. He said that the people of our caste in Pune had gathered for an agitation. All the soldiers dismissed from the army had come together to send a petition to the queen. They are getting organized. You must get more information on them,' said Warren.

Their faces lit up.

'Such questions had never arisen in our minds earlier!' Balbhim said as he was leaving.

'The Company Raj was good. It gave opportunities to the untouchables. But the British government is on the side of the upper castes,' said Lakshman.

Balbhim and Lakshman looked like uprooted trees. There was fury in their eyes. They looked at Warren, who appeared like a church gate to them.

The people of Hindustan are illiterates. They need to be educated and civilized. This was the British government's patronizing attitude towards them. There were debates about how Indians should be educated. Should they be given a Western education or traditional Sanskrit education? Social reformers were in favour of Western education. The British wanted to create a class of servants who could perform the duties assigned by the government. The power of guns was giving way to the power of socio-cultural change. The age of consent for the girl child had been raised to ten in 1860. In 1868, Mahatma Phule opened the doors of a house for the untouchables to draw water from the well. In 1871, the Criminal Law was passed, making allowances for the rehabilitation and training of 'criminal tribes'. They built 'open prisons' in places where 'criminal' people were huddled in and 'reformed'. This kind of life was unbearable for those who had always led a free life; now they were being trained to lead a so-called civilized life. Those who were considered to have been sufficiently trained were released to go and live in the free settlements, but they had to report to the police station twice a day. The authorities wanted to prevent crimes, but they did not know that keeping people confined within four walls was itself a crime. The Special Marriage Act was passed in 1872, and in 1874 a law was passed regarding married women's right to property. On the one hand, social reform was making its presence felt, while on the other, general discontent was being channelled by the Indian National Congress into a national movement.

Balbhim had built his house on Chambhar Tekadi, just below the Maharwada. Lakshman had built his beside the Pir Dargah of Daval Malik. It was only the family members of Dhondnak Mahar who came to the dargah for prayers. No one else went there. Balbhim had got his son, Manik, married to Lakshman's daughter, Durga. Their friendship was now strengthened by kinship ties. Balbhim's wife, Bhama, and Lakshman's wife, Bhima, were from the same village, Pitapur. The two families were very close.

Both Balbhim and Lakshman were alcoholics. Balbhim would not talk at all when he was drunk and lie down quietly, while

Lakshman became very quarrelsome after a few drinks. No one came to his house after dark.

One night, Balbhim went to sleep after drinking and never woke up. He died in his sleep. When Manik tried to wake him he found that the body had become rigid. Bhama began to wail. People gathered. Lakshman came running. Jaya, Mohan, Bhima—they all came. Everyone was shocked at the sudden death. A crowd gathered. Mahars from Sonai and Pitapur village had come. Warren had also come for the funeral.

After this, all responsibilities fell on Manik. He was a guide. Guides were employed to accompany people on dangerous journeys through uncharted territories. The British had built a dirt track between the villages of Rampur and Saykheda. An earthen dam was being built close to this road, at the *sangam* of Tapi and Falguni rivers. There was no other road except this dirt track. Bamboo forests encircled Rampur and Jhol on all sides. Travelling from one village to another through the Satpuda range was an arduous task. It was very difficult to cross the Tapi and Falguni due to the dense forests and deep valleys. The roads were winding, dacoits roamed the area and then the fear of ghosts! The forests were laden with footpaths, tunnels and hidden passages. When a bride was to go to her in-laws or when a pregnant woman had to come to her parents' place for childbirth, the Mahars would be employed as guides. They would accompany the army, the Christian missionaries and government officials. They would carry official documents.

Manik, Khandnak, Mohan were all guides. Their employment was the direct result of the thick, dangerous jungles. The cutting of forests worried them. What would they do once the land was cleared and roads built? Who would give them work? What would the coming generations do? It was a matter of life and death for them. Many Mahars had lost their jobs. Work was unavailable.

A wind blew from the chasm. A stench emanated from the Chambhar Tekadi. One could hear the hissing of vultures. Even animals don't die in as great a number as they used to. The Mahars were worried. The British had put up barriers in everyone's way.

* * *

Lakshman had become lonely after Balbhim's death. He suffered bouts of madness and lost his memory. He stopped recognizing people. He spoke only about the past. Childhood. His days in the army. He had lost all connection with the present. At times he made sense. But at other times he was completely insane. He went to Balbhim's place. Balbhim's wife, Bhama, was sitting in the courtyard and Durga was combing her hair. Seeing Lakshman, Bhama covered her head. Lakshman stepped into the courtyard.

'Where is the man of the house? I haven't seen him lately. When will he come?'

Hearing Lakshman's voice, Manik came out. Lakshman was inquiring about Balbhim. Manik held his hand and helped him sit. Durga brought him some water to drink.

Lakshman said, 'The laws are very strict in Malabar. The untouchables are barred from wearing new clothes. Even if we had new clothes, we would dip them in mud to make them dirty. We would then wash the dirty clothes and wear them. If anyone was caught wearing new clothes, he would get a good thrashing. His clothes would be ripped off. The laws are strict in Malabar. You can come to Malabar. We have a house there. Our town is called Calicut. It's big. Do you want to see it? You have to go via Bombay. It takes a long time.'

Manik looked at Lakshman with tears in his eyes.

Durga interrupted, 'Who am I?'

Lakshman smiled at her and went on, 'There is a big sea in our Malabar. Vasco da Gama came there. We played on the beach. He was not a good player. I taught him. Have you ever seen a beach?'

Lakshman kept talking nonsensically. Without a break. He was now foaming at the mouth. He spoke about whatever he remembered, whatever came to his mind. He either did not understand or did not hear what the others were saying. He was lost in himself, in his past. He would sometimes laugh. Sometimes he became quiet all of a sudden.

He said, 'In Malabar, all our people are Christians. They would have to wear dirty clothes when they went to church. They would take out their new clothes only when they came near the church. They would wear the dirty clothes again while returning. It was impossible to walk on the streets wearing anything but dirty clothes. The laws are very strict in Malabar.'

Lakshman's wife, Bhima, came there in search of her husband. She said to Bhama, 'He has gone crazy, you know. He talks of his childhood days all the time. He talks of his village, his days in the army. I have to listen. He has no sense of anything else. I have to manage everything. Sometimes, when he is in his senses, it is good.' She was clearly worried.

'There are quite a few churches in our Malabar. The churches have godowns. People are kept imprisoned in the godowns. Anyone walking alone on the street would be put in the godowns. Eight to ten godowns were filled with slaves. They were taken to work in the plantations. They could not refuse. If they did, they would be flogged. They would be trampled by bulls. I opened the godowns. "Run away," I told them. But no one ran. Where could they go after having spent nearly a decade trapped in the godowns? I locked the godowns again.' He laughed.

He was now back to his senses. He asked Bhima, 'Have you cooked? Has Mohan eaten? Let's go home.'

He got up to go.

Manik, his son-in-law, walked along with him.

Lakshman assured him, 'Don't worry. I am fine. I will not abandon you like Balbhim.'

He was speaking confidently. Manik smiled.

Durga said, 'You were telling us stories about Malabar.'

Lakshman replied, 'Malabar is close to my heart. I remember my army days. Wearing the uniform filled me with vigour. I spent my life in the army. I had to eat rice and fish. We did not get our food there.'

He was very excited.

'Wherever you go in the world, our people are always discriminated against. Our people suffered in Malabar, Travancore, Cochin . . . everywhere. The women suffered the most.' Lakshman entered the courtyard and sat down to resume his story. The others had no option but to listen to him.

'Our women do not have the right to wear a blouse. They have to be bare-breasted. If someone dares to wear a blouse, her breasts are cut off. She is severely beaten. Sometimes hung upside down from a tree. The other women of our caste must see her suffer and never dare to wear a blouse. It is the upper-caste man's right to stare at the bare breasts of the untouchable woman. If she wears a blouse, it is considered an insult to upper-caste men.' Lakshman cleared his throat.

'When the king would walk to the temple from his palace, bare-breasted untouchable women flanked the road and showered him with flowers. Men thronged the streets to look at these women. Our women were not spared even after we became Christians. The resident of Travancore, Colonel John Munro, issued an order in 1813, stating that "lower-caste women who converted to Christianity are permitted to wear an upper-body garment". This enraged upper-caste men. The king himself did not want to oppose the order. The upper-caste men complained against this and protested strongly, because of which the king revoked the law. Lower-caste women had to keep their breasts bare once again.' Lakshman scratched his head.

'Everyone knows the story of Nangeli. The untouchable women there had no respite even after being bare-breasted. They had to pay a breast tax. Women with larger breasts had to pay a higher tax. When the tax collectors went to Nangeli's house, she cut off her breasts gave them to the tax collectors. She died of bleeding. When her husband, Chirukandan, came home to see the ghastly sight he was devastated. He jumped on to the funeral pyre of his wife. This incident led to protests against the breast tax. The breast tax was abolished, but women were still not allowed to cover their breasts. There were more protests. The governor of the Madras Presidency, Charles Trevelyan, complained to the king. Finally, on 26 July 1859, the king of Travancore passed a law allowing untouchable women to cover their breasts. I know all this so well. I have repeated it to many . . .'

He kept talking. Manik and Durga listened.

Warren came to Lakshman's house in search of Manik. Lakshman was happy to see him.

Warren said, 'Christian missionaries have come from Pune. They are going to Rampur. You must come early tomorrow to my house in Lal Dongar. We will go to their office, and I will introduce you to them.'

Warren began to take his leave. Lakshman wanted to stop him, but Warren was in a hurry.

'I have to go tomorrow,' said Manik, sounding content.

Durga watched the glow of satisfaction on Manik's face.

* * *

Father Anthony and Father Simon, both of whom were Christian missionaries in Pune, had been sent to Jhol. Father Anthony came to visit the churches in Rampur. He had been invited to the palace by the king of Rampur. There were three churches in the princely state of Rampur princely: in Rampur, Devgadh, Saykheda; but there was only one in the princely state of Jhol. Since Jhol was a Muslim-majority province, the Christian influence was limited there. Sanatani Hindus routinely attacked Christian missionaries. The nuns and fathers were anxious for their safety.

Manik and Father Anthony left for Rampur in the early hours of the morning. Father was on a horse and held a copy of the Bible in his hands. Manik was a guide—it was his responsibility to look out for thieves, and to keep the father safe. Manik was walking ahead of the father. There were shrubs, cliffs, insects, streams, forests, open spaces, birds and animals. Finally, they reached Rampur, where Father Dibrito was waiting for them. Father Anthony had to go to the palace.

The king of Rampur was childless. He had married many times in the hope of a child, but to no avail. He finally married Taramati, who was only thirteen. She gave birth to a child, but it was very weak and slept all day. The king had tried all medicines. Father Anthony had been called to bless the child.

Father Anthony and Father Dibrito reached the palace, where the raja welcomed them. The two missionaries prayed and gave the child their blessings. The raja gave them handsome gifts in return. Father Anthony presented the king with a copy of the Bible and a cross to be tied around the child's neck. The king was surprised to hear that Father Anthony had made this journey in a day. The father said that all credit for it should go to Manik Mahar, the guide.

The king asked Manik Guide to stay the night. Manik slept with his head resting on the steps of the dharmashala. He seemed like he had been sculpted on the steps. His youthful, dark-skinned body was well-built. He had big eyes, muscular arms, a broad forehead and an unattractive face—every aspect of his face and body proclaimed his racial origins. His face was stamped with helplessness. The tired body slept soundly under the open sky.

Manik woke early. He went towards the lower ghat of the river. The upper ghat was reserved for the upper castes, and the lower castes were barred from coming here. The untouchables could fill water only at the lower ghat. It was one river, it was the same water, but the upper castes had divided it. The place where the upper castes came for water was pure, while the place where the lower castes came was unholy. Manik went to the unholy part of the river and took a bath.

As the sun rose, Manik came to the Palace Square. The palanquin was ready to leave. Manik joined the procession too. The palanquin stopped at Khwaja Bhil's pada. The khwaja's daughter-in-law had just given birth. The Adivasis were overwhelmed to see that a palanquin had come from the king's palace for Najuka.

Najuka came out and was asked to sit in the palanquin. She refused. 'How can I sit there? It's the queen's rightful place!' But the palanquin could not go back empty. A coconut was placed inside the palanquin, and Najuka began to walk behind it as the palanquin was turned around to be taken back to the palace. Manik Mahar walked in front of the palanquin as it made its way back to Rampur.

Najuka sat on the steps of the palace. What a big palace it was! Najuka's skin was the colour of ripe jamun. Her lips were like the kadli flowers, her eyes like musk melon. The king arrived. The queen too. Behind the queen, a dasi stood with the prince glued to her breast. The king pleaded with Najuka to feed the prince. The dasi handed the prince to Najuka, who hesitated for a moment. But she complied. The king's wish was her command. She breastfed the child. The little prince drank the milk happily. A smile formed on Najuka's face. The dasi looked at Najuka as though she were a milk-laden cow. The king was happy.

'The prince has drunk a Bhilni's milk. He will be as strong as a Bhil now.'

An Adivasi woman's milk was precious but not the Adivasi woman herself! Her place was on the stairs.

The torture of British rule was on the rise. People wanted a solution. The kings had been defeated. The army had been defeated. The soldiers' revolution had been in vain. God was not showing up as an avatar. People were out on the streets. They were unarmed. They sang folk songs to organize a movement. As more and more people gathered, all fear was gone. When people come together, power is in danger. It becomes a signal that power is in its last stages. Such a movement of people symbolized non-violence—the kind of non-violence that can combat violence. For its part, the Indian National Congress was trying to motivate people to come together against British rule. Social reformers were raising consciousness among the lower rungs of society. The Sanatanis were engaged in the sublimation of the past and history, while the social reformers were trying to explain its true meaning. They were engaged in showing the path to social reformation. Winds of change were blowing. It was time for real social change. Civil society had become like a huge elephant stuck in a mire.

* * *

The king of Rampur had arranged a yagya in the hope of a bright future. Brahmins from various villages thronged Rampur. Brahmins of Pitapur, Pimpri, Sonai came together with those from Jhol and prepared to go to Rampur. Moropant had gathered all the Brahmins. His wife, Padma, prepared meals for them. Saraswati's head had been shaved. She sat quietly in a corner, wearing a red *alwaan* sari. She was the widow of Narsopant. The Brahmins looked at her as though she was a bad omen.

The Brahmins of the neighbouring villages, on their way to Rampur, had gathered in Jhol to rest there for the night. They were to go to Rampur the next morning. A message had been sent to Manik Guide. They slept early that night. Moropant was supervising everything. Everyone in his house was awake. They had lots to do. Except for Saraswati—she was not allowed to take part in any activity. She was continually reminded by one and all that she was an ominous woman. She was not allowed to participate in anything good or holy. Her widowhood had marked her as forever unholy, inauspicious. When Narsopant was hanged she was only twenty-five years old. She had been following the rigours of widowhood for thirty years now. She spent her days in utter solitude. Her youth had been burnt to ashes, wasted. Her daughter, Yamu, had been married off at the age of fourteen and lived with her in-laws. Her younger son, Vedant, was sent to study in the ashram. She spent her nights in wakeful anticipation. She would lie awake waiting to hear the sound of Moropant's footsteps. Sometimes she would wake up to the sound of rustling leaves. She would sit up. All her nights were lonely. Her fate was like a barren womb. She had seen Moropant's naked body many times. When he was bathing, for instance. Or changing his clothes. Many times, in many contexts. She could reach him only through her gaze. He never looked at her. Never spoke to her. Never even acknowledged her presence. Only Padma spoke to her. She would be given the leftovers to eat. She accepted it as the widow's lot. She was a bad omen in the house of Moropant, an illustrious kirtankar. She had no human identity. She was so immersed in the thoughts of Narsopant that these ideas had raised a mountain of sadness around her. Her shaved head, red alwaan sari, bare neck, white forehead and unholy presence! She looked like a fossilized tree.

When Saraswati woke up that morning the house was empty. Moropant had gone to Rampur. She wondered why she woke up. For whom? What would she do? Her existence had no meaning. This house got its identity from Moropant, while she bore the brunt of a life without a man. Narsopant had become immortal, and she had become garbage. She wanted to ask, 'Has Moropant left?' but couldn't gather the courage to do so. Padma would always rebuke her. She would say, 'Be quiet. Don't interfere. Eat what you have got!' A plate would be thrown in her direction as a bundle of hay before a cow. But there was a difference: the cow was holy, whereas she was unholy.

Moropant had gone to Rampur. The house would be quiet for eight days. She got up. Padma was looking at her.

* * *

Showing the way to the Brahmins, Manik Mahar started for Rampur. He had chosen a safe, short route, which was well lit by sunshine and yet had shadows, where drinking water was available and where there were spaces to rest. The other road was infested with ghosts and dacoits. He avoided the road where whirlwinds and Vetal, the god of the ghosts, wandered. He thought that even if the dacoits spotted them, they would be respectful seeing that they were Brahmins. The dacoits would touch their feet and be blessed in return. Their sins would be washed away. At this point he was not scared at all, neither of ghosts nor of dacoits. He was with the Brahmin gods on earth.

The Brahmins were having fun on the way. But they didn't forget to intermittently chant 'Har Har Mahadev'.

Manik would turn to look at the Brahmins. On seeing them he would start walking again. He had to maintain a distance from the Brahmins at all times. But he would have to wait till they caught up with him. As he walked, he picked guavas, jamuns and berries from the trees. He would drink water from the streams. He would look up at the sun to make sense of time. The laughter and gossip of the Brahmins entertained him. Sometimes they sang hymns; at other times they made fun of each other. They cracked jokes. After going through various ups and downs and turns, they were finally out of the mango forest. From the hilltop of Shingnapur he could see Rampur Palace, which meant Rampur was now less than three miles away.

As they approached Rampur, the landscape became more and more beautiful. The houses nested in the lap of hills, deodar trees that stood like soldiers on the slope of hills, the hilltops that seemed to reach the sky, the meeting of the sky and the earth, the troops of monkeys, the Shiva temple on the hill, the sun peeping through the trees, the whirling water of the Falguni River, the solitude of the deep blue sky, the sheep-like clouds floating in the sky . . . and Manik Mahar was in the midst of it all, like a glow-worm in a bamboo forest!

Rampur was here.

The Brahmins jumped into the Falguni River. Moropant was piously doing his ablutions. He was chanting mantras. After their bath, the Brahmins completed the other rituals, such as Pranayam, Achman, Suryanamaskar and chanted the Gayatri Mantra. They worshipped the sun god with the utmost seriousness.

Manik Mahar felt envious. He could not do what the Brahmins could. 'The Brahmins should be Mahars, and the Mahars should be Brahmins. If I were to become a Brahmin, I would go to the Himalayas, do penance and attain consciousness of God!' Manik thought as he looked at the Brahmins frolicking in the water.

Moropant shouted out to Manik, 'Mahar, you have done your job, you can go now!' Manik felt relieved.

The organization of the untouchables had raised the question, 'Without social reform, what is the use of political freedom?' Moropant had taken these words to heart. He was a studious man. Sir Herbert Risley had studied Hindu rituals and sent a list of questions to Moropant through Father D'Souza.

Rishi-munis had come for the yagya. The yagya mandap stood on pillars made of gold. Everything was golden—the yagya kund, the *bedi*. The Brahmins who chanted the Vedas were welcomed. The puja started. The holy fire was lit in the hom-kund. The sky echoed with the chants of the mantras. Sacrifice and offerings were made. The yagya started with all the rituals. People crowded the place—the householders, students, brahmacharis, sanyasis. The idol was bathed in flower water. The sound of conch shells, drums, bells and other instruments filled the air. Women sang hymns. Munis were chanting the Vedas and mantras. The Samveda songs were sung. 'Donate . . . feed . . . respect . . .' one could hear these words often. The king sat rapt in attention.

Moropant's seat was beside the Brahmins from Kashi. The Brahmins blessed the royal family. The prince was placed at the

Brahmins' feet. The king and queen sat before the Brahmins with folded hands. Eleven queens stood behind the king. The dasis showered flowers on the Brahmins and the royal family. A Kashi Brahmin blessed the prince.

'The tongue that sings the glory of God is fortunate, so is the mind that is immersed in God. The ear that is restless and eager to hear the name of God is blessed, and so are the hands that worship God. Blessed are the eyes that lower before God, and blessed are the feet that move respectfully in the temple. He whose five senses are aligned with God crosses this world to go to the next.'

The royal family was joyous to receive the blessings of the Brahmins. They donated handsomely to the Brahmins. After the rituals, all the Brahmins went to the Falguni River. The sumptuous luncheon began: the Brahmin *bhoj*. The aroma of the food filled the air. The untouchables waited eagerly for the Brahmins to finish their lunch. They had gathered in large numbers. It was after a long time that so many Brahmins were here. The Brahmin bhoj was not so common any more in these days of British rule.

The Brahmin bhoj ended. Leftovers lay scattered on banana leaves. The untouchables lunged at the leftovers. They rubbed the food on their bodies. It was believed that this would make their unholy bodies holy. The untouchables felt grateful as they rubbed the leftovers on their bodies with great vigour. They imagined that by doing this their next lives would be better. They were excited.

Manik was fortunate. He had served the Brahmins. He felt indebted. He remembered his wife, Durga. He remembered the naughty little one in Durga's womb. He was lost in thoughts of her. He floated like a cloud as he moved towards Jhol.

* * *

Father Simon went to Khwaja Bhil's pada. He had brought sweets for the Adivasi children. The children had never seen these things before. They looked at them in awe and surprise. The father offered the sweets to the children. He patted their backs. A crowd had gathered to see Father Simon.

He spoke lovingly. He would take the children in his lap. Some cried loudly, afraid that the father would kidnap them. The father went to many huts. He sat with the Adivasis and drank water. He gave medicines to the sick, and promised to come and meet them again.

The Adivasis took Father Simon to the Chennayya ghost temple. The khwaja pujari of the ghosts was angry when he saw the father. The father calmed him down, patting his back gently. The khwaja's wife, Mariamma, was busy filling up a basket with the severed heads of hens and goats. The father looked around the ghost temple. A wide stone marked with haldi-kumkum and bloodstains caught his eye. There was no light in the temple. Flies were buzzing all around. The father looked at everything carefully and keenly. He was eager to know the place well. Khwaja and Mariamma looked on as the father observed everything minutely.

Warren was beginning to feel anxious. He was worried about Father Simon. But Father Simon was relaxed. He had no qualms about the great danger he was putting himself in by interacting with the Adivasis. Some Adivasis were afraid of the father, some suspected his motives. But those who interacted with him closely were deeply touched by his affection.

Father Simon went to Pinya Pawra's house. Pinya was Chennayya's son. Pinya's wife was Margi. She was feeding her child. Pinya Pawra had a stern face, like that of an exorcist. His wife was much younger than him. Pinya's elder son brought home a jar of tadi. Pinya had seven children. He stayed home all the time and drank tadi. Margi did all the housework by herself. Father talked to Pinya and asked him many questions. But Pinya kept quiet. He looked at the father, unaffected. Margi came and sat beside Father Simon. The children stood behind her.

'Why doesn't he talk?' Father asked Margi.

'He speaks very little. He only speaks to his family. He is a ghost.'

'How can he be a ghost?'

'He is a ghost.'

'He is human,'

'No! He is a ghost.' Margi was upset now. 'I told you he is a ghost. Don't you understand? How can you insult us poor people? You may be a big man, but in your own home. We have not come to your house. You have come here. And you dare make fun of us?' Margi said whatever came to her mind.

The father apologized with folded hands. Warren was scared.

The Adivasis who stood there shouted, 'He is a ghost, he is!'

The father was puzzled. This was his first experience of seeing a live ghost. He kept his patience and tried to win Margi's confidence. Warren asked Father Simon to leave, but the latter was in no mood to listen. The Adivasis surrounded the father.

Margi was wailing now. 'Chennayya is my husband's father. He is the panch! He will give us justice. He owned land near the Biruba Plateau. Hindurao Patil snatched our land. He made my father-in-law sign a blank paper in return for a little jowar. There was a banana orchard in one part of our land. He usurped our fields. He said he had proof that the land was sold. But that was a lie. My father-in-law had never sold the land. He was tricked. One had to respect the Patil, because he is the head of our village. But this was what we got in return. The fields were taken away.' Margi narrated her painful story.

Pinya was still sitting with his head buried in his knees. His wife's pained voice made him look up. His face had changed.

Margi's throat was parched now. She coughed. But she kept talking. 'My father-in-law came to know about the villainy. He was the panch. He made petitions, but it came to nothing. Everyone supported Hindurao. He even went to the diwan, but that did not help in any way. One day, Hindurao sent his goons to silence my father-in-law. My father-in-law was a huge man. He ate half a deer in one go. He thrashed the goons. They ran away. We thought that was the end of the matter . . . But . . .'

Her voice changed. It was her soul that was speaking now. Pinya got goosebumps. He was trembling. Father looked on, closely observing Pinya, whose inert body was beginning to show signs of life now.

Margi continued her story. 'Three days later, the goons came again. They were fully prepared for an assault. Fully armed. They caught hold of my father-in-law, laid him on the ground and sat on his huge body . . . I shrieked . . . but to no avail. They gouged his eye out . . . I was at their feet . . . begging for mercy . . . there were fountains of blood . . . no one came to help . . . they carved his eye out . . .'

Pinya's body was reeling now. The father listened on. But this was not a new thing for Warren. He knew that this kind of torture was a part of life for the Adivasis and untouchables.

Margi went on, 'The goons were now going for his other eye. He was screaming in pain. Pools of blood . . . screams . . . help me . . . our people ran away scared . . . I was the lone woman there . . . I kept begging for pity . . . They placed his eye on my hand . . . I froze in fear and helplessness. My father-in-law was on the ground, writhing in pain. But the goons weren't done yet. Now they came to me. They stripped me naked. They violated my body . . .'

It was getting difficult for Margi to speak. Pinya began to yell. The Adivasis brought their drums and started to beat them loudly. Pinya was dancing to the beats.

Margi continued. The pain was evident in her voice. 'We tried a lot of cures for my father-in-law, but it was all in vain. His wounds were infested with worms. He would scream like an animal . . . he was overridden with pain. We would make him drink alcohol. That would quieten him for a bit. As soon as the effect wore off, he would start screaming again. He couldn't even sleep. He died a month later. We couldn't save him.' Margi wept.

Pinya's screams were scary.

The Adivasis murmured, 'The ghost is on him. He is possessed.' They beat the drums.

'My father-in-law, Chennayya, is back here—as a ghost!' murmured Margi.

Warren's head was spinning. The father, too, was dazed. He stared dumbfoundedly at Pinya. Warren was worried about the consequences of this news reaching Hindurao Patil. He wondered what would happen then.

Hindurao Patil got the news that very night. The Adivasis had told him. 'The European father was here. He sat all day before Pinya's house. He heard Pinya's story.'

Hindurao Patil was scared when he heard this. He knew the power of the British. 'The British will attack me now,' he said, sounding worried. This disturbing thought did not let him sleep.

A wave of awakening, of self-consciousness, swept through the untouchables. They began to organize themselves to demand their rights. Shivram Janba Kamble established the Anarya Rectification Association. In 1903, he organized a public meeting of Mahars from fifty-one villages in Sasvad village near Pune. He praised the courage shown by the untouchables. He raised the demand that untouchables be given suitable jobs by the government, which should also take responsibility for the education of children. A total of 1588 Mahars had signed a petition that was sent to the British government with the help of P.V. Mahadev Govind Ranade. Lakshman was present at that public meeting. For a moment, he felt as though he was standing with a rifle.

Chatrapati Shahoo Maharaj worked for the upliftment of the lower castes—he started the reservation system. In 1906, Maharshi Vitthal Ramji established the Depressed Classes Mission to strengthen the untouchables. Sant Gadge Maharaj, Bhaurao Patil and Sir Narayanrao Chandavarkar also worked for the welfare of the untouchables. If the British gave the reins of power in the hands of upper-caste Hindus, the untouchables would continue to suffer. Discrimination would not come to an end. If the thought that untouchables should get adequate representation in the government began to take root, it would mean trouble for the upper castes. Winds of change had begun to blow, and it bothered Hindurao Patil. He was worried.

* * *

Hindurao Patil sent his servant Karim to Pinya's house. The Adivasis were scared to see Karim in their pada. Karim began to sing praises of his master, 'He is godlike, my master. He has never cheated anyone. The Patil is ready to pay you compensation. Please forget all that happened. Don't listen to the father. He will baptize you. He will pollute you.'

Pinya was immobile. He stared at Karim blankly.

Hindurao Patil had usurped the lands of many Adivasis. People were worried that he was going to come to the pada. Everyone had decided that they would not speak or protest. Pinya sat with his head buried in his knees.

Margi was angry. She cursed the Patil. 'The Patil will be destroyed. He has tricked us. He usurped the land, blinded my father-in-law and stripped me naked. I curse him. He will suffer for all he did. Someone will take revenge . . . strip his daughter-in-law naked, like his goons did to me . . . I curse him . . .' she went on blabbering.

Pinya looked up. 'Don't stay in the hut today. Go out somewhere. Anywhere. But don't stay here. The Patil will be here with his men . . . Go . . .'

Margi was upset. 'What will the Patil do? I will take off my clothes myself and stand naked before him. Let him see my ass.

His mother's ass must also be the same. Let him see where he was born from.'

Pinya shook vigorously. He screamed.

Margi said whatever came to her mouth. 'Let him come. Am I afraid? I will shove my ass in his mouth. I don't care . . .' Margi was bubbling with rage.

She hadn't noticed that Patil was standing right before her.

Pinya began to dance. Margi put the dhol around her neck and began to beat it loudly. Pinya was angry. Hindurao Patil had come alone. His horse stood some distance away. Patil was scared. He had thought he would see a scared Pinya. He had thought Pinya would be waiting for him. But here was Pinya and his wife, mad with rage. How could they be so insolent? Patil was in deep thought.

Pinya's lips began to quiver. 'Oh, Patil! I am Chennayya! Recognize me. You took all my land. You blinded me. You disrobed my daughter-in-law. Now I will destroy you. No one can save you. I am a ghost!'

Margi made strange noises as she beat the dhol. All the other Adivasis who had been wronged by Patil now came forward. Patil was terrified by the ghost. The Adivasis took Patil towards the Chennayya temple. Patil felt nervous and agitated.

Hindurao Patil was now at the Chennayya temple. Khwaja Bhil sat there, scratching his head. He folded his hands when he saw Patil. The Khwaja's wife greeted Patil and bowed in obeisance. Patil was quiet.

Khwaja Bhil explained to Patil, 'There are seventeen ghosts in our pada. Chennayya is one of them, and a dangerous one. He has injured a few people. Wherever he goes, there is destruction.'

Hindurao Patil was too scared to listen any further. He interrupted Khwaja Bhil, 'We need to take care of this one. Tell me how.'

Khwaja smiled. 'We could arrange a *bhoot-shanti* and appease Chennayya's ghost. It won't be too expensive. What will the ghost ask for at most? Maybe a chicken, or a goat or a buffalo. We will give him a chicken.'

Patil was impatient. 'When can we get it done? I am ready to spend what is needed.'

Khwaja was happy to hear that. He said excitedly, 'The full moon night was four days ago. Let's wait till the new moon, the Amavasya night. I shall send an invitation to the ghost. It's good that you came on a black horse. The ghost is afraid of black horses. Else it would have caught hold of you. Go home in peace. We shall meet on Amavasya.'

Patil nodded and sat on his horse. The horse galloped away. Hindurao Patil was gone. The Adivasis were happy. Dhols were still being beaten in front of Pinya's house!

* * *

Patil was more scared of Pinya than Father Simon had been. He was unable to forget Pinya's dance. He called Karim and said, 'We shall do a bhoot-shanti on Amavasya to appease the ghost.'

Karim nodded silently.

Suddenly, there was a scream. It was the voice of Patil's daughter-in-law, Lalita. Patil ran hurriedly. He saw his wife, Uma, lying on the ground. She was shivering. Patil was scared. The servants came running. Uma had had a stroke. Her face was contorted. The right side of her body was paralysed. She was looking at Patil. Her lips were trembling. Lalita sat near her mother-in-law. She was dizzy. They tried to make Uma sit up, but her body sank. She was unable to talk. Hindurao Patil remembered Pinya's tremendous dance.

Patil was overcome with fear. He felt helpless. He was sad to see his wife in this condition. His life seemed desolate. His marriage of 40–45 years seemed to lay scattered. Uma used to run around the house busily, but now she lay still, helpless, glued to the bed. Looking at her was like a punishment. He cried silently. His splendour was all gone. Relatives came to visit Uma. But after they were gone, it was desolation all around. Nothing could lessen his anxiety. Different people suggested different cures. He tried them all. But Uma could not be made to sit up. Every time he looked at Uma he wanted to die. He felt guilty that he could not do anything to save her. His wife was paralysed, but it was he who felt all the pain. The mansion felt cold. A mountain of sadness had descended on it.

Today was Amavasya, the night of bhoot-shanti.

Pinya wore the garb of a ghost. He was dressed in black robes. A necklace of red and black beads hung around his neck. He put on a white moustache like Chennayya. Red vermilion smeared his cheeks. There was a stick in his hand and a crown of coconut leaves on his head. Pinya, Margi and their eldest son all went to the Chennayya temple. They worshipped the ghost. The Khwaja blessed him, saying, 'The ghost resides in your body. May it become even more dangerous. May you remain restless, unsettled. May your soul be taken over by the ghost. May the ghost wreak havoc.'

Pinya looked at the Khwaja. His eldest son hung a dhol around his neck. Margi hung a loose sack-like bag around hers, to hold her little child. They set out for Patil's mansion and reached just as the day was about to break.

Seeing them, Karim went inside to announce, 'The ghost is here.'

Pinya's son began to beat the drum. The Khwaja was marking off a space in the courtyard. Margi was breastfeeding her child. Pinya sat with his head buried in his knees. He scratched the mud with his toes. Margi was unhappy to see him sitting silently.

'How will it work if you stay so quiet? Let the ghost come!'

Pinya grinned. 'The ghost doesn't come to me.'

Margi got even more enraged. 'At least you can pretend to do it. If the Patil comes, we will be in trouble. How will they do the shanti if there is no ghost?'

Her anger only amused Pinya. He laughed.

Margi was furious. 'You dead man! You have come to Patil's mansion. Don't be crazy now. Let the ghost take hold of you. Don't insult the ghost.'

Pinya looked at her, unaffected by her pleas.

Margi felt helpless. She was confused. She began to rouse the ghost in him. 'Patil has usurped your fields. You were the panch of your wadi. Have you forgotten everything? Try to remember. Patil sent his goons. They gouged your eyeballs and placed them in my hand. You screamed and shrieked like an animal. How can you forget the wrongs? Are you a eunuch?' Margi was screaming while Pinya listened in silence. The little baby cried in Margi's *jhola*. The elder son was beating the drum.

Margi went on, furious, 'They stripped me naked. But perhaps you did not see that, because they had already taken out your eyes. They violated my body. Maybe you could not see, but you must have heard my screams.'

Hearing Margi's pained voice, Pinya screamed. He sprang up.

Margi kept on inciting him. 'They cheated you. They asked for your thumb impression, and you gave it. Our field was taken. Our source of food. And when you protested, what price did you have to pay? Remember, remember your ghastly, painful death. Aren't you angry? Don't act dead, say something!' yelled Margi.

Pinya was shaking. The ghost was dancing. Margi kept breast-feeding her child. As she fed her child, she screamed, 'Our house is graced by the presence of your ghost, and that is why people respect us! Don't deny us your blessings! We have no one else to turn to. Do come as soon as you are invoked. We respect you. Don't forget us. We are your children. I don't let Pinya do any work because you reside in his body!'

The drum was being beaten loudly. The Khwaja was waiting for Patil, with a whip in his hand.

Hindurao Patil's daughter-in-law, Lalita, came down the stairs holding an aarti thali. She wore a pink sari. Hindurao Patil and his son, Ramrao Patil, held Uma, as she could not walk properly without support. They brought her down the stairs. She had been made to wear a parrot-green sari. Ramrao's children were at the mansion, but they were not brought here because the sight would be too frightening for them. Patil's servants stood at the back.

The Khwaja whipped the ghost. He threatened it. The ghost glared at Khwaja, who stood beside him. It showed its tongue. Roared. Patil's servants gave sacks of grain to Margi. She kept those. Lalita was afraid to go near the ghost.

Hindurao Patil tried to comfort his daughter-in-law. 'Don't be afraid,' he said.

Lalita murmured, 'I am very scared . . .'

Margi looked at her. Patil said to Lalita, 'It's our Chennayya . . . He used to come to our house . . . He would sit at the door . . . He was a poor man . . . Don't be scared. Do the aarti. Come on!'

Margi was lulling her baby to sleep. Khwaja lashed his whip in the air. Pinya sat there looking ready to attack. The drumbeats were getting loud. Pinya roared. Lalita did the aarti. Pinya screamed. The aarti thali fell from Lalita's hands. Khwaja whipped Pinya a couple of times. Lalita moved away and stood in a corner.

Hindurao Patil greeted the ghost with folded hands. Ramrao did the same. They helped Uma fold her hands in a namaste too. Khwaja spoke to the ghost in a loud voice: 'Chennayya, Patil is the king of the village! What can we do if the king beats us? It is his right. He is ready to take care of your children's upbringing. He will help them. Please be calm now. You can ask whatever you want. Patil will fulfil your wishes.' Khwaja lashed his whip.

Pinya roared, 'I won't calm down!'

Khwaja said to Patil, 'Please go inside. I will take care of him. Don't worry. It will all be well.'

Patil went inside with his family. The servants left too. Khwaja came and sat beside Margi. Pinya's son stopped beating the drum. Pinya had calmed down a bit. They sat under a tree. Karim brought them food and they all ate from one plate. After they finished eating they picked up the bag of grain given by Hindurao Patil and started to walk away. Karim cleaned the place where the ghost had danced.

Lalita looked at the ghost from her window. She was Hindurao Patil's second daughter-in-law. His first, Kamala, had given birth to six daughters. After the birth of the sixth she had jumped into the well at the back of the mansion. Patil got his son married a second time. Lalita was from a poor family. She had a pretty face and was sixteen years younger than Ramrao. Her parents had agreed to the match because the proposal had come from a rich family. Ramrao's daughters never allowed Lalita a moment of peace. They always complained about her. Lalita was afraid of the room in which Kamala used to live.

Ramrao Patil was to go to Lal Dongar. He wanted to visit the palace. He wanted to report to the king that Father Simon frequented the Adivasi areas. The mahout was ready with the elephant. Ramrao went near it. The mahout signalled the elephant to get up, but it did not budge from its position. The mahout struck the elephant with his stick. Still, it didn't budge. The mahout began to beat the elephant, and it suddenly sprang up. It held Ramrao by its trunk and threw him on the ground. Then it trampled on his head. The mahout shrieked. The elephant now turned to the mahout. Karim ran inside screaming. The mad elephant wreaked havoc, until some people tried to bring it under control.

Ramrao's corpse lay on the ground. Hindurao Patil was shocked. He felt that the mad elephant and the ghost were similar. Lalita came out screaming. Hindurao Patil was heartbroken when he saw his son's corpse. Lalita was traumatized to see her husband's dead body. Her screams worsened Hindurao's state of mind.

* * *

Days passed. The mansion was filled with a pall of gloom that could not be lifted. There was no peace. Lalita had completely withered. Hindurao Patil thought of sending Lalita to her parents' house for a few days. He called for Manik Guide. Lalita prepared to go to her parents. Earlier, whenever she visited her parents, she was always accompanied her by husband, Ramrao. This would be the first time that she would be going there without him.

Manik Mahar stood in front of the mansion. Karim sent word inside that Mahar was here. The horse was ready. Lalita touched her in-laws' feet. Her eyes were filled with tears. It was difficult for Uma to talk, but her voice was affectionate when she said, 'Come back soon. You know my condition. You are young, but you have to take responsibility now. You are our son now . . .'

'Have you taken all that you need? Is anything left behind?' Hindurao Patil asked his daughter-in-law.

She wore a pink sari when she left the mansion.

Manik Mahar ran in front of the horse. A stench filled the air near Chambhar Tekadi. The horse turned towards the Biruba Plateau. Though Manik ran in front of the horse, his mind was with his wife, Durga, who would be giving birth any day now. When he was leaving she had told him, 'Come back soon!' Her voice echoed in Manik's ears. The horse moved at a leisurely pace. Sitting on it, Lalita was lost in thought.

Manik Mahar had been given a lot of instructions before the journey. He was an experienced guide. He spoke very little. He ate only when he was given food. He didn't ask for anything.

He never cheated, never caused any trouble. He never misled people. But today, Manik Mahar was unmindful. His head was full of thoughts about Durga. It was her first delivery. He felt somewhat reassured to think that his mother, Bhama, was with her.

Lalita felt restless, lonely. She could not forget the time spent with her husband. Ramrao would say, 'These are our lands . . . they are barren . . .' A little later he would say, 'I killed a deer here.' Sometimes he would say, 'It was here that the dacoits surrounded and threatened me. They ran away when I fired a shot in the air!' Or, 'Once we saw a big snake here.' He shared his memories of Kamala when they had travelled together on this way. Once it had rained very heavily . . . He would speak of many things. She remembered it all. She remembered tiny details of their journeys together.

Manik, too, was lost in thought. And he lost his way. The horse stopped. It was unwilling to go ahead. Lalita screamed. Manik shouted, 'What is it?' when he suddenly noticed the way. He had unknowingly walked into dangerous territory. It was a hilly area known as Khandoba Pathar. It was a place infested with ghosts who lived on trees. Manik realized he had made a mistake. He had lost his way. He felt afraid. It was midday, and he saw a storm approaching. There was so much dust that one could not see the sky.

'Let us wait till the storm passes,' said Manik.

'Doesn't the storm have ghosts?' Lalita asked.

'There is a Vetal in the storm, it is going to visit Mari Ma. There are ghosts with them.'

Lalita alighted from the horse. Manik Mahar tied the horse. Lalita looked at the storm. It was approaching in their direction. An amaltas tree had been uprooted by the strong winds. The thunderous winds were slapping it. All the trees shook wildly. Manik Mahar could sense danger. An old mango tree fell with a thud. Lalita was scared. Her pink sari fluttered in the wind. Her hair was all scattered. The storm intensified, it was furious now.

'I am very scared. Please hold my hand,' Lalita said.

'I am a Mahar. You will be polluted.'

'The wind is pulling me back.'

'Hold the tree.'

'I am afraid of the tree.'

'Don't be scared. The storm will pass.'

The horse neighed loudly. Lalita felt even more frightened. She ran to the tree and hugged it tightly. The tree shook dangerously. It was a strange tree, possessed by ghosts. Its branches stooped to the ground. It seemed as though the tree was touching the ground with its thousand hands. Lalita realized that it was dangerous to hold on to the tree, which was shaking violently. She left the tree and ran to Manik Mahar. Manik stood with his face towards the storm. Lalita's *pallu* got entangled in a branch of the tree as she ran towards Manik. Her pallu was so badly stuck that she could not get it off. Instead, her whole sari came off. Overcome with fear and shame, Lalita clenched Manik from behind. The storm changed its direction. Lalita saw her sari being carried away by the wind. The sari was twirling in the sky.

Manik's touch had polluted Lalita. He was nervous. He did not turn to look behind him. He was looking at the strong current in the Tapi River. She still stood glued to him.

* * *

Moropant was tired. Now it was Narsopant's son Vedant's turn to observe Brahmin dharma.

Moropant advised Vedant on the things he should follow, 'This veena is now on your shoulders! Take responsibility for it!'

After Father Edmund was murdered and Narsopant hanged, Moropant had decided to raise Vedant with the love and affection of a father. Vedant addressed him as Baba.

Vedant kept asking one question after another, and Moropant answered them as well as he could. Moropant once explained the age-old Hindu tradition to him: 'High–low in this life and heaven–hell in the afterlife—this is the foundation of the Hindu religion. The concept of *paap–punya* is central to it. The Hindu religion stands on discrimination. The concept of purity is behind it. It cannot tolerate any hybridity. At the head of this religion is the god who killed the non-Aryans, including the Dravidians, Dasyus and Danavs.'

'But how should we behave with the progeny of the Asuras and the Dravidians?' asked Vedant.

This was Moropant's favourite topic. He said, 'The clash between the Vedic and the non-Vedic is ancient, and it will continue in the days to come. These are two different traditions. But we have to make sure that the Hindu dharma reigns supreme. It is our prime responsibility. We must try and fuse the non-Vedic into the Vedic Hindu way of life. They should assimilate with the Hindus. This is our stand.'

Moropant added, 'If the non-Vedic do not want to come to the right path, we must force them. We must teach them a lesson. If any Vedic stands with or supports a non-Vedic, we must punish him. He is our enemy. We must not spare him.'

'In the Hindu religion, the Brahmin is supreme, and the others are beneath him. So what should be the relationship between the Brahmins and the other castes?' Vedant had come to the point. Times had changed. This was an important question.

Moropant weighed his words carefully. 'You are right. In the days to come, there may be a clash between the Brahmins and non-Brahmins. We need to preach the importance of Sanatan dharma. It is our mission. We need to place one hand on the Bahujans and one hand on the backward castes. We have to step into politics. Only religious preaching won't do.'

Moropant excitedly went on, 'This is Kaliyug. The day Krishna left this earth was the advent of Kaliyug. Our society today is like a chariot without a charioteer. Thieves will take over such a society. People will fight among themselves. There will be debauchery and crimes of all sorts. Men will be worse than animals. Men will be robbed. Women kidnapped. Religion will change its very nature to suit the modern times. The Varnashrama system, based on the division of the four Varnas, will be demolished. The purity of race will be destroyed. People will crossbreed, like dogs and cats.'

Vedant kept asking one question after another. Moropant tried to answer as sincerely as he could. He felt it was his responsibility to answer Vedant's questions.

Vedant finally asked, 'Tell me about the untouchables, the Christians and the Muslims.'

Moropant's face fell. He knew he had to answer this question very carefully. His voice changed. 'The untouchables, Muslims and Christians are the minorities. We need not pay much attention to them. We need to worry about the majority. Touch their hearts. We should build unity by playing on the sentiments of the majority. We can build a strong foundation by opposing the minorities and appeasing the majority. In the coming days we must assume the role of God and use religion as a weapon. Remember that the Hindu religion destroys the irreligious. We must stand up and defend Ram Rajya.' Saying so, Moropant patted Vedant's back.

Vedant was confused. He fell silent, as if a mountain had descended on him.

As he rose to go, Moropant said, 'Circumstances teach a man what he needs to do.' Then Moropant went into his puja room.

When Vedant started to walk towards the tulsi Vrindavan, Saraswati, his mother, called out to him. She looked at him with fiery eyes. 'Don't you feel like asking me? I am your mother.'

'Why do you speak like this, Ma?' Vedant said.

'I heard all that he told you. It was completely wrong. Be a human being first. Behave like a human being! Everything else other than humanity is false. Pay heed to what I say. Do you understand? See my tonsured head. My white forehead without *kumkum* . . . My empty neck without a mangalsutra.

My appearance is disfigured and hideous because I am a Hindu widow. I am a human being, but I am treated as a bad omen . . . He died . . . but I had to live through tortures worse than death . . .'

'What are you trying to say?'

'That you must treat everyone as human. Behave humanely. That's all.'

'Hindu dharma stands on the foundation of humanity, doesn't it?'

'No. No religion stands on the foundation of humanity. They all stand on the concept of God. We talk so much about gods. But do we ever talk about humans? We must! We talk a lot about heaven. But how much do we talk about the society we live in? The life I lived as a widow has given me this insight, my own perspective. Forget me. Think of the untouchables. If not today, they will ask for an answer a hundred years later. You think you are such a wise pandit. What do you feel when you look at your mother as a bad omen? I have given birth to you, hence I have the right to ask.'

'You live all alone by yourself. That is why you think like this.'

'Whoever has been isolated like me, they all think the same way, remember that.'

Moropant looked angrily at Saraswati. Saraswati turned away from him. Vedant was feeling restless. Conflicting thoughts engulfed his mind. His mother's widowhood and the pain it caused bothered him deeply. Moropant went towards Saraswati and stood in front of her. He asked affectionately, 'What do you want to say?'

Saraswati kept her eyes averted from Moropant but said in a calm voice, 'Until and unless the untouchables write their own history, they will have to sing the glory of Brahmins. But the untouchables will write. Today, or tomorrow!'

As Saraswati stopped, Moropant felt terrified. He could never have imagined that a widow like Saraswati could speak in this way. There was truth in Saraswati's words, though. There was experience. Moropant felt strangely undermined, despite all he had learnt, studied or shared in speeches. He had always spoken about gods, never about humans. He had no knowledge about humans. He turned around and left. Saraswati watched his receding shadow.

Vedant was getting ready to go to Hindurao Patil's mansion. Saraswati looked at him. He was just like his father. Hindurao Patil had arranged for a tulsi marriage. Father Simon had been invited. Hindurao Patil was more concerned with the father than with the tulsi marriage. He wanted to be in the father's good books. The father had agreed to attend; he wanted to see the rituals of the tulsi marriage. Though Moropant was opposed to the father, he did not want to anger Hindurao Patil, and so he'd sent Vedant. This was the first time Vedant was in the Patil's mansion.

A big tent had been built in the courtyard of the mansion. Many well-known people of Jhol were in attendance. The news that Father Simon, too, was going to be there had caused a lot of excitement. A crowd had gathered to see him. They all wanted to shake his hand. They wanted to sit near him, talk to him. No one paid much attention to Vedant. He was simply a preacher. The main attraction was Father Simon.

Father Simon was eager to witness the tulsi marriage. He had been a priest at many weddings but had never seen the marriage of a tulsi plant with a shaligram stone. He watched the rituals and left soon after.

Pinya and Margi, too, had come to attend the tulsi marriage. There were arrangements for food after the rituals. Hindurao Patil, the diwan of Jhol and Vedant were on the stage. The diwan of Jhol inquired after Moropant's health. Vedant told him that

Moropant was not keeping well. Uma could not climb the stairs, so she was seated below, in the front row. Lalita and Ramrao's daughters sat near her.

Vedant began to narrate the story of Tulsi's marriage, as described in the Vishnu Purana, in his honey-sweet voice: 'In the ancient days, there was a Rakshasa named Jalandhar. His wife's name was Vrinda. She was a faithful and dedicated wife. Everywhere people sang about her virtues. Jalandhar was a majestic king. He declared war against the gods. He began to torture them. He had never lost a battle against the gods, defeating them every time. The gods were helpless in front of his might. They got together and sent a petition to Lord Vishnu, who promised to help them. The battle was on. The Rakshasa could not be defeated. The gods felt that they would lose again. Lord Vishnu disguised himself as Jalandhar and went to his house. Vrinda was happy to see her husband. She welcomed him. Lord Vishnu violated her. At that very moment, Jalandhar died on the battlefield. The gods were victorious. They sang praises of Lord Vishnu. Vrinda wailed in sorrow. She could not decipher how this had come about. Finally, when she came to know of Vishnu's treachery, she cursed him. "Oh Lord Vishnu! You shall fall to the earth like a stone!" Vrinda's curse turned Vishnu into a shaligram stone, and he fell to the earth in the holy place of Vrindavan. He cursed Vrinda: "Oh Vrinda, you have made me a stone. I curse you that you shall be born as a tulsi plant in your next life. And you will be married to a shaligram stone."

'Vrinda climbed the funeral pyre of her husband and became a sati. In the ashes of that pyre was born a tulsi plant. Tulsi was married to shaligram. We celebrate that marriage to this day. It is the symbol of the marriage of Lord Vishnu and Goddess Lakshmi.' Vedant ended the mythical story.

The story—about killing a Rakshasa by violating his wife's modesty—had scared Pinya and Margi. They were sitting far from the tent, but they had heard the entire story.

'Not only humans, but the gods too are unjust,' Margi murmured.

Hindurao Patil came up to meet Pinya in spite of the crowd. He called for Karim and said to him, 'Give them some food.'

Karim went to get food for them. Margi laughed. Pinya was happy that Patil had walked up to them. When Patil started to walk away Margi asked him to stop and took out a pink sari from her jhola. She said, 'I was cutting grass when I saw this sari lying on the field. I have seen your daughter-in-law wearing this sari. Who else can wear such an expensive sari? I brought it back as I was coming here.'

Patil listened to Margi's words in silence. Karim had returned with the food.

Hindurao Patil could not sleep all night. He had not eaten. People thought that Hindurao Patil was angry because Father Simon had left early, or perhaps because Moropant had refused to come. But something else was on Patil's mind . . . Lalita was wearing this sari when she had left for her parents' place . . . How did the sari end up in the field? Who took off her sari? Ramrao had brought this sari for her from Pune. Hindurao Patil woke Lalita up and showed her the sari. Her face went pale as soon as she saw it. She started to cry. She said, 'It was stolen when I was at my father's place. A thief took it away along with other things. I didn't tell you because I thought you would get upset.'

Patil was furious. Her words didn't ring true. A cyclone of doubt tossed his mind about like a dry leaf.

'How could the Mahar forget his status? How could a lower-caste man have such audacity? Didn't he feel afraid to touch Patil's daughter-in-law? Why do I carry the sword? Is it for this? Do I have no value?' Patil was as restless as a tiger in its cage. He felt his dignity was lost. He was determined to find out the truth. He sent for Karim early in the morning. When Karim came he saw that his master's eyes were bloodshot. Patil's face was swollen. He asked Karim to fetch Manik Mahar. He emphasized that it was very important that Manik Mahar be brought to him. Karim said 'Yes, sir' and left. He was scared.

Karim went to the Chambhar Tekadi. Manik Mahar lived there. Manik's mother, Bhama, was sitting in the courtyard. Durga sat beside Bhama.

Bhama asked Durga, 'Do you feel any pain?'

'No, Mother, not yet.'

'Let me know if you feel any pain. The count is over. You should give birth anytime now, maybe today or tomorrow. I know it will be a boy. As soon as Manik comes home we shall give him the boy!'

'First let it be born, Mother!'

The women's conversation made Karim feel uneasy. 'Where is Manik? He has been summoned to the mansion,' Karim said to Bhama.

'He went at night with the soldiers. Where have they gone, when will they come back? I don't know . . . The soldiers keep these things secret . . . Manik usually informs me when he goes out, but this time it was different.'

Karim heard Bhama's reply and left. Manik's broken hut, his simple-minded mother, his wife's ragged sari—it was all part of the naked dance of poverty. Karim remembered his own pregnant wife and her mother . . . He remembered his own poverty and wondered, 'We belong to two different religions, but is there any difference between us really? We are both poor, the same as each other.' Karim reached the mansion lost in thought!

'Manik Mahar is not at home!' Karim said to Hindurao Patil.

Patil was confused. His face was contorted. Karim felt scared looking at it. He had known his master a long time, but he had never seen this face. Not even when his son Ramrao died. Karim left quickly, without another word.

Patil began to think, 'Either Karim is lying or he has been told a lie . . . Karim did not search the hut . . . There is no point in sending him again . . . I must go myself . . . or he will run away . . .'

Patil was miserable. He could think of nothing except Manik Mahar. He kept imagining the look on Manik's face when he would be shown the sari. Patil felt vengeful and pitiless. He imagined that Manik would start crying on seeing the sari. He thought, 'I have to check if his answer matches what Lalita said about the sari . . . Unless he blurts out the truth, I will chop off his limbs one by one . . . I will stuff his body parts in a sack!'

He also fantasized about cutting Lalita into pieces and putting her body parts in a sack . . . She was treacherous, unfaithful . . . She had tricked him and stained his family's honour . . . But then, he thought practically. 'She takes care of the household . . . Uma is sick . . . Ramrao's six girls have not yet grown up . . . Let me keep her as a servant in the house!' Hindurao Patil's mind was plagued with such thoughts.

Lalita came in with his plate of food. Hindurao refused it, and looked at her with spite and hatred. Lalita noticed her father-in-law's expression and knew that he doubted her. She shuddered. She walked away with the plate she had brought. She felt insecure. She thought Manik Mahar would be called. What would he say? Who would believe him if he told the truth . . . that the storm had carried the sari away? She had clenched him from behind, like a little child clasps its mother. Manik Mahar had felt a young woman's body on him. His body must have felt the sparks, but he had not turned back, not once.

Lalita had worn another sari from her luggage and climbed on to the horse. The horse started to move, with Manik running ahead of it. Manik did not turn to look at Lalita. When they reached her parents' place, her mother gave him some food. He ate, drank water and then stood at the door for a while.

Lalita's mother asked, 'What do you want?'

'The stale roti and pickle you gave me were very good. Can I take some for my wife? She is pregnant.'

Lalita's mother gave him the roti and pickle, and he went away. All he wanted at that moment, Lalita thought, was to go home and feed his wife. Then Lalita remembered Ramrao's words: 'Whoever speaks against the mansion, we call for him. Once he is summoned, there is no going back . . . he will be chopped into pieces, put in a sack and thrown into the chasm of the Chambhar Tekadi . . .'

Lalita felt faint. Her consciousness was slowly slipping away. She could hear the calls of vultures . . .

* * *

Manik Mahar had gone to Rahimpur with the British Army. Havildar Dharyasheel Dabhade and fifty soldiers were in the troop. They had received an urgent order. It had to be followed that night. Manik Mahar was called to show the way, and so he went with the troop. It was a moonlit night; they did not need torches or mashals.

The tehsildar of Rahimpur had sent a message, 'The Bhils are getting ready to loot the treasury of Rahimatpur in a day or two. They have gathered in large numbers on the hill of Jyotiba. The news is confirmed. Send the army immediately. Rahimatpur's army has been sent to Sultanpur for immediate action. We cannot call it back!'

The lieutenant colonel of Jhol decided to send the battalion urgently. The battalion reached Rahimatpur in the morning. The sepoys were bathing in the Tapi River. Manik stood on the edge of the river. The army was ready for Rahimatpur. Havildar Dabhade called for the Mahar. As he came close, Manik's shadow fell on the havildar. He was annoyed and moved away. 'Your shadow shouldn't touch me.'

The havildar's annoyance made Manik recoil a few steps away immediately.

'I have come here many times from Jhol, but I did not know this way. It's good that we brought you. You know the roads well. You can go now. Rahimatpur is near. We can find our way ahead. Go now.' Dabhade thus freed Manik from his responsibilities.

Manik smiled and got ready to leave.

'Where is Jyotiba Hill?' Dabhade asked as an afterthought.

Manik replied, 'That's the road I brought you by. We crossed the Bhairab stream as we came here.'

Havildar Dabhade was shocked to hear that. He had kept the task a secret. He was surprised that the Bhils did not stop them on their way. He was happy that the guide had ensured a safe passage for them.

Manik Mahar bowed to the havildar and left. Dabhade asked the battalion to move ahead. They crossed the Tapi River. The havildar suddenly stopped. He called two soldiers, Tanaji More and Dhanaji Jadhav, and said to them, 'The Mahar is going back. He will go by the Jyotiba hill. The Bhils are there. They will stop him. He will inform them. He can say anything. Kill him. Hurry up!'

Manik Mahar was walking towards his home, carefree as a bird. He was happy that he was relieved of his duties early. He sang and breathed freely in the open air. He thought, 'If Durga gives birth to a boy child, I shall name him Dhairyasheel, after the havildar. If it is a girl, I will name her Lalita! After Patil's daughter-in-law!' Manik Mahar whistled as he walked.

An array of bullets pierced his body. He fell with a thud.

Tanaji More and Dhanaji Jadhav checked his body for any signs of life and on finding none, they left.

The battalion entered Rahimatpur. The havildar went to meet the tehsildar. He had to report to him. The tehsildar asked him to be alert. The havildar saluted him and left.

Tanaji More and Dhanaji Jhadav came to Rahimatpur and met the havildar.

'What happened?' the havildar asked.

'We shot him. He is dead. We checked,' Tanaji More responded.

'Good. He might have opened his mouth. We can't trust the Mahars.'

The news of the army's presence in Rahimatpur was no secret now. People were scared and could sense that something was about to happen. The roads became deserted.

* * *

Karim went to the Chambhar Tekadi twice. Each time the answer was, 'Manik Mahar is not home.'

Patil's doubt deepened. He was annoyed with himself. He could not sleep. His face was swollen, his eyes bloodshot! He felt as though hot oil was bubbling in his head.

The diwan came early in the morning. Patil was happy to see him. The diwan asked about Chennayya's land and its cost. 'Father Simon is about to sell his London house. He will buy Chennayya's land for Pinya with the money. He asked me if you would like to sell the land. I did not give an answer, but I think he wanted me to speak to you about it. He knows that you and I are close.'

The diwan waited for Patil's reaction. But Patil changed the subject. 'Where is the battalion?'

The diwan understood that Patil was more interested in talking about the army than about the land. He answered, 'The battalion has been sent to Rahimatpur. The tehsildar had called for it. Manik Mahar Guide was sent with them.'

Patil fell into deep thought. The diwan felt that perhaps Patil was not well. He said, 'The tulsi marriage was a grand success. A large crowd attended it. Moropant should have come.'

Patil kept silent. The diwan rose to go and left.

Patil was still lost in his own thoughts. He had not even asked the diwan to stay back for a while, as would be normally expected of him. The diwan, confused by Patil's demeanour, couldn't make sense of the matter. He had no clue what was going on in Patil's mind. Maybe Father Simon's interest in the Adivasis' land was what bothered Patil, he thought. The diwan's visit was unusually short. No gossip. No exchange of news. No arrangements for food and drinks.

Karim was feeding the elephant when he saw the diwan leave. He couldn't help asking, 'Are you leaving early today?'

The diwan smiled. 'The weather looks rough today. There's thunder and lightning. I should go.'

Karim was confused. Something was surely wrong, he thought as he went on feeding the elephant.

Hindurao Patil got ready. He picked up his sword, Lalita's sari, got on his horse and started for the Chambhar Tekadi. He had never been there before. Thunder clouds darkened the sky. The wind was fierce. Lightning bolted in the sky. People were surprised to see Patil headed towards the Chambhar Tekadi.

Patil climbed the slopes of the Chambhar Tekadi. A deep stench filled the air. Dogs barked. Vultures screeched. Patil bubbled with anger. 'I will kill him in broad daylight. It's a question of my honour. I will hack him to pieces.'

He was furious. The stench was maddening. 'How can they live in this stench? They eat dirt and live in dirt. It's their habit!'

The dirt and squalor were too much for Patil to bear. All around him were ramshackle huts, naked children and ditches filled with dirty water. Old, skeletal people and sleeping dogs . . . Patil was irritated. To think that these lowly people could protest! Rebel! He increased the horse's pace. 'These people look like mere insects.' Hindurao Patil was seeing broken people at the Chambhar Tekadi.

Thunder roared in the sky. The winds blew wild. An old woman was trying her best to light a fire. A beggar practised his song to the beat of his dafli. Potraj was back in his hut with the alms he had received. A woman wailed in her hut. Patil was amazed to see such poverty and such dirt. He wondered, 'After staying in such dirt, how can the Mahar still dare to look at an upper-caste woman?' He was furious thinking that a man from such a squalid setting had stripped Lalita naked. The thought almost killed him.

The news of Hindurao Patil coming to the Chambhar Tekadi spread like wildfire. People came out of their huts to see Patil. They whispered excitedly, 'So far only the father had come here. Now that Patil is here, our fate shall smile.'

Patil's horse stopped in front of Manik's house. Karim had told him, 'It is the last house in the Maharwada, at the edge of the slope. There is a peepal tree in front of the house.'

Patil alighted from the horse. Manik's mother sat in the courtyard. She was waiting for Manik. Day and night! She was restless for him. She wanted to happily shout, 'A son has been born to you! Your father has come back to us!'

The moment she saw Hindurao Patil, Bhama greeted him warmly. She touched her head to the ground as a mark of respect. She then sat at the door. The cheerful expression on Bhama's face confused Hindurao Patil. The sword hung from his waist, and in his hand was the pink sari.

'Where is Manik?' he asked.

'We are waiting for him. He hasn't come back. It has been eight days. I don't understand what happened . . .' Bhama said.

'Don't lie.'

'Why should I lie?'

'Is he home?'

'If he were home, you would have seen him by now. Why would I hide him?'

'I want to search the house.'

'My daughter-in-law is inside. She has just given birth. The infant is five days old. Please don't go in.'

Bhama stood in front of the door. Hindurao Patil was getting angrier. Bhama had hurried to stop him. Patil's doubt thickened. His hand reached for the sword.

'He must be inside. I will kill him just there,' he thought and, pushing Bhama aside, stormed inside.

He was seething, but as soon as he went inside the hut he shivered to see what was before his eyes. He did not know what to do. He could not believe his eyes. He felt ashamed. His hand loosened its grip on the sword. Bhama came rushing in and stood in front of him.

'She is my daughter-in-law. Manik's wife. She is like your daughter. Kill me if you want but spare her,' Bhama pleaded in a sorrowful voice. 'The baby is five days old. It's a boy. We have named him Neminath!'

Durga was naked. She sat with her baby in her lap. She had no sari on her. The only ragged sari she had was out in the sun to dry. The baby was breastfeeding. Her long hair cascaded across her body. Bhama had been sitting guard at the door so that no one could go inside. But Hindurao Patil had ignored her pleas. He had pushed her aside in rage and suspicion. But Patil felt repentant now. He cursed himself. He gave the packet containing Lalita's sari to Bhama.

'Give it to your daughter-in-law!' he almost screamed out.

Bhama went to Durga with the sari. Durga sat stupefied as Patil retreated in haste.

A crowd of Mahars had gathered outside the hut. Dark clouds filled the sky. Lightning flashed threateningly. The wind shrieked. Seeing Hindurao Patil standing in the courtyard, Lakshman saluted him. 'I was in the British Army,' said Lakshman proudly.

Patil felt sorry thinking that the army had come to such a sorry state! Perhaps his poverty egged him on to fight for his life! Lightning struck again. The rain fell heavily. Children started getting drenched.

'O lord of the clouds! O Meghraj! Stop! Have mercy! My hut will crumble to the ground,' Lakshman pleaded to the sky.

Durga came to the door. She was wearing the sari that Patil had given her. Patil looked at her, and his eyes watered. Bhama was carrying the little one, trying to put him to sleep. The child, named Neminath Mahar, was born to serve the Patils.

Lingnak Mahar of Rahimatpur came to Manik Mahar's house. Lingnak was dripping wet. He did not know how to break the news of Manik Mahar's death.

The heavy rain continued. Water leaked into Manik Mahar's hut. The rain showed no signs of stopping. It poured on. Relentless.

Six

The sea was at full tide. There was water all around. Waves seemed to touch the horizon. Ferocious, angry waves. Strong winds. The gossip of middlemen kept pace with the fierceness of the sea.

'You will be rich. Poverty will be eradicated. You will earn a lot! There are no limits for hard-working people . . .' The middlemen had deceived everyone.

And now, there were foaming waves all around. Sparkling water. Crashing waves. Thunderous, ear-piercing noises! The ship tossed.

'Come back rich and spend the rest of the life in leisure.' This was the dream with which people had boarded the ship. The slave ship! The captain started the ship, and everyone paid their respects to the shore.

The past was coming back to Bhimnak now. Eyes watered. The ground seemed hazy, unclear. The head reeled at the sight of water. The vastness of the sea all around overwhelmed the mind. A month-long ship journey. After stopping at many ports, the final port was here. One of them had died within the first fortnight. His body was put in a sack and thrown into the water. The 300 Indian coolies on the ship looked on in pity and disbelief.

Peter was shaken. So was Barbara. Carter and Jack stood quietly. Their sorrow was like the sand. Their dejection was limitless, like the sea itself. Bhimnak's body looked like the giant dead fish that floated on the waves.

The sails fluttered in the wind. The cold wind pierced their skin. The sound of the waves numbed the mind. Everyone tried to hide the helplessness within. They did not know each other. Yes, they were Indians all right. But they were different from each other. Language, clothes, food, traditions—everything was different. Some were Tamil, some Malayali, some Kannada, some Bihari . . . some from Pune, Bombay. They were not the same in any way. Except in their poverty.

Then, a fourteen-year-old died. His body, too, was thrown into the sea. How many more would be thrown away? Everyone was now afraid of death. How many would reach the shore alive? They still had quite some distance to cover. Everyone had left their homes and families behind for this difficult journey. It was better to ask Bhimnak than to ask the captain. So they all asked him the same question:

'When shall we reach? We cannot take it any more . . . The cough is worsening . . . the feet are paralysed . . . the wind slaps the face mercilessly . . .'

Bhimnak tried his best to console everyone.

Ram Prasad was frightened and restless. He knew that he had left his motherland forever. The guilt of an overseas journey burdened his mind. His poverty had made him go against his God and religion. But now, his mind was heavy with regret. He had found out about Bhimnak's caste. The thought of living with an untouchable shattered him. He felt afraid that he would be going to hell. He wanted to kill himself. Perhaps that would absolve him of his sins, he thought. The sound of the coolies snoring was like the sound of toads on a rainy night. The fierce wind seemed to be rebuking the waves.

The sin Ram Prasad thought he had committed rampaged his mind with a force fiercer than the waves. He got up. He folded his hands to pay his respects to the gods in the sky. And he jumped into the sea. The ship lost another coolie.

The labourers—available for cheap in India—were sent to the colonies of the British Empire. They were sent to Ceylon, Burma, Mauritius, Malaya, South America. The slave trade had been banned, but it was very much a practice still. It had taken the form of indentured labour. Labourers were needed for sugarcane and cotton plantations. Manual labour was in short supply in the colonies. So Indian labourers were sent there. After all, they were all citizens of the British Empire!

They boarded the ship from Mazagon Dock. The sergeant superintendent filled out everyone's migration form. Name, age, father's name, wife's name if married, names of relatives, name of the native village, mohalla, tehsil and zila, birthmark and thumb impression. Man immigration pass, woman immigration pass, boy immigration pass, girl immigration pass . . . The Sergeant wrote 'Healthy Immigrants' on each document and signed it. Everyone was given an ID number. The immigration officer issued passes for all. He made a list of passengers. Bhimnak's ID number was 9863. It was the first time that they were going on such a long journey, which seemed like a punishment meted out at Kaala Paani.

Bhimnak was quietly helping everyone as best he could. Peter called out to him. Bhimnak's eyes were half open. His eyelids closed, and he was unable to open his eyes.

The waves were like a hooded cobra. The sound of the roaring, crashing waves . . . his consciousness was slowly fading away, like the dead bodies thrown into the water. His face looked bleached of colour. Peter saw his father dying. He was with his father in his last moments.

The English slave ship was filled with men, women, children and cargo. Bhimnak remembered Sidnak. He remembered Sonai, Jhol, Devgadh . . . Parbati . . .

The ship was stationed at the dock. The police came on board and took the Indian coolies away to Baraki. The coolies shivered as they set foot on this new land. New people! New language! New climate! It was Liverpool!

There were clusters of indentured labourers from many countries in Baraki. They were of different nationalities, spoke different languages, came from different cultures! Bhimnak felt like he was standing in a slave market. The government itself depended on this market! Bhimnak had been tricked. Labourers were sent according to their ID numbers. Sugar plantations, mines, construction work, cotton plantations, tea plantations, railway lines . . . Bhimank's chest reverberated with a grinding sound. Where did the ship from India with its human cargo go? Who knows! He was sent to work on the railway line. He tried to fight with the British police. The labourers were attacking them! They shrieked and yelled as the police rained lathis on their backs in a bid to keep them under control. As a lathi came down heavily on Bhimnak's back, his eyes floundered.

In India, the first question people asked when they met anyone was, 'What is your caste?' Here, they asked, 'Which country are you from?' South Asians were easily recognized. So were the Chinese. The White master was the figure of authority for his coloured labourers. His was the final word. One word from him, perhaps even half a word, could destroy a coolie. The coolies were scared of their masters. They showed him respect. No one dared to talk back to the master. The master had rights over the women labourers. He believed he was a superior being. He would tell the labourers, 'You have no brains, you understand nothing. So don't try to use your empty heads. Do as you are told!'

The White people thought that the coloured people were fools. The pride of being White ran in their veins. Bhimnak was beaten up quite a few times because of this. His back bore many scars. Peter knew that Bhimnak's life had been one of pain and suffering. All his life, Bhimnak had worked very hard. His lips trembled! He tried to utter a prayer to Mari Ma. Barbara stood like an anchor in the sand. Carter and Jack stood desolate. Carter was his eldest grandson! Very dear to him. Bhimnak used to narrate stories of his village to Carter. He would play with him. After Carter, three more granddaughters and two grandsons were born . . . but they died of malnutrition. Jack was the youngest. There was a ten-year difference between Jack and Carter.

Peter gave Bhimnak a sip of water, which trickled down his parched throat.

'I am Indian . . . Your mother is Caribbean . . . Where are you from?' Bhimnak would joke with his son, who would say, 'I am British!'

Father and son were good friends. Bhimnak would tell everyone, 'I am Indian by birth.' Whenever he met an Indian he would greet them with, 'Ram Ram!' He always said, 'I will go to Sonai once! Offer prayers to Mari Ma.'

Now he was past all this. Peter felt restless. His father was going away from him forever . . . His father would never speak to him again, never see him again . . .

Bhimnak was a soldier at heart. He never bowed before anyone, nor listened to anyone. Perhaps he lived for a hundred years. Whenever he was drunk on rum, he would say, 'I will go to India!'

Peter was crying loudly now. There was no one before whom he could be a child. The thought of loneliness scared him.

After his father's death, it was unbearable for Peter to live in the house with his father's memories all around. He went away to his father-in-law's house to live with them.

Sugar plantations! They were labourers from Fiji and Nigeria. There were Indians in only two houses, and they were Biharis: Ramkisen and Makhan Lal. Peter started working at the sugar plantation. It was the right environment for growing sugar. Thousands of acres of sugarcane plants. Sugar was sold like gold! No one could leave the place without the permission of the plantation manager.

A White man would come at dawn to wake up the coolies—with a whip! They would get up in a daze, writhing in agony. They would then take a bath, cook and leave for work. The coolies did all the work—they worked on the land, planting seeds, watering plants, weeding, fertilizing, cutting, reaping, harvesting . . .

Those unwilling to work were severely punished. There were no locals in that group. The very fact that they were migrants had lowered their self-esteem and confidence, and this was a good thing for the masters. The swords of helplessness, restlessness and insecurity hung over their necks. The Whites prospered and became wealthy on the daily and unending sacrifice of the Black and coloured people. Millions of coolies worked day and night to strengthen the British economy. They were abducted and forcefully brought to the plantations from various colonies. The 'goods' they produced were traded by many shipping companies engaged in export–import.

The coolie had no identity of his own. He was identified by the name of his master. They were given numbers to wear on their arms or around their necks. The difference between a White man and a Black man was the same as that between a human and an animal. The latter were like insignificant leaves on a shrub. Barbara would sometimes joke, 'By the time we reach the last days of our life, we will start to comprehend the language of animals.'

They had nothing they could call their own—no relations, not even a place they could call home, no village . . . All they had was a master. 'Hurry up, you Indian pig! If you don't work, you will be back in the garbage heap where you lived.' The coolie was used to such abuse and curses. Peter's back bore whip marks. Carter would shriek when he saw the scars on his father's back.

The children of the coolies were playing and talking among themselves:

'I am a Nigerian!'

'My mom is from Fiji! Father Caribbean! I am Black British!'

'I am Black!'

'I am an Indian coolie . . .'

Carter's head reeled as he heard the children's voices. He had inherited the fierceness of his grandfather. His father, Peter, was of mild disposition. Carter looked Indian, but on closer scrutiny, his Nigerian features would be evident. His curly hair, thick eyebrows, broad lips, swollen nostrils—he had inherited these from his mother. But he also resembled his grandfather Bhimnak closely. Bhimnak had given Carter much love because he was his first grandson. Carter now knew the difference between Whites and Blacks. He also understood the misdemeanours of the Whites. The lives of the Blacks were like the skeleton of a house destroyed by an earthquake. No matter if the fellow was an upper or lower caste. For the White man, he was an 'Indian pig'.

'Which country?'

'What race?'

'What language do you speak?'

'When did you last visit your country?'

'What culture?'

'Which country do you like? The one where you live or the one where you were born?'

'Where is your mother from? Where is your father from?'

His name was Carter Peter Mahar. A Christian by birth! He did not have a birth certificate. He could not decide where he was from. None of them had citizenship. They had no citizen rights. Nor did they enjoy any facilities. Their identities were as scattered as the rusted parts of an old ship. He often wondered where he was from. From the land he was born in, or from the land of his forefathers? He loved fish curry. He loved Indian white rice. He was raised in a multilingual and multicultural environment. A single caste culture was beyond his comprehension. Racial superiority, caste superiority—these concepts were nightmarish to him.

The prevalent sentiment regarding indentured labourers was that they should be got rid of as soon as their work was done. Or else they would stay back and demand habitation, work, citizenship, etc. The country could not take this burden! They were a hindrance to the country's economic stability and would impede its development. Those who nourished such thoughts had completely forgotten that their capitalist society stood on the foundation of the hard work of these very coloured workers.

It was nighttime. Peter and Barbara were talking to each other. Carter was glued to Peter's body and Jack to Barbara's. Peter said to Barbara, 'Here, the upper castes are in higher positions, and they help the other upper castes. They ask about caste and then decide whether or not they will help someone. The Indian coolies don't talk to me properly. They think I am an untouchable. Ramkisen runs away whenever he sees me.'

Barbara was angry. She said, 'Let us not keep any relations with him. How does it matter that he is from India? What does he understand about Indianness? It is better to have relations with my Nigerian people. My brother is here. You can spend time with him. Talk to him. He is a don. If he finds out about this discrimination, he will beat Ramkisen black and blue.'

Carter was quietly listening to his parents. Sleep had deserted him. Ramkisen's daughter, Vaishali, had been stealing glances at him recently.

The plantation manager had sent Ramkisen's wife to work in a friend's house. There was some event there. Ramkisen's wife did not return even after the event ended. Ramkisen inquired with his manager a number of times, but the manager evaded him. One day, the manager's goons beat up Ramkisen badly on the pretext of something minor. That night, Ramkisen left his house. He took everyone with him, including Vaishali. She was seventeen! Carter was twenty-one! Vaishali had once told Carter, 'My uncle works in construction at the Liverpool dock.'

She cried when she was leaving. 'I will come back and meet you.'

Carter waited for Vaishali, but she never returned. And Carter could never forget her. He became restless thinking about her. One day, he ran away. He left for Liverpool. The Port of Liverpool, Princess Dock . . . he searched every corner. No one spoke to him. Vaishali was nowhere to be found. He saw some Indian coolies at a spot and approached them. He spoke to Hariprasad, who was also a runaway.

'All coolies here are from Calcutta. I have been working here since I was your age. Now I have a son like you,' Hariprasad said to him kindly.

Carter was a good-tempered boy. Well-built, tall and strong. He was fluent in English, like the Whites. In a crowd, he was sure to get all the attention. Hariprasad took him to his house. He worked as a labourer loading and unloading goods on ships. It was a hazardous job. There would be about ninety ships on the dock at any given time. Every day, 15–20 new ships arrived from various countries and about the same number left the dock. Liverpool was one of the most famous and busiest ports in the world. A small village, famous for fishing! Its fortunes had risen because of the slave trade. Indian ships often came to Liverpool. This news made Carter happy!

Goods were being packed into the shipping container. The label 'Buy British Class' was being pasted on the packs. Hariprasad was dejected. 'Our lives are like bricks—they have no function but to be useful to the system. I have been a coolie for so long . . . I am a skeleton now . . . No one cares.'

The labourers, whether on the ship or off, hardly ever got a proper wage. The master would be at their backs, rebuking and abusing. There was no job security. It was a precarious existence. After such hard work throughout the day, they could not even afford a proper meal. Their living conditions were pathetic. Dirt all around. Unhygienic.

Hariprasad's brother worked at the docks as well. His job was to burn the garbage. The ships' horns were being sounded, the coolies were hurriedly finishing their tasks. A cacophony of voices, howling, bawling. Goods had arrived on horse carts from the godown. Cranes were lifting containers on to the ships. Containers were being unloaded from some ships. The coolies were sweating. There were a hundred coolies for each ship. The ships tossed in the water. Papers were being readied at the port. Everyone was busy playing their part!

Carter was unable to sleep. He was gazing at the sky. He was used to sleeping glued to his father and would have done it even at this age. Now he lay on the hard ground. Some waste papers were all he had for bedding. A ragged sack was his blanket. Mosquitoes bit him. The sea wailed. He was tearful as he remembered his parents and his brother, Jack.

Thoughts of Vaishali distressed Carter. He felt restless. Then, at some point, he drifted off to sleep. In his dream he saw his grandfather Bhimnak.

'I must offer a prayer to Mari Ma!' Bhimnak was saying while laying down the rail lines.

Carter's grandfather was in his dreams all night long. He did not budge from his bed all night, not even when he felt an urge to pee. He did not want to wake up from this beautiful dream. Bhimnak was like a mountain in his life, the sky above which seemed magical.

* * *

The waves gurgled. The foaming water danced rhythmically, reflecting the blue sky above. Seafowls hovered around. A month had passed. After stopping at various ports, they had now reached the port of Mazagon Dock. He jumped with joy as they neared the dock. He looked at the land with longing in his eyes. The ship stopped. It had been tied up like an animal. A ship from London was of great significance to everyone. For the natives, everything that arrived on a ship from London was special. Carter looked keenly at the natives. He was searching for glimpses of Bhimnak, Peter, Jack and Vaishali in them.

Carter got off the ship with Cook Mike Cullen, who knew Bombay quite well. He had been here many times. The Chinese third engineer went towards the cargo control room. The captain greeted the immigration officer. The maintenance team walked behind the captain. The port officials got busy with documentation. Cadets unloaded their luggage. Carter felt confused. What should he do now?

He came out with Cook Mike Cullen. They reached Nagpada. Cook went into a club. He gave a packet to a European man, who recognized him. The man gave him a hundred rupees. They came out of the club. They drank kawa. On one side of Nagpada was the Chor Bazaar and on the other was Kamathipura. Kamathipura! The infamous red-light area! The two of them crossed the Irani hotel to reach Fors Road. Horse-drawn carriages roamed the streets. The two of them settled down to have a few drinks. The locals stared at them. Carter had never had a drink before. This was his first time, and he was gulping them down quickly. Oh, the joy of having reached India! Cook was in no hurry. He was enjoying his drink. Looking at Carter, he said, 'Go slow, brother!'

But Carter had already had a bit too much. He was feeling dizzy. He felt like vomiting. He went to a corner of the road. A hooker stood nearby, bargaining with a prospective client. She looked so similar to Vaishali. He was drawn to her. By the time he was near her the client had walked away. Carter spoke to her, but neither of them understood each other except for the word 'sex'. Carter followed her to the brothel. He saw the other women there. As he stared at them in astonishment, she became angry. This was her client. She had fetched him off the road. He had no business looking at the other women now. She began to curse him in a foul language. He did not understand a word of what she said and grinned. This irked her more. He was in a drunken stupor.

She pushed him, and he fell to the ground. He could not get up. He lay there on the road. The pimps came out and kicked him. A woman spat on him. 'What kind of a client have you fetched for yourself? He cannot even sit straight!' They mocked the girl who had brought him there. Carter lay on the ground. Cook called out to Carter, but he was in no situation to reply. He fell asleep.

Someone woke him up at midnight. Business had closed for the day. He went to sleep at the door of a brothel. Someone covered him with a cloth. A dog slept beside him.

Soon it was morning. People were beginning to wake up. The women were cleaning their courtyard. Some were still asleep, having completed their late-night business deals.

Many tried to speak with Carter, but they didn't understand him, just as he didn't understand them.

'He is speaking in English. We should send him to the Englishman, or else people will take advantage of him,' suggested a well-meaning eunuch.

Naughty kids surrounded him on all sides.

'He hasn't eaten since night. Let's give him something to eat!' said a pimp.

'He must sleep with one of the hookers! Isn't that why he came here?' joked another pimp.

An older woman came up to him and said, 'He should be sent to his people.'

'The British live in Mahalakshmi Hill. Let's take him there. They will arrange something. We cannot understand his language.'

Someone offered him water. He washed his face. Some children held him by the hand, and he walked with them. He looked at all the people around him; it felt right to be in India. He reached Mahalakshmi Hill and saw a bungalow at the top.

The bungalow was built in the British architectural style. Carter smiled and went inside, where he met Bernard. 'Good morning!'

Bernard was pleased to hear the British accent. He called Carter near and asked who he was. Carter told him that he had come from England but was of Indian origin. Bernard was happy to find such a worker and immediately hired him as a butler. Carter was glad that he had found his footing now. He decided that he wouldn't budge from there until he learnt Marathi.

1918. The South Bureau Commission had come to Bombay. It toured the important areas of India to gather testimony of representatives of Indian people. The 1909 Morley–Minto Reforms had failed to appease the people. There was political dissent in the country. The reforms had granted a separate electorate to Muslims, who wanted to weaken the political might of the majority Hindu community. They raised the demand that the untouchables not be counted among the Hindu population. The South Bureau Commission wanted to know the opinion of the Hindus on this matter. Maharshi Shinde and Sir Narayanrao Chandavarkar opined that the untouchables were to be regarded as Hindus and should not be given a separate political identity. At that time, B.R. Ambedkar was a professor at Sydenham College. He had sent a petition to the governor stating, 'I should be chosen as a representative of the untouchables.'

The governor accepted his plea. Ambedkar told the commission: 'The untouchables must have voting rights. They must have the right to contest the elections and choose their own representative from their separate electorate. They should get representation in proportion to their population.'

India's existing social order was melting like ice. The three new social orders—comprising the Hindus, Muslims and the untouchables were now in motion.

Bernard had invited the members of the South Bureau Commission to his house for a meal. He knew these members. Bernard treated them to lunch. He gave them gifts. Carter listened attentively as they talked. He could well grasp the conversation that was going on in English. 'If the Muslims and the untouchables unite, the significance of the Hindus will decline, but this is not going to happen. The untouchables won't side with the Muslims. They will remain with the Hindus,' Bernard expressed his thoughts. Bernard had been living in India for the last ten years. His insights were important. Carter heard the name of Ambedkar again and again. In his mind there arose a keen desire to meet Ambedkar.

Bernard had two strong interests. One was brandy and the other was betting on horse racing. Every Sunday, Bernard would send a servant from Bombay to Pune with a packet of money to Michael. Michael and Bernard were good friends. Michael lived in the Camp area in Pune. He, too, loved horse racing. He had previously worked as the tehsildar of Jhol. He had got himself a transfer from Jhol to Pune because of his love for racing. Michael was a close aide of the governor. Bernard had to send the money to Michael through Carter because the usual carrier had not turned up this time. This was all to the good, because it gave Carter the opportunity to go to Pune. He asked for permission to visit his ancestral village for a couple of days. Bernard agreed.

Carter reached Camp, where he met Michael and gave him the packet of money. Michael was surprised at Carter's British English. As Carter narrated his life story, Michael was struck by Carter's journey, his boldness, his courage, which reminded him of racing. Michael decided to help Carter. He knew Jhol quite well and also knew that the Scottish missionaries were due to go there. Michael wrote a letter in praise of Carter and asked him to take the letter to the missionaries immediately, so that they would take Carter with them. Michael also gave him fifty rupees as tip. The boy had impressed him.

* * *

Carter reached Jhol with the Scottish missionaries. He slept in the church that night. During the journey, Father Brudo, who was from Liverpool, had been kind to Carter. He felt an emotional connection with Carter because Carter had come from his native place. Father Brudo gave Carter some clothes and a pair of boots.

'If you want to become a priest, I can arrange for your training. You will have to work in the Adivasi area. There are forests near Jhol. Many Adivasis live in those forests. Helping people is doing God's work. We must serve people. Think about it. There is no compulsion.' Father Brudo patted Carter's back affectionately.

Carter laughed. 'The upper castes in India do not want to convert. They are worried about the status of their high caste. The untouchables and Adivasis are ready to convert. They want to bring an end to their status as low castes.'

'You work with the Adivasis!' Father looked at him sympathetically.

The next day, Carter went to the Chambhar Tekadi. He saw a potraj approaching from the other side. His strange appearance amused Carter. He stopped him and asked, 'Did you know Bhimnak and Sidnak? They were in the British Army.'

'Go to the very end. Someone from that house was in the army. Ask him. The last house. I would have come with you, but I am getting late. Go straight and ask for Neminath's house. Anyone will show you.'

Carter followed the directions and went straight ahead. Dogs were barking. They were shooed away by some children playing on the streets.

'Where do you have to go?' the kids asked him.

'Neminath's house.'

'The last house,' they said.

Carter walked on. The Tekadi was an empire of stench. It was filthier than the sugar plantations and Princess Dock. Carter pressed his nostrils shut as he walked on.

Neminath was working with animal hide. He stopped when he saw Carter.

'Did you know Bhimnak, Sidnak?' Carter asked.

'No. Who were they?'

'They were in the British Army. It's an old story.'

'My grandfather was also in the army. I heard the names of Bhimnak, Sidnak and Philip from him.'

'Bhimnak was my grandfather. I have to go to Sonai. Is there anyone from Bhimnak's family here?'

'All the old people have died. I go to Sonai sometimes. But none of the people from the older generation are there either.'

'My name is Carter, and I am staying in the church.'

'Sonai is close by. A four–five-hour journey by foot.'

'I won't go back to London. I will stay here. I will work for the church.'

Carter and Neminath became friends. Carter sat for a long time in the Chambhar Tekadi. He spoke with Neminath about a lot of things.

'Once we make a decision, nothing is impossible. Not even the journey from England to Sonai,' thought Carter as he bade goodbye to Neminath for the day.

He was elated that he had finally found his way. At least he knew someone in Jhol now. He walked down the Chambhar Tekadi, towards Lal Dongar.

Vedant stopped Carter on the way. 'Hindustan is not a place where anyone can just walk in. We won't allow outsiders here. This is the land of the Hindus.'

Vedant was on fire. He had found out that the missionaries had come to Jhol. The Hindu Vahini workers were active here, and Vedant was their leader.

Carter did not understand the import of Vedant's threatening words.

'The missionaries are working with the Adivasis. And now they are eyeing the Chambhar Tekadi as well. They are a danger to Hindu religion,' Vedant added.

The Hindu Vahini youths surrounded Carter. He stood quietly. They seemed angry.

'Why did you go to the Chambhar Tekadi? Do you want to convert the untouchables?'

'I want to convert. I want to become a Mahar. Will you help?'

'We will make you a Hindu. Purify you.'

'After you purify me, will I remain pure?'

'No. The Mahars are untouchables.'

'I will let you know!'

Carter walked away from the young men.

'Illegal migrants are in danger in England, and the same can be said of the untouchables here in India. The White men and the upper castes are similar.' Carter sensed danger. He would have to stand firm.

Native Christians who walked past Carter looked at him respectfully. Carter waved at them. The church was busy today because of the presence of the Scottish missionaries. A felicitation ceremony had been organized here for the Mahar soldiers who had fought in the First World War. Several Mahar soldiers had gathered in the church.

* * *

Carter reached Sonai with Neminath. There were some 40–50 huts in the Maharwada of Sonai. Neminath took Carter around the Maharwada. There was one main road and three alleys. Carter felt as though he was in a dreamland. His grandfather was born here and had lived here. And now Carter was in the same Maharwada. His grandfather's Maharwada.

Carter's mind churned like a sea storm. He felt like he was floating in the air. The Mari Ma temple lay in ruins. Bhimnak's hut was deserted. No one lived there any more. The roof had caved in. Carter went down on his knees and touched his forehead to the ground as a mark of respect. This was holy land for him. He felt thrilled to think that his grandfather Bhimnak had once lived here. Carter remembered his parents. He remembered the sugar plantation. He trembled to think how far he had travelled.

'He doesn't look like a Mahar.'

'He was born in England.'

'His hair, his features . . . so unlike ours.'

'His mother is Nigerian.'

'He is not a pure Mahar.'

'What do you mean by pure Mahar?'

'I mean son of a Mahar mother and a Mahar father—pure Mahar.'

'No, he is British.'

'What's the use, then? He is not one of us.'

The Mahars went on questioning Neminath. Carter could understand their emotions. His face fell. He was trying his best to express solidarity with the Mahars. But the Mahars were not ready to accept him. They thought he was contriving tricks to deceive them.

Carter reached the tamarind tree. Bhimnak would often sit under this tree, eat its fruit, hang animal hides to dry on its branches. The tree had given shade to generations of Mahars. The generations changed, but the tree remained the same, as did the circumstances. The distance between the village and the Maharwada had not changed, had not lessened.

Vedant and the workers of the Hindu Vahini came to Sonai. A Hindu Navjagaran Sabha was being held in the village. News of Carter's arrival had spread everywhere. The village was keenly observing the Maharwada. The villagers were angry. They spoke of coercive conversions.

Carter, Neminath and the young Mahars sat under the tamarind tree. Carter watched the Falguni River flow. The Mahars had brought a dead animal with them. Carter got up immediately. Bhimnak had told him about this. Carter went forward, moved one of the Mahars out of the way and carried the dead animal on his shoulder. He felt strange. He was doing the same work that his grandfather had done. Such filthy work! The Mahars will trust me now, he thought. He was not used to all this. His shoulder ached. The carcass seemed to slip from his shoulder.

'What more proof can I give?' he asked himself.

The Mahars placed the carcass behind the Maharwada, on the rubbish heap. It was a cow. Carter held the front leg of the cow. The Padewar Mahars started to skin the carcass. Crows and dogs had gathered. The Mahars had come to take the meat. Carter remembered the foaming waves. He remembered the ship anchored at Princess Dock. He remembered the Indian coolies. The Mahars had skinned the animal now. They had cut open its gut. He remembered the hooker in Kamathipura. He remembered the children of the hookers. He remembered the pimp who took him to Mahalakshmi Hill. The Mahars came near the animal. They were eager to collect the meat. Carter remembered the South Bureau Commission members. He remembered Ambedkar, who had testified for the untouchables and defended their rights.

The Mahars held out their utensils. But Carter stopped them. His voice thundered loud and clear, like a ship's siren. 'Don't eat this carcass!'

The Mahars angrily responded, 'We eat dead animals' meat. Who are you to dictate what we should choose to eat? Go back to England!'

Neminath was waiting to take the hide. He had to give it to the Dhor in Jhol. The Padewar Mahars stood at some distance. Carter was desperate now. He took some shit lying nearby and flung it at the dead animal. This scared the Mahars.

'He has ruined our food!' They went away, saddened.

The Maharwada debated the incident. The Padewar Mahars were in favour of Carter. 'Good that someone has come forward to say that eating meat from carcasses is humiliating for the Mahars. You never listened when we said the same thing.'

They tried to explain why Carter was right. They held bloodstained knives and hide in their hands. They were near the tamarind tree and wanted to go and wash their knives, and their hands and feet in the river.

People could be seen coming from the direction of the village. They were heavily armed with lathis and axes. News had spread like wildfire that Carter had insulted a dead cow. A huge crowd surrounded Carter. He was confused. He didn't understand what was going on. What had fuelled this anger? The Padewar Mahars begged the villagers for mercy.

'Didn't he throw shit on the cow? Tell us the truth!' demanded one villager.

'I didn't mean to insult. I wanted to stop the Mahars from eating the dead animal's meat.' Carter was trying to make his point despite the fear.

'You have hurt our sentiments!' shouted someone.

'I am sorry. I got carried away. Please try to understand,' said Carter politely.

'Now you will see our sentiments! Catch him. Don't let him go!'

By now, more people had gathered. Carter was beaten up. He was attacked with sharp weapons. He lay on the ground, near the place where the Mahars would ignite the Holi. The Padewar Mahars stood some distance away. Neminath was shivering. He had also been beaten up. Carter's body trembled. There was a fountain of blood. Someone in the crowd urinated on him.

Vedant came running with his Hindu Vahini activists. He was shocked to see Carter writhing on the ground.

'Don't punish the Mahars any more. They have been through a lot already. If you don't stop now they will convert. Be humane. Or there will be revenge!'

Vedant raised his hands to bless the Mahars. The Mahars bowed to show their respect.

Carter's body appeared contorted. Waves were rising in the sea. It was full tide. The reflection of the blue sky fell on the water. Peter was eating his food. He had brought white Indian rice. It was Carter's favourite. Barbara couldn't eat. The food was bitter.

Putting a morsel in his mouth, Jack asked, 'Where is Carter?'

Peter's eyes overflowed.

Life slowly dimmed in Carter's body. The attackers had left. A distant noise could be heard from the village; people were raising slogans against conversion. The waves had calmed down now.

A whirlwind arose near the Falguni River. The Vetal and the ghosts danced in it. They wanted to dance in front of the Mari Ma temple. They had come to fetch Carter's soul. Right at the front of the procession was Parbati's ghost. To the left of Vetal was Chennayya's ghost, on the right was Manik's. With skulls around their necks, the ghosts danced in gleeful abandon. The sight of the whirlwind unsettled Vedant. His distress worried the villagers.

'We must do a bhoot-shanti, or the village will be ruined.'

The Hindu Vahini activists were worried to see their leader Vedant Guruji's anxiety-ridden face. The whirlwind was moving towards the Maharwada. The tamarind tree shook violently. Its branches appeared strange. Yallamma, who was sitting under the tamarind tree, looked like a witch. She was coughing. Her old nerves made her head shake, just as it made the lathi shake in her withered hand. She asked Vedant, 'You are talking about ghosts. You just killed a young man. Why don't you talk about his murder?'

Yellamma's question shocked everyone. Vedant felt pressured to give an answer. All the villagers were looking at him hopefully.

Vedant gathered up his courage and said loudly, 'Whoever opposes the Hindu religion will be killed!'

'But the Hindu religion is against the untouchables. What about that?' asked Yellamma.

This Mahar woman had the courage to question Vedant? The villagers were enraged at this. Vedant did not know what to say.

This old, fragile woman, with a wobbling head on her frail shoulders, was outright insulting him! The thin branches of the tamarind tree quivered. Dust flew. Some garbage that had been carried by the wind now settled on Carter's corpse. The whirlwind was gaining in strength. Dry leaves circled in the air.

'The lower castes can be punished by the upper castes. So says the Hindu religion. The untouchables have no value before the gods.' Vedant had finally found some words.

'If you keep punishing us, we will go elsewhere.' Yellamma's reply had silenced Vedant.

His fear that the untouchables would convert was now coming true. He shivered at the thought. How dare the old hag speak in this undaunted way? The whirlwind intensified. It was scary. The clothes on Carter's corpse fluttered in the wind. Roofs blew off the huts. Garbage wafted across. Vedant's voice changed. A storm rose in his mind. The Sanatan door in his mind was now half closed. Vedant said with emotion, 'All Hindus are brothers. We should be proud to say that we are Hindus.'

Vedant's emotional tone astonished the villagers. Something must be wrong with Vedant. Perhaps it was the ghosts! The untouchables and the upper castes could never be brothers! The young activists of the Hindu Vahini wondered what 'brotherhood' meant.

'Fraternity means justice based on the principle of coexistence. It means the relationship between men and life, the splendid symbiosis between human beings. It is a divine form of equality. Fraternity is at the heart of a culture. In fraternity lies the chemistry of a nation. Fraternity celebrates freedom! It is the dream of democracy! All this is fraternity.'

The skies had delivered an oracle. The whirlwind quietened. But the air was still rife with dust and loose dry leaves.

The Mahars lifted Carter's corpse. They placed it in front of Bhimnak's hut. Many years ago, Bhimnak's mother's corpse was laid in the same place, in the same way. The villagers left. Yellama went towards the corpse. Vultures descended on the dead cow. Crows and dogs also lined up to get their share. Cacophony. Stench.

Mahars gathered near Carter's corpse. Yellamma said, 'The villagers attacked him, but he did not hit them even once. He will be reborn as a cow.'

Carter's corpse lay on the ground like a ship anchored at a dock.

A new whirlwind started to emerge from the Falguni River.

Glossary

Aarti: A form of worship.

Achman: Prayer.

Adharmi: Irreligious.

Alwaan: A type of red sari worn by some Hindu Brahmin widows. It is compulsory for widows of a particular community to wear it. It is an identifier/mark of such widows.

Ashada: A month marked by heavy rain.

Ashram: Hermitage/place of religious retreat.

Asura: Demigods. The term has a complex history, and carry varying connotations and significance. Often, and commonly regarded as the manifestation of evil, the opposers of the devas, in traditional Hindu thought, the asuras have been reclaimed as non-Aryan heroic figures.

Batu: A young Brahmin boy, 8–10 years old, who has started wearing the janave.

Behrupiya: A nomadic tribe of folk artists who entertain villagers and use their art of singing, dancing and acting to beg for alms from the upper castes.

Bhajan: Devotional songs.

Bhakt: Devotee.

Bhangi: An untouchable caste comprising those who manually clean toilets of the upper castes. They carry buckets of faeces on their heads. Manual scavenging has now been banned by the Indian government.

Bhoot-shanti: A ritual to pacify ghosts. It involves the ritual of sacrifice animals and chickens on a new-moon night.

Bhumi puja: A ritual that involves the worship the land.

Chawadi: A village office where the patil, head of the village, sat for village administration purposes. This was where the village's records were kept. It was usually a big room, which only the upper castes could enter.

Darshan: Glimpse of God/the holy one.

Dasi: A female servant.

Devi: Goddess.

Dhor: An untouchable caste.

Dhoti: Loose loincloth.

Fatwa: A legal ruling on a point of Islamic law (Sharia). It is decreed by a qualified jurist in response to a question posed by a private individual, judge or government.

Gayatri Mantra: A highly revered mantra in the Rig Veda.

Haldi-Kumkum: Turmeric and vermilion, symbol of a married woman.

Haldi-smeared rice: Rice mixed with turmeric powder. In the old times, there were no wedding cards. So people would invite guests by sending them some yellow-coloured rice.

Hom-havan: A Vedic ritual where offerings are made to a consecrated fire.

House Mahar: A Mahar who is bound to work in a particular house, of village heads, landlords and upper-caste people.

Janave: Holy thread worn by Brahmins.

Jogteen: A Mahar devotee woman who sings of the Goddess and lives by begging alms.

Kaala Wada: *Kaala* means black, and Wada is a mansion/palace.

Kaala Dongar: Black Hills.

Kansa: Krishna's maternal uncle and the king of Magadha in the Mahabharata.

Kasar: A artisan caste known for making bracelets for Indian women.
Khalita: Letter, order, message sent by the king.
Kirtan: A form of devotional song and preaching.
Kirtankar: One who sings kirtans or devotional songs and tells stories.
Kuladevata: The family deity.
Lal Dongar: Red Hills.
Lathi: A stick.
Mahadev: Also known as Shiva and Maheshwar, one of the tripartite godheads of Brahma–Vishnu–Maheshwar in the Hindu religion. Mahadev is regarded as the 'destroyer' in the cycle of creation that involves birth, death and rebirth.
Mahapuja: A special or big worship ritual.
Mahar: A caste cluster or group of many endogamous castes, living chiefly in Maharashtra and the adjoining states in India. They mostly speak Marathi, the official language of Maharashtra. They constituted the lowest social class in the Hindu caste system and had been branded 'untouchables' before the Constitution of 1950 outlawed discrimination against them. Social discrimination, however, is rampant even today. Traditionally, the Mahars lived on the outskirts of villages and performed a number of duties for the entire village. They chiefly worked as village watchmen, messengers, wall menders, adjudicators of boundary disputes, street sweepers and remover of carcasses.
Maharwada: Where the untouchable Mahars live. This place is on the outskirts of every village.
Mahishasura: Half-human, half-buffalo demon. Regarded as a villain by the Aryans, and his death is celebrated as the victory of good over evil. Mahishasura is celebrated as a hero by certain tribes in India.
Mangalsutra: A thread that is a symbol of marriage. Hindu men tie the mangalsutra around their wives' necks as a wedding ritual.
Mari Ma: Mother goddess of the Mahars.

Marwari: An Indian ethnic group that originates from the state of Rajasthan.

Mashaal: A torch.

Murli: A Mahar woman who is a lifetime devotee of the Goddess. She doesn't marry and lives by begging for alms. She spends her life singing devotional songs and dancing to them.

Narad Muni: A divine sage and among the sons of Brahma, he travels between the worlds and sings the glory of Narayan.

Narli-punam: A full-moon night celebrated by Hindus in the Shravan month.

Nirmalya: An offering to the gods.

Pada: Area/settlement.

Padewar Mahars: A Mahar man. He is bound to work for upper-caste people. He has to do menial jobs in the village. For this work he gets leftovers from the upper-caste houses. If he is unable to do his job on a particular day due to sickness, he must send his son or wife to fill in for him.

Param Brahma: The supreme Brahmin beyond all thought and conceptualization. Formless. Eternally pervades everything in the universe and all that is beyond it.

Pardhi: A tribal people who are dacoits by profession.

Parvati/Parbati: Parvati has been used in the book to refer to Goddess Parvati, and Parbati to refer to the character.

Patil: Chief of village.

Potraj: A Mahar devotee who keeps long hair and lives on alms. He is not allowed to cut his hair.

Pranayam: Breathing exercises.

Puranas: Holy scriptures of the Hindu religion. There are eighteen Puranas. The texts are based on stories of Hindu gods and preach moral values.

Purusha Sukta: A hymn in the Rig Veda. The Purusha Sukta describes the spiritual unity of the universe. It presents the nature of

Purusha, or the cosmic being, as immanent in the manifested world and yet transcendent to it.

Pushpak Viman: An airborne vehicle mentioned in Hindu texts, something like the modern-day planes/helicopters.

Ravana: The ten-headed heroic warrior king of Lanka. The antagonist in the Ramayana, the one who kidnaps Sita and whom Rama beheads eventually. Ravana was known for his wisdom and his capacity for severe penance. Although he was seen as an evil incarnate by the Hindus for a long time, alternative narratives now claim him as a representative of the marginalized and those whom the Aryans wanted to destroy to expand their kingdom.

Shaligram: A particular kind of stone collected from riverbanks, used as a representation of Vishnu by some Hindus.

Shloka: A poetic form used in Sanskrit.

Shradh: Funeral rites.

Shravan: The month of Shravan follows Ashada and is also marked by heavy rain.

Stick-with-bells: The Mahars were made to carry a stick with bells attached to it, so that the rattling sound alerted people that a Mahar was nearby.

Suryanamaskar: A ritual used in the worship of the sun god.

Takya: The community hall of the Mahars. They would rest here during day and sleep here at night.

Tapasya: Penance.

Tati: A bier, a frame made of sticks to lift a dead body.

Tehsildar: Head of the town, appointed by the East India Company. He would be a White man, responsible for the town and villages in his jurisdiction.

Teli: A caste traditionally associated with oil pressing and trade in India.

Thali: A plate.

Thekedar: Contractor.

Tulsi: Basil plant, regarded as holy by Hindus; a symbol of chastity.

Vaghya: A Mahar devotee of god Khandoba.

Varna: A social class within a hierarchical caste system. The four varnas are: Brahmin, Kshatriya, Vaishya and Shudra.

Vidhata: Another name for the creator or Brahma.

Village Mahar: A Mahar who works for the entire village.

Scan QR code to access the
Penguin Random House India website